CAMP COTTONWOOD

Rose Giacomini

For Cherry.

2019

Tara Ayala is almost packed. Her chipboard bookcase, stuffed to bursting only days ago, slumps from its phantom burden. The contents of her desk have been dumped across her hand-me-down mattress. She sifts through bone dry pens and stumpy erasers, on her knees in the ratty carpet to divvy important documents from the useless looseleaf.

She's put this off long enough. If she doesn't have her room packed away by Friday, she won't make it in time for orientation.

She stuffs the salvageable office supplies into a plastic grocery sack. Next week, she'll be settled in Eugene. University of Oregon is expensive to attend, but her parents just so happened to have enough from a fund they forgot they'd put aside. It has enough to cover her tuition until 2021, on top of what she's scraped together through FAFSA.

Four hundred miles should be enough. That's what matters to Tara. Not the degree in communications, chosen since it sounded just vague enough on paper to be worth something when she graduates. She's not going for her parents, for their pride she'll be headed for university instead of trade school or the community college she's opted for the past two years. The first bigshot state grad in the family, they say, something bittersweet in their tone.

With those two years of community college complete, Tara is ready for a change. Goodbye Del Bosque, goodbye rainy northern California, goodbye apartment she's grown up in and can never convince her parents to move from. They used to move every couple years when she was younger, but they've been adamant on staying here, even with the cracks and the leaks and the shitty complex management.

Her dad Tom was a mechanic before he got injured. Her mother Rebecca has been a medical assistant since before Tara was born. Her brother David is extremely, painfully fifteen and pretends he won't miss her. Her brother Alex is thirteen and clings to her as she crosses off calendar days and crams clothes into bulging garbage bags.

He stands there on the curb and watches her load up her thousand dollar Nissan. Pieces of her life fill up cardboard boxes, pilfered from the nearby retailer she cashiers at. Alex stares, not sure why her moving six hours away scares him so.

But Tara understands. Someone else should be packing for university right now. Someone else should be getting crushed in hugs and cried over, ordered to call daily, to have fun but not too much fun, yeah?

Tara can't wait to get out of here, so she won't be reminded another day what's been taken from her family.

Just the desk to go. Tara opens the bottom drawer, emptying its contents onto a heap of drained markers and crunched receipts she should have tossed months ago.

She braces for what's inside. A cheap, ruffled polyester flower crown from Pixieland. Crumbling rocks and shells from the coast, still sandy. Three sweatshirts, pilled from daily wear, half the size she is now. A box made of uneven scrap wood, clunking when it collides with the other offal on the bed.

CW is scribbled in Sharpie on its side. She swats it off the pile.

The box rattles to the floor, knocking against the peeling bedpost on its way down.

Tara frowns at it.

She opens it.

Inside, a hemp necklace knotted with colored plastic beads. A map. A stack of letters, all but one sealed. She lets her thumb arc over their address.

She closes the box. She stomps down the stairs.

Alex is talking to her, asking about someone he sees outside. We live in an apartment complex, Lex. There's going to be strangers outside the house. Don't you remember the time that kid from 204 was running amok with a steak knife last spring? Just stay inside and keep your head down.

He peers out the blinds as Tara makes her march to the communal dumpster. The box is smaller than a loaf of bread, heavier than a cinder block on her mind. The wood grain burns its pattern into her palms. The unopened letters, preserved in the dark of the drawer like brand new, shuffle across each other with each step.

Tara reaches the dumpster. She wrinkles her nose. Stinks with late summer heat. Is she really going to condemn the box, for all its sins, to such a fate?

Yes. She's held onto its contents long enough. Nothing good has ever come of them. She lifts the lid.

A hand takes her arm.

She flinches. The hand belongs to a girl, standing at her side.

The box clatters to the concrete.

The girl recoils. She can't be older than eighteen. Her skin's the brown of dry dust, her russet hair in a tousled bun, her chestnut eyes blurred with tears as they search Tara's own. An oversized beige shirt and khaki shorts hang off her skinny frame.

Tara wants to sink into the sidewalk.

"Tara," breathes the girl, grabbing Tara's shoulder like a cliff's edge. The girl smears her wrist across her eyes. She sniffs up snot. "Sorry," she says. "You have to remember me, don't you?"

Tara hears her family's van rumble up the lot. Tom and Rebecca have pulled up from their monthly shopping trip.

They shout for the boys to unload the trunk. Where's your sister? Stacks of bulk pasta and rice, bags of frozen vegetables, a box of popsicles that their mother insists the kids only eat once of per day, please. David doesn't even acknowledge the girl at Tara's side. Alex smiles an apology and follows to help heave a chuck roast into the kitchen for their dad to butcher.

Tara watches her family. She turns to the girl, Leah Ayala, who hasn't been seen for ten years.

Leah lets go of Tara's arm. She stumbles over the lawn. Tara stares after her sister.

Tom Ayala hefts a box of Costco chicken onto one knee. He cocks a brow at the girl running up to him.

"Dad?" Leah asks, grasping her father's arm. Her nails bite into Tom's tattoos. It's the same sleeve he had when he'd married her mother, the ink having since run his roses and skulls into barely decipherable smudges. His jet black hair has long since grayed at the temples.

He wrenches away. Rebecca Ayala calls after the boys to be careful with those eggs. Seeing her oldest daughter doesn't even register for her. She mutters after Tom. Tom just grumbles about weird kids these days. Maybe this is a new YouTube challenge he's not hip to?

The trunk closes. The van is empty. The boys and their parents go inside the apartment where Tara lives in a room far too large and lived in for just one kid. An apartment where there are pencil marks on the door frame that none can claim, because they were taller than any Ayala child in memory had ever been. Halls where there are photos of a smiling girl no one but Tara can seem to see.

"It didn't work," Leah says.

"I know," Tara gets out.

"I thought it might work."

"I know," Tara repeats. Tara has always known. She's the only one who's ever been able to know.

She takes her shivering sister by the elbow. She walks Leah to the overflow parking.

On their walk Leah picks up the box, now splintered on one corner.

Leah's index traces the letters. CW. Tara takes the steering wheel, her Nissan idle.

Tara had almost made it out. Maybe she'll never be free from what happened, not really. But she might have driven far enough away it couldn't reach her anymore.

Instead she's still in Del Bosque, mere hours' drive from Camp Cottonwood. Instead her sister, last seen as a counselor at that camp, shudders out silent gasps and chugs a stale water bottle from Tara's center console.

Their parents are peeking through the kitchen blinds. They begrudgingly accepted Tara when she informed them she's a lesbian. The thought of them arguing if the supposed stranger in the car is her secret girlfriend or not makes her want to spit out the car window. She rolls one down and does so.

Her mother's eyes vanish behind the white vinyl slats. David and Alex need supervision. Tara does not. Tara's an adult now.

Not that this means her parents don't insist she can stay home as long as she likes. Her parents can't bear to part with her, though she doubts they can tell her why they hold on so tight. That's why she's learned. They can't see or remember what's missing from their lives. But they can still feel the hole.

Leah digs a bandana from the glove compartment. She blows her nose. She drops it into a wad to the floorboard.

She sniffs. "I'm okay," she manages. "I'm just glad you never moved. I can't believe you're older than me," she chuckles. Her eyes are red and puffy from crying, clearing as they examine Tara head to toe. "So, 2019? This is the future."

Tara nods.

Leah laughs, voice thick. She's got the same bray belonging to their mom, to Tara herself.

"And no one else remembers me?"

Tara sighs. She squeezes her eyes shut. "How are you back?" she asks. "How are you… you?"

Leah isn't listening. Leah's opening the box.

Tara reaches over to stop her, too late.

Leah twirls the hemp necklace around her fingers. She looks at the folded map, crunched and crinkled. She squints at a letter's address. Bug Nursery. 1315 Dianthus Drive. Bonny, California.

Tara presses into the scratchy seat cover. She can't meet Leah's eyes. Can't accept she's real, not yet. Leah looks too unaltered, too much the same when Tara's older than her sister's body ever got to be.

She really thought she could get out of this. She really thought she'd be able to put this all behind her, regret in the rearview as the past shrank in her wake.

She did it before. Look how that's turned out.

The name above the address turns Tara's stomach.

"Tara?" Leah asks. "Does June remember?"

2

June Bug bounced down from her Grandma Betty's Ford, suitcase rattling over the gravel road. Tara and Leah Ayala, ten and eighteen, waited among the crowd of other kids bidding their guardians goodbye. You could tell campers and staff from their families by their matching Camp Cottonwood sweatshirts. 2009's were deep brown, the camp's puffy cloud logo embroidered on the right breast. June's hemp necklace swung under her collar, laden with plastic and clay beads for every adventure in '07 and '08.

She recognized Tara by how she wore her own sweatshirt: a size too large, big and baggy as possible, hands disappeared into the sleeves unless she was drawing. She waved her sleeve at June and tugged Leah toward the Ford.

Leah and Betty exchanged hellos. Both chuckled as June tackled Tara with a hug.

"I missed you so much!" June squealed.

Tara laughed. June squished their cheeks together. She could feel Tara's blush, even if she couldn't see it on her face when she drew away.

She sized up how Tara had grown. "I'm taller again! Ha!" June crowed.

Tara blew a raspberry.

"Can't believe you're taking on both of them this year," Betty said to Leah, shaking her head. Her eyes sparkled. She didn't mean nothing by it, bending over the passenger's seat to see the gathered girls. "Are you sure you can handle my Junie?"

Leah smiled. "Definitely, Ms. Bug. You're going to want to keep moving. See you in August?"

Betty nodded. She saluted to June, who saluted back. Then Betty continued up the drive, though not without calling for the kids to behave themselves. Her truck rumbled down the gravel before any impatient parents could honk at her.

June couldn't help watching until the truck's bumper disappeared into the trees. Tara nudged her. "Come on," she snorted. "We've still gotta pick our bunks. Do you want top or bottom?"

"Ooooh," June said. She tapped her chin, wiggling the handle of her suitcase in thought. "You like to read at night, so maybe I take the bottom? Then the ceiling light will be right there for you."

"Or," Leah said, "you can both be top bunks." She winked. "You get your own room. No need for applause, please. How was your year, June?"

June jumped in place. "Did Tara tell you? We live on a farm now," she said proudly. "I get to help grow the lavender."

"What variety?" Leah asked. "Royal Velvet? Melissa? I bet she does Buena Vista for the you picks."

"Nerd," Tara fake coughed.

"What?" Leah said. She smirked at her sister's ribbing. Her hands fell on Tara's shoulders, her smile mischievous. "This one has a looooot of art to show you."

"I have a normal amount," Tara mumbled from behind her sketchbook.

June was leaning on Tara's shoulder. "Show me when we get to our room," she said. "Who else is gonna be in Madrone?"

Leah vogued. "Other than me?"

"Other than you!" Tara said, giving her sister a playful shove. Leah tugged her into a side hug. Tara scowled, her long hair mussed from its ponytail. Leah's taut bun didn't lose a single, severe strand. But Leah smiled until Tara smiled back.

They ambled past the mess hall to the cabins, their own bubble in a sea of kids. Camp Cottonwood held activities for Grades 3 through 5. The rest of the year, the property hosted a conservation center for the purposes of building biodiversity in the Pacific Northwest. No loggers or lobbyists permitted, and enough underbrush management that there never seemed to be wildfires in these woods. For years, all campaigning to get the conservation status revoked had failed to stick. Talk would trend, then die off with the next crisis of the week.

At least according to June's grandmother, who worked at the center before she planted her nursery. In 2007, when June came to live with her, she sent June here to make friends. Grandma Betty would be right up the hill, diagnosing pathogens on various plants and pests.

In her first week here, June had been recruited by Haylee Pierce. The Bugs living in Bonny made June the prime target for the tyrant of Amarante Elementary. Children outside Del Bosque didn't know Haylee Pierce's game, so they quickly caught her interest before her ire. Her and her cohorts, Mandy and Tyese, would snap up every new kid. Sit at their tables. Help them in games and crafts. June was eager to please and excited to play with girls her age.

Of course Tara had already learned to keep to herself at Amarante. She may have grown up with Haylee Pierce, immune to this particular dumping cycle. That didn't mean she was safe, though. Haylee Pierce had a habit of stealing whatever was in your hand and putting it on display for all to mock, so Tara guarded her sketchbook zealously and stayed far from the line of fire.

Haylee Pierce's backhanded compliments failed to land at first. Day after day, June's optimism couldn't be tarnished. Tara sighed and bet June would be discarded by July. Maybe they'd get to know each other once Haylee Pierce dropped the new kid from her jaws. Or, worse, brought her fully into the fold.

Their fates met at the zipline.

Tara had known there would be a zipline. The brochure her sister brought home had said so. It never said the activity was mandatory. The other kids queued up and chattered like zooming hundreds of feet down a stretch of forest was the most ordinary ritual in the world. Before she saw it in person, Tara thought she could handle it.

Standing below the climbing wall, she couldn't handle it. Her hands cupped her elbows. A's always had to go first. Jake Adderly and Zoe Atkins climbed without complaint. When they jumped off the edge, they were whooping and howling with the thrill. If jumping off the edge was all it took, Tara might have been fine.

But they harnessed her up, and she saw how scuffed the chains were. The straps were frayed. The ladder to take her up was patched where rungs had broken, repaired by black electrical tape and two by fours.

Tara's eyes welled on the first step. She hiccuped, climbing higher and higher. If she got far enough from the ground, no one would see her losing her nerve. She wouldn't be embarrassing Leah, for being a coward wussing out of something everyone did no matter their misgivings.

There was no escape, though. Mandy pointed up and said, "Are you crying, Tara?"

"Ugh, what a wimp," Tyese groaned.

"She's going to make the line even longer now," Haylee Pierce said. "They should get her down. She's not gonna make it."

June Bug, tucked in the B's, was visible even from this high up.

"You guys suck," June said.

"What? She's the one bawling like a baby," Haylee Pierce scoffed.

"She's scared, you jerk!"

"You don't have to defend her," Tyese stagewhispered. She wanted Tara to hear this. "We all know she was too poor to get in."

"Maybe she'll go home. She shouldn't even be here," Haylee Pierce laughed.

June's face was red as a tomato. Haylee Pierce waited for June to give in and agree.

June pushed Haylee Pierce to the ground.

"Bitch!" Haylee Pierce shrieked.

The counselors smelled blood in the water. They were upon Haylee Pierce, dusting her off and completely distracted by the sound of a swear.

June was being told she didn't get to have a zipline ride. She would go to the bottom of the hill and wait for people who had already jumped. If she behaved herself, maybe she'd get to try again later that summer.

Tara smeared a hand across her dripping nose. She couldn't stifle her laughter.

When Tara reached the bottom, flying through the foliage like a snotty blue jay, June was down there to hug her. Tara would never forget it.

Unfortunately, neither would the other campers. June was in trouble, though she didn't act like it. Haylee Pierce refused to go anywhere near her, already spinning the rumor mill. June Bug was fat, anyway. She was a hick who couldn't even tell when she was being made fun of. Haylee Pierce only snickered when June cracked jokes because she thought June was stupid. June was a trusting idiot, being openly merciful in a treacherous pecking order. When she learned what a creep Tara Ayala was, they'd both be joyless and alone for the rest of the summer.

But Tara had never had a friend like June. Someone who wasn't friends with her out of proximity, like the kids in her apartment complex or the ones she sat beside in class. June had chosen to be her friend. For all Tara's fear June would drift away to the next reject who caught her eye, June never did.

And June was funny. The ornithologist from the conservation center brought owl pellets for the kids to dissect. He'd claimed you could eat them, swallowing what appeared to be a log of bones and fur to a chorus of ew's. June spat out her own pellet when he panicked and revealed he'd just eaten an Almond Roca as a prank. Tara was slapping the picnic table to hide her giggles.

It wasn't perfect. Haylee Pierce's terrorism was petty but effective. June could hang out with Tara all she wanted, and she did. But the other kids from Del Bosque knew the consequences. They'd only loosen up as the summers passed, though assured there would be no second chances if June defied Haylee Pierce again.

By 2009, it was mostly forgotten what made June a pariah. The stain on her reputation remained, but it was fading. She planned for her Cottonwood career to go out with a bang. What could go wrong? Leah would be here to protect them. She and Betty had vouched for the friends sharing a cabin, so they'd stop sneaking out to visit each other at night like they'd done the last few seasons.

The cabins at Camp Cottonwood were named after trees. There was the Cottonwood cabin where the directors, Tino Medina and Marydale Barlowe, stayed. No doubt the two of them would be drinking on the porch swing after a long day corralling wards for the summer. In a ring around the campfire were the camper cabins: Alder, Beech, Cedar, Maple, Oak, Rowan, and Madrone.

June followed the Ayalas to Madrone. A few campers were waving to them. Next to willowy, quiet Tara, June always caught attention first. She had an orange mass of curls like a lion's mane, big round glasses, and a smattering of freckles like she'd just been splatter-painted. At the friendly faces she waved her whole arm, threatening to throw it out of socket.

Tara kept to Leah's shadow. She actually looked like Leah in shadow, her skin tawny and her hair so dark it shone black. Her eyes were just as dark, like damp soil. June fell back to grasp her hand through her sweatshirt sleeve.

Leah introduced them to the rest of their cabin. June mingled with Gabi Lorenzo, Vanessa Schmidt, and a girl in her first year who they knew to be Brody C's sister.

Tara got to work setting up her bunk. She had her special Pokémon blanket, one of those tie-together fleeces Leah helped her make. Her dingy stuffed rabbit, Villain, was placed on the pillow. Before being squashed under the pillow, set on the pillow, then finally settled in a hard to see corner of the bed by the wall.

Force of habit, given she and June were getting this bunkbed and two whole others to themselves. Leah mentioned a slow season due to the recession, so she could dole out such a treat.

June was sitting on the bottom bunk, kicking her legs and shouting into the bathroom at the other girls. They'd be sharing a toilet and shower like usual. The bathroom connected the two bedrooms, which were in turn connected to a common room no one really used aside from counselors or visiting parents.

While the other girls unpacked, June rambled to Brody C's sister- Grace C, because there were at least two other Graces- about how she once bit Brody in a food fight gone awry. Gabi and Vanessa paired off on their bunk and cut June a wide berth. They'd tell Grace C how June was weird and not to be engaged with later.

Leah was bopping her head to the radio as she restocked toilet paper. Her own bunk had been set up for a week now. Staff came early to train and prepare curriculum. Leah made the drive even earlier than the other teens. More than once in the last three years Betty spotted Leah hovering around the conservation center, hassling biologists and botanists to let her in for hands-on experience.

Her plan to be a park ranger honestly gave Betty hope, she'd confided to June. Most other counselors were aspiring actors, comedians, or teachers. Leah could build connections here to get into the center once she finished her time as counselor. Plus Leah's benefits included the family discount. If not for Leah being on payroll, there was no way the Ayalas could have sent their second daughter along.

When Tara finished her blanket nest for the night, Leah was standing in the doorway. She shut the door to the bathroom behind her.

June had gotten distracted. She was clipping pieces of Game Informer to be taped to the walls. Neither of the girls had ever played the grownup games depicted in its glossy magazine pages, but they liked the RPG monsters contained within. Leah sat on the bed and began braiding Tara's hair while Tara knelt on the floor.

"I wanted to ask you something," Leah said.

Tara nodded, not really listening. A creature design caught her eye and she pointed for June to clip it free. June grinned and did so, tongue sticking out in her focus.

"Do you remember Mr. Valdez?" Leah asked. "The groundskeeper?"

Tara shrugged. June frowned.

"What do you remember about him?" Leah's voice was low.

"Um," Tara said. She really wanted to help June decorate. Sure, they had all summer to make their room perfect. But this was a rare time the campers weren't expected at mess or demonstrations or any other scheduled activities. June even brought a Nintendo DS this year, too. A gift from Betty, with the new handheld Guitar Hero and Super Princess Peach.

But Leah was looking at Tara, and Tara wracked her brain. "He's nice?" she tried. "He speaks Spanish." Their dad did, too, even if Tara didn't know all the words.

"Anything else?"

"He's got a cowboy hat," Tara recalled. "And a mustache. Why? Did he get fired?"

"No," Leah said. "No, he didn't. Thanks, Tara. I was starting to think I was the only one who remembered him."

Tara grimaced. She didn't want to be talking about this. She wanted her summer with June, in their same cabin with their same classes. All the kids who tolerated Tara back home couldn't afford Cottonwood. June's mom had ditched her to live with Betty, something that put her on the wrong foot with kids back in rural Bonny. They were the bright spot in each other's lives, and they only got three months aside from letters during the school year to share it. Tara was determined to make the most of it.

Leah heard bickering in the other room. She sighed. On her way through the bathroom, she reset her loosening bun in the mirror. "Make sure you're ready for dinner on time," she called behind her.

Tara gave her sister a raised brow.

June tugged on her sleeve. "Hey! I still wanna see your sketches," she said.

Tara pulled out her sketchbook. She flopped down beside June.

They flipped through the slightly rough pages reverently. "These are amazing," June said.

"No, they're not. See all the erasing?"

"You're getting really good!" June insisted. "This one? I like her face. Did you freehand all these?"

June was pointing to a fairy drawn in pencil. Tara had mirrored it from the cover of a book she'd checked out from the library. This particular artist always made Tara long for watercolors, though she didn't feel as confident in her strokes as the illustrator must have.

Still, Tara tried. Along with the beasts she found in books or magazines, she'd made up a few of her own. June loved her little gnome with a tail, like a mouse in a conical hat and ragged clothes. "He's so cute! What's his name?" June asked.

"Her name is Lucinda," Tara said softly. "She's a girl gnome. All gnomes have beards."

"I want a beard," June whined, yanking on her curls. "I like her braids."

On and on they talked. They'd annoyed many a counselor and fellow camper. But whenever they got together like this, shame couldn't penetrate their fortress. It couldn't at the mess hall, and at the welcome bonfire, and late into the night.

In their beds, catching up on everything they didn't say in their letters, they did not hear Leah leave.

3

Bug Nursery is hard to miss. First off, it's the only business on Dianthus Drive, surrounded by sprawling fields and sturdy greenhouses for over a mile in every direction.

Second, it's the only business where a giant welded T-Rex stands sentry over the main off-ramp. Its lime green metal scales are eye-searing enough to see through freeway traffic. Frilled around its neck are the petals of a spray-painted tin daisy. If Betty Bug wants to draw in roadside looky loos, she's crafted quite the spectacle.

Tara pulls her Nissan into a sea of sedans and SUVs, broken up by cages of dirty plastic carts. Along the asphalt paths are even more sculptures. A junkyard centaur, hoe and rake in either hand, guards the entrance. Flocks of technicolor parrots and flamingos are mounted over long tables of starts and sprouts, their wings and claws flared open wide.

They park in the rear lot. Leah stirs, having dozed on the ride over. She'd been so exhausted, she didn't tell Tara anything aside from how she hitchhiked to Del Bosque. Within five minutes Tara glanced over to see her sister sacked out in the passenger's seat.

Tara had tossed a blanket over Leah and let her sleep. At least the silence meant Tara didn't have to explain why most of her room was packed into this car.

Now Leah yawns. "This is it?" she asks.

Must be. Maybe June's gone off to college or moved out on her own. Maybe she's states away.

Tara sighs. Maybe she won't have to do this at all. "I'll go in," she says.

Leah nods. The barn, painted in peeling magenta, awaits.

Tara climbs out. She knocks an old coffee cup from the Nissan to the weedy pavement. She tosses it back in through the window, taking one last glance at Leah rubbing her eyes in shotgun, and walks for the entrance.

It's been long enough that a bouquet or bed of roses shouldn't bother her like they used to. Yet she barely keeps from bristling at all these plants on display tables, lining the walkways, reaching down from hanging baskets to brush the top of her head.

She holds her breath and twists her hoodie's drawstrings, grounding herself in the fabric's fibers. There's a lot of crowd to push through, not to mention dodging clay

gnomes in sunglasses or teetering towers of terracotta pots.
She almost trips on a birdbath before she makes it to the barn's
double doors.

Within the barn there's even more to overwhelm her
senses. She stumbles past a cafe nook, where people line up
for ice cream to beat this heat. Its tables and chairs are shoved
to the corner by racks of every sort of trinket and tchotchke
under the sun, which shines through the plexiglas skylights
spaced evenly in the roof. Flags embroidered with sayings like
"fall down six times, get up seven" and "I love my gourden"
sway from the ceiling between. Trees of greeting cards,
stickers, magnets, and postcards dance left and right as tourists
select their obligatory souvenir from this stop.

At the head of the barn is the sales counter. Tara
almosts breaks a teapot shaped like a frog, rattling its matching
set of tadpole teacups, to reach it.

She cuts to the front of its zigzag queue.

The woman being checked out stops mid-rant. The
employee opens his mouth to tell Tara off, but she shouts over
the din. "I have someone I need you to call for me," she says.
"June Bug. Is she here?"

"Who wants to know?" barks an old lady, filling a
lavender sachet. She wears a muddy apron over a shirt with the
Bug Nursery logo. Her hands go to her hips, looking down her
nose at the line-cutter.

"Betty?" Tara asks. She shakes her head. "I need to
talk to June."

Betty furrows her brow. Tara waits for the recognition to enter her eyes. Then Betty's speaking into a walkie unclipped from her waist.

She beckons Tara into the backroom behind the counter.

The backroom may be a maze of boxed knick knacks, but it's better than the pandemonium of this farmstand in August. Tara ducks out of the fray and pants against the door, gripping her hoodie.

Her relief doesn't last long. What's she going to say if June is here? Hopefully Betty's sent her here to say June is miles away, beyond the grasp of Cottonwood.

Part of Tara would be disappointed, but that's for the best. Leah won't let it go so easily, though. Why? Does she actually believe June will want to see them after all these years? Whatever she thinks, Leah will just have to give it up if there's no June to be found.

"Excuse me!"

Tara presses to the wall, narrowly ducking out of an employee's path.

"I'll be there in a minute, gran," she hears. The woman striding by, sacks of peat over her shoulder like they're full of feathers, pivots and offers Tara a grin. "Sorry," she adds. "You lost?"

Tara can't move. That carrot orange hair, buzzed to a pomp. The round glasses, magnifying brown eyes, on a pale freckled face. She's bigger, older, more butched out in her denim boilersuit and hardy boots than she'd ever been as a rambunctious child.

Thick gloves patterned in bees cover her fingers. She lowers the peat onto a pile of others, letting her hands rest at her hips. "Oh!" she says. "Are you the one who asked for me?"

Tara nods.

June wipes sweat from her forehead. "Great," she says.

She's giving Tara the once over. Twice over. She whistles. Her eyes flicker to the doorway, like she's waiting for Tara to introduce herself or step aside. Is Tara really so unrecognizable? She never got over her lack of style, donning baggy jeans and a comfy hoodie. She fiddles with the drawstring on the hoodie she's wearing now, an emerald U of O swag sweatshirt.

Maybe it's the hair? Unlike Leah's russet curls, Tara has their father's jet black color and slightly wavy texture. She has it clipped short, kept to an inch-long ponytail at the back of her head.

"Wait," June finally says. Tara freezes. "Tara?"

Tara nods again. She brushes a loose strand behind her ear.

June shakes something from her pomp. The muscles in her raised arm draw Tara's eye, how the bicep bulges and works against the hem of her short sleeve.

"I didn't think you'd, uh," June says. "What have you been up to?" she asks.

Tara plucks the cartoon duck on her hoodie. "School, mostly. You're still here."

"Yeah," June says. She slouches against the pile of peat, arms crossed. Oh god, has she seen where Tara's looking? "My grandma's got her hands full these days. People found out we exist, I guess."

"Right." Tara averts her eyes. She's definitely staring. If she keeps staring, she's just going to make this more awkward than it needs to be.

Like this was never going to be awkward. She almost gulps when June makes eye contact again.

"What about you?" June asks.

Tara can do this. All she has to do is say it. Leah is in the car, right now.

"Me? School, like I said." Great job, Tara.

June stands there, hands in her pockets, grin frozen to her face. "Your brothers must be pretty big now," she tries.

Tara rubs her eyes on her hoodie cuff. She just has to say it.

"Look, June. I need you to come with me."

June peels up from the peat.

Tara walks farther into the backroom. Does it matter who hears what Tara's about to tell June? No one else can remember, June included if her first letter could be called confirmation. There'd been nothing in it, no reference to Leah or camp or more than just miscellany. Normalcy. June deserves to keep it, instead of joining Tara.

If she even can. If she can't, then what Tara says won't make a difference. No harm, no foul. So why can't she dig the words from her chest?

Tara paces. June is staring now. Tara stalls before she can kick over one of those wet foam bricks you stab flower arrangements into.

"Um. Okay? Just so you know, I never got any of your letters," June admits. "Alex and David, are they okay? You never said if your mom and dad-"

"I didn't send any letters," Tara says.

"Oh."

Fuck.

"That makes more sense," June says. "I know mine never got anything back. Which is totally fine, you have a life and all. Thanks for coming here on your way to Oregon! I hope you like it there."

"June," Tara says.

June's hands go behind her back. She's already walking away, stepping further into the stacks. "I think Betty's calling me. Good luck with school."

Then June turns a corner and she's gone. There's no relief, no untangling the knot in Tara's chest. If anything it wads up tighter, threatening to choke her. She can't get the truth to come up from the pit of her stomach, to call out what's changed.

But nothing has. Tara lets her go. Better to cut June off than drag her deeper down.

June's legs were falling asleep.

She shifted in her crouch behind the cottonwoods, watching a small opening in a thicket. This thicket lay just at the end of the creek that ran a jagged vein from here to the lake southwest. The zipline lay north, the entrance of the camp dead south, and the conservation center campus another few miles further down. Camp Cottonwood connected them all with gravel roads and well-tended hiking paths.

None of these paths crisscrossed northeast, though. No one maintained this side of the woods, so June had to trample ferns and bramble to keep up with Tara.

Who had gone through the thicket, into whatever lay beyond. June had followed her here.

From the moment they woke up, on day two of their summer, Tara had been acting off. She'd been asking for someone named Leah. The other Madrone girls, Gabi and Vanessa and Grace C, made fun of her. June told them to shut up, but she admitted herself that she didn't know Tara had a sister. She sounded nice! If she was half as cool as Tara, Leah had to be awesome.

Tara had looked at her like a wounded animal. She seemed so betrayed. What a peculiar prank. Her and June spent a week last year pretending they were aliens from another planet, but June had been in on the bit.

And it had been a bit. They'd dropped the joke once they got bored.

Instead Tara accused June of being mean to her. Of getting the other girls in Madrone in on it. But when she asked Tino where their counselor was, the director realized he hadn't assigned them one.

June couldn't deny it was weird. Why didn't they have a counselor? Must not have been enough staff this year, what with the economy Betty kept lamenting. June didn't quite know how the economy affected this just yet. She did understand it to be why she hadn't gotten the same hubbub around birthday and Christmas this year, and that adults blamed money when they lacked enough people or supplies.

Money had nothing to do with why Tara didn't talk to her anymore. They got a new counselor, breezy Britney, to fill the empty position. Britney let June and Tara keep their separate bedroom all to themselves, though she stored some of her luggage on one of the unused bunks.

They were in the same room. They could have been in separate dimensions for how Tara ghosted her. When they would usually be up through the night talking, Tara would be shining a flashlight on a planner she'd dug from the counselor's nightstand. She would be tracing the lines of a map, annotated at the margins in a scrawl June didn't recognize.

At activities, Tara was sullen and silent. She wouldn't be cajoled by June. Wouldn't show June her art. Wouldn't bray at June's antics. Wouldn't even react to Haylee Pierce calling her a schizo for pretending to have a secret sister who worked here.

June stood up, fists slammed on the fold-out table they used for demonstration. Haylee Pierce was a bully. June had shut her up before for Tara, and she'd do it again.

But Tara didn't even care. She just kept studying the map under her worksheet. She pulled it out on hikes, when she could pass it off as checking for directions, yet June could make out a few of the words. *Mower found here. Possibly N?* When June looked over Tara's shoulder, Tara would fold the map up and jog further down the trail.

The cabin should have been their reprieve. Whenever Haylee Pierce and Mandy and Tyese picked on them, Madrone was supposed to act as sanctuary. June laid in her bed below Tara. Was this going to be their whole summer?

Friday night, June woke to Tara's feet fumbling down the ladder. June stayed quiet. She could feel the air tense, Tara letting the room and the bedframe settle before slipping her sneakers on over her pajamas.

June waited. She watched Tara slip out the window.

She wiggled her fingers at each other. Had she just seen Tara sneak out? But they shared a room now! They didn't even have to sneak out to see each other anymore!

Which meant that unlike in '07 and '08, they didn't have anyone expecting them to escape their bunks.

June slid on her boots. She climbed out to follow Tara with no trouble at all. Guards did not patrol the night. Camp Cottonwood was no troubled teen ranch. Still, she crept like a thief along the cabin walls, employing her practiced stealth from midnights past.

It'd taken a half hour of walking. June was honestly more sore from the lurking, staying out of Tara's flashlight beam. If Tara refused to tell her what was wrong, June would have to do this in secret. It added an air of adventure to the whole affair, anyway. Maybe Tara had a good reason to be acting like they didn't know each other.

That had been around 4am. Now light sparkled over the creek's burbles, streaming through the trees in beams. Only cottonwood seeds, drifting the air like late spring snow, broke up the rays.

June was drooling on her fist, scrunched up in the bracken below the cottonwoods, when Tara finally emerged from the hole in the thicket. June managed not to make a sound.

Tara didn't linger. She was already treading the creek, headed back towards camp.

June waited until Tara was out of sight. She didn't dare ask about it, not after how Tara had been acting. What if Tara thought June was gonna snitch on her? Like she would ever, since they had the same record of daring escapes. But that had been before, when Tara would tell her things.

This had to be a solo investigation then. June stretched her pins and needles away and approached the hole in the thicket. She climbed through.

Thorns caught on her fleece pajama pants. Her middle almost got stuck like Winnie the Pooh, then she tumbled to the grass. She spat out a twig and huffed. Adventuring was not as glamorous as she'd imagined.

When she staggered up, the grass was up to her stomach. A meadow of bee balm and bluestem swayed in the morning chill. This meadow extended into a dense treeline.

How had she not seen these trees from the other side of the thicket? They were papered birches, gargantuan as redwoods, the crown shy canopy stories high and blotting out the sky. She touched one as she delved deeper, spreading her hand over the flaking bark. In '08 a dendrochronologist had shown the kids how to date a tree by its rings. Would this tree have a blackened core, to be so big?

June's scalp prickled. As she pushed on, the trees seemed to be hemming her in. If she looked behind her, the meadow faded to blotches and smears. She wouldn't even be able to see the thicket anymore.

On and on she walked. She walked until the trees parted.

At the end of the birches was a clearing, where a hedge sloped and swirled through a wrought iron gate, threatening to spill from its fence. An exuberant garden flowed from the hedge to surround a house that soared into the branches above like a castle, made of seamless stucco and two cylindrical stone towers. To its left, a domed greenhouse of iron and frosted glass.

She didn't see any signs of life aside from the plants. If this house was abandoned, no one would mind her going in and looking, right?

While she couldn't squeeze between the gate's bars, she found they were spaced out wider on the rest of the fence. The hedge was dense, but not enough to stop her entry. Her sweatshirt snagged on the arborvitae, and then June was through.

She had to army crawl to get under the roses just beyond. Her orange hair got petals in it, curls tangling on the thorns above her head. Something else snagged on her hair, too. It tickled, tapping her like little legs.

She reached up and hoped it was a spider.

The something else wound itself around her hand.

June's knees were starting to ache again. She paused mid-crawl in the rose bushes. What had looped her finger was a root-like appendage. Connected to it were a dozen others, radiating from a central bulb with flowers atop its knobbly head. Its two beady black eyes blinked at June.

When another root wrapped around her finger, it was warm. These limbs reminded her of carrots she'd seen Betty yank from their yard once, the asymmetrical ones that were pink and peach and thinner than she'd ever seen in a produce section.

She slid all the way down to her belly. Slipping through gaps in the bushes were more and more of these fairies. They had to be fairies, didn't they? No wings, their roots grappling from stick to stick or over the dirt clods to get around, but what else could she call them?

One, a butterfly-sized fairy with closed white hypericum buds sprouting off its head, lassoed itself to her hair. It nestled on her head like a crown. June nodded so the fairy dangled before her eyes. The fairy stayed tethered where June could see it.

"Nice to meet you," she told it. "You're beautiful. Can you understand me? Beautiful?"

"What are you doing here?" the fairy asked. It spoke in a whisper.

June froze. "Ah."

"Ah?"

June's mouth opened, closed, twitched with the urge to squeal. Fairies! Talking to her! She began to eee until a leaf pressed to her lips.

"Now you stop that," another fairy, this one grown from a pink tulip, told her.

"Eeeee," June repeated, quieter.

"He's going to hear you," the hypericum fairy warned. On its tiny face were those beady black eyes, its words spoken from a thin mouth like a cut in the bulb given motion.

June rested her cheek on her palm. "Who?"

"The master."

"The gardenkeeper," said another fairy to her right.

"He lords over this place," said another voice in the bush above.

"Oh," June says. "Is he nice?"

Laughter filled the rose bush. Fairies of all species of flower and weed, of lichen and moss and even pebbles strung together like a beaded necklace. June wanted to hug all of them to her chest. Her legs kicked behind her. The surreality of it all was making her giddy.

A fairy over her ear said, "He is."

"To us," the tulip fairy scoffed.

"The master hates humans," a fairy wearing a stargazer lily like a tutu said.

"Steals them," grumbles a mossy stone.

"Not anymore," the tulip said, rolling its eyes.

"I'm getting mixed signals here," June said. "But you guys are nice, right?"

"Oh, yes!"

"Very nice!"

"You seem nice, human,"

"Awww, thanks," June replied. She gently scooped up the fairies in her hair and rolled over, careful not to crush anyone. The fairies examined her.

"Interesting," the hypericum breathed.

"Your face."

"Hands."

"Humans are funny things, aren't they?" the stargazer murmured.

June spread the hand that held this fairy. "Right?" she told her. "Super weird. I like you guys. Could you tell me more about this master, though? He's good to you?"

"Very good."

"Very kind."

"But not to you."

"Go!"

"Out!"

"You're not safe," the stones managed.

"What about Tara?"

"What's a Tara?" the stargazer asked.

"Tara?" the hypericum cried.

"Never mind," June told them. She sat up, her curls even more ensnared in thorns. She winced and tugged them out. "I'm probably wrong. So you don't get a lot of humans here?"

"No."

"Never."

"You should leave."

"Go, human."

The fairies were pushing against her, their appendages fighting June into the eaves of the bush. Roots were surprisingly strong! June's cheek got scratched on a thorn and she flailed out of the flowers. She sat sprawled, legs out in front of her. "Hey! Rude!"

She hadn't been shoved back through the wrought iron gate, though. She was now on a pebble path. On the path were two clawed feet.

She looked up. The creature standing above her was very much not a fairy she'd have seen in watercolor illustrations.

Not in Tara's drawings, either. It was a lizard on its hind legs, equal parts rock and wood. Two arms and a leg made of a sturdy black rock, its second leg and torso made up of a dark oak tree. A mossy cloak adorned its shoulders, its long tail lashing, its crystalline eyes flashing in its snake-like skull. A viney tongue crossed the shards of its teeth.

It rumbled. June skittered back.

A claw plucked up the back of her sweatshirt. She was getting carried toward the greenhouse. The cold crystal eyes of the creature barely regarded her, but June swore she heard a disgusted sigh from it.

And behind it she heard the rabble of fairies in the foliage now. Some clung to the creature's mossy cloak, eyes disapproving.

"Invader."

"Trespasser."

"What can the master do?"

The creature opened its other claw. The frosted greenhouse window cleared, swinging open.

June didn't get to peek inside before the fairies were protesting.

"You mustn't!"

"The deal."

"The game."

"Will all of you hush?" the creature rasped. With a flick of his tail, the lot of them were cast back to the bushes. "I don't have time for this. What's your excuse, human? Lost? Selling… what is it you sell?"

"I don't sell things. I'm a kid."

"Right," the creature said, voice clipped. "Fine, sprout. What is your reason for coming upon my property?"

"Your garden was pretty," June said. "I love flowers. I didn't know there were people here until I got in the bushes."

"So chatty. They don't know how to keep to themselves."

"They called you the master?" June's sweatshirt still hung in his grip. He carried her collar like the tail of a snake that might bite him, those shining black teeth held in perpetual grimace. "Can you put me down? I can walk."

The creature dropped her.

He grabbed her arm and hauled her to her feet. His silence allowed her to watch as the house beside the greenhouse passed. There were no doors on it, just open archways and empty stoops draped in ivy. The creature walked and walked and she stumbled along until they came to a pond. Green fish swam among hyacinth and frogbit. Lilies danced on the water's surface.

Then the creature jerked her to a stop.

He growled. He lashed his tail back and forth.

"Uh, I can leave," June said.

"No, you cannot," the creature intoned. "Let me make this plain to you, human. You are a nuisance to me. I cannot allow you to tell anyone what you've seen, yet I cannot make you forget it. So what do you propose I do with you?"

"Let me go?" Sunrise had gone beyond suggesting morning, a now bright blue sky visible here in an island where the trees didn't drown it out. Then again it was a Saturday morning when the campers were allowed to sleep in, but

Britney was going to discover she was gone if she didn't hurry back soon.

The creature curled a lip. His stone face was weirdly expressive, even more so than the stone fairy she'd just encountered. He leered over her. He prodded her side, lifted her arm, sniffed at her hair which she found unnecessary because of the stone face part. There were notches for nostrils that moved like he might be able to breathe, kinda, but could he even smell things?

He dragged the end of a talon down her hairline to the tip of her nose. She crossed her eyes following it. "No. No, I cannot do that. And I cannot do what I would with the rest of your kind, either."

"What's that?"

The creature's mouth took on a sharp smile. "I am called Weiss. What are you called?"

"Wise?"

"No."

She tasted the word. "Wait. Wice? Like edelweiss?"

"I am no flower," Weiss hissed.

"If it's edelweiss, you say it like vice. With a V."

Weiss seemed to be reconsidering his decisions. "Just tell me your name already."

June shook her head, raising her index. "Nuh uh. Aren't you a fairy? If I give you my name, you own me or whatever. Not gonna happen."

Weiss's eyes bored holes into her. "What gives you the impression that I'm a fairy?"

It was June's turn to stare.

"Do I look like a fairy to you?"

"Well, I mean. A troll. Or something." He was stone and wood, not flesh and blood, yet he had touched her. His supple claws wrapped around her wrist like a living gargoyle's. She rubbed her arm. "Alright. I don't know what kind of magic thing you are. But you're magic."

"Yes," Weiss agreed. "What told you that? When I opened the door without touching it?"

"More like your… you-ness." She waved to all of him.

"My what?"

"I don't know how to put it! You're magicky. Sorry."

"Very. And you should be. Is it out of fashion to ask before entering the premises in the human world?"

"No."

"Then why did you believe your rules did not apply?"

"I don't know! I thought no one lived here. Sorry," she repeated. "I only wanted to see your flowers. That's it."

"You enjoy them?" Weiss asked, bending down. He took a curl of her hair between two talons. Glassy obsidian shards tipped each.

June didn't let her eyes leave the sight.

"I like flowers a normal amount," she said.

"Pity," Weiss huffed, and tossed the curl back.

He turned and faced the water. His claws met behind his back, beneath his cloak. They were like a bearded dragon's, the fingers too long and short in the wrong places to be human hands.

He gazed into the pond.

June waited to be dismissed. But she'd been told she couldn't leave. "The camp's gonna notice I'm not there."

Weiss stilled his sweeping tail. "Yes," he said. "You are from the camp."

"See my sweatshirt?" June said.

Weiss glanced over his shoulder, as if trying to hide he was checking. Then he said, "So be it. I'll allow you to leave on one condition."

"Why do you get to pick?" she asked.

Weiss rumbled. June staggered.

"Because you snuck onto my property. I have a right to keep or remove you at my prerogative. Is that understood, sprout?"

June picked at her fingers, needling the dirt from under a nail. She nodded. She had trespassed, not that she thought that was wrong but there was a gate. Closed gates meant don't come in.

But she'd been following Tara! She didn't add this, however. She didn't want both of them in trouble.

"Okay," she said. "I'm ready to go then."

"You haven't heard my condition," Weiss snarled. He sighed. "You must return here tomorrow in the daylight. If you do not, I will seek you out. Do you understand?"

"Why?"

"It is none of your business why. I gave you my terms."

"That's not fair," June said. "I'm not doing that unless I get a reason. Do I get to play with your fairies if I come back?"

Weiss looked at the greenhouse. "Fine," he bit out. "You can entertain them while I work. You will assist me when you visit. Are we done here?"

June pumped a fist. "Yeah! I'll be back tomorrow," she told him.

"You are not to tell anyone where you've been," he added.

"Got it!" June called back, throwing a thumbs up behind her.

Weiss's heavy steps did not follow her out. Fairies poked their heads from the shrubs as she passed. She found the exit, unlatching the gate and running through the trees until the meadow rose into clear view.

So this had been the treasure Tara had been hunting on her map? Whatever her justification for keeping June in the dark, June would keep coming here. Maybe this was how June would learn what had gone so wrong between them.

5

Tara storms out. She won't let anyone touch her, bobbing and weaving through the crowd until she reaches the double doors and escapes the humid, human-filled barn. Doesn't matter that she keeps thinking she sees an orange pomp among the horde.

The surrounding plant life blurs by, then the parking lot. She's making a beeline for her Nissan. The lemon car can't do much, but it can get her out of sight so she can stew in how ridiculous she feels in peace and privacy.

She gets in. She turns the key. The car shudders alive, at great effort.

"She's not here?" Leah asks.

Tara shuts her eyes, arms hyperextended at the wheel. What does she do now? Even without June in the picture, she's got to go.

Leah takes her bicep. "Tara?"

"She's not coming with us. Okay?" Tara bites out.

Leah's grip loosens. "She's here?"

Tara gives a single nod. "And she's not coming with. She told me to get lost. Can we please go?"

She opens her eyes. Leah is shaking her head. "No. You two were best friends. You literally could not be split up. We put you-"

"On opposite ends of the mess, and we'd still be in each other's laps, anyway. We were ten, Leah." Tara feels the engine growl, her toe feathering the gas even in park. Leah hasn't been here. It's not her fault, but of course she's not going to understand that they aren't children anymore. "We grew up."

"I wanted to thank her," Leah says softly.

"For what?"

"You really told her about me," Leah says, "and she said no?"

Tara flinches.

Leah blinks.

Tara sputters, then presses her lips shut. She looks out the window. Her face burns.

"You didn't tell her?" Leah cries.

Before Tara can form a response, Leah is out of the car and slamming the door shut.

Tara checks her rearview. Leah's striding to the barn.

Shit. Tara shuts off the car and hops out, only to trip on the coffee cup again. She swipes the gravel from her palms and gets on Leah's trail.

As Tara braves the displays once more, Leah marches through them all resolute. Until she reaches the double doors. The crowd within mills and moves.

She's shaking. "We can just go," Tara tells her. Leah's face is ashen. She has to be struggling with so much stimulus. At least that's what Tara assumes. It's only fair if she can't handle all these people.

But then Leah takes a step forward. She plunges in.

Tara manages to get a grip on her sister's shirt, letting Leah lead them to the sales counter.

Betty sees them. At her side stands June, pinching her nose bridge and thumbing her eyes under her glasses. Betty pats June's arm. Her shoulder is out of Betty's reach, since June didn't get the little Bug genes. Instead of a hobbit, June is more of an Amazon.

Still June enough, though. Leah clocks her instantly.

She laughs, triumphant. "I can't believe she didn't tell you," she says, waving an arm for the Bugs' attention. "You're so big now!"

June looks between the Ayalas. She didn't even recognize Tara at first. Here's hoping Leah takes June forgetting her a bit better than she did their parents.

June vaults over the counter, knocking an earrings rack and a bucket of mints to the concrete. Leah is snatched off the ground in June's embrace. Leah shushes June. She squirms a hand under June's armpit to tap her back.

"You're big, too," June says, lowering Leah to the floor. She absorbs Leah as she did Tara. "Well, kinda. Bigger, but not older?"

"Yeah," Leah drawls. "It's not ideal. But, hey, 28 and I've still got this body? I have those secrets doctors don't want you to know about."

Betty comes around the counter to join June's left. She takes June's elbow in both hands. She boings a little on her feet. "Oh, Tara," she says, breathless. "I can't believe it."

Tara fidgets, strangling her drawstrings and glancing for the doors.

"I couldn't tell it was you, sweetheart," Betty says. "If I had, I… and this is…"

So Betty didn't recognize Tara either? She does now. She sidehugs June. June flushes. Leah gets the same treatment.

Tara tries to skirt the PDA, but Betty's orbit grows and she brings the other Ayala sister in. The old woman has lost weight in her age. She'd been larger than life when Tara was a kid, now barely coming up to Tara's chin and at least a head shorter than her own granddaughter. The hug's less soft than Tara remembers.

She's still paralyzed inside Betty's skinny arms. Tara doesn't deserve this reunion. Leah does, but from their own parents, not this acquaintance. Leah lets her chin rest on Betty's shoulder, though. Seems like she takes this as an acceptable substitute, if not the teaser trailer for familial hugs in future.

"Hold on," Tara realizes. "How do you remember Leah?"

Betty releases them after a kiss to each of their temples. Tara dodges the floral scented affection. Betty smiles and gestures to June. "I see you three have some catching up to do," she says.

June's face is bloody beet red, blotting out her freckles. A man grouses something at the counter, to which Betty scowls. She gathers the fallen earrings and mints into her apron. Cheerfully she tells the customers to simmer down now.

The line resumes, a few of them glaring at the interruption. Tara's body retreats into her hoodie.

June won't stop staring at her and Leah.

Leah loops her arm in June's. "You told her and it worked?" she asks.

"Yeah. Gran remembered when I told her," June says.

Tara's jaw pangs from clenching so tight. She chews her cheek. Amazing. Wonderful. Fanfuckingtastic. "She can know, but not our parents?" she asks.

June frowns. "But you're back," she says to Leah. "You're back, but they can't…"

Leah scratches the back of her neck. She shakes her head. "That's why we're here. They don't remember, but I knew you would have to. It's really good to see you again, June. You're so cute! I mean, you were always cute." She shimmies in place. "I can't believe you got Betty to remember me!"

June grins. She shows too many teeth. "Yup," she says. "I'm sorry to hear about your mom and dad. So you just want me to talk to them, or?"

"You don't have to," Leah says. "And you don't have to come back with me either. But it's changed. I promise. I mean, look at me!"

She spins. Leah's oversized shirt twirls like a floor length ball gown.

Tara avoids June's searching eyes. June is trying to suss out what Leah is saying, where any of this is leading to. But she has to know, right? Tara braces for June to duck out on Leah like she did Tara in the backroom.

June says nothing. She just reaches onto a shelf for a bundle of purple yarn. She tosses it to Leah, and it flops into a chunky knit sweater. Leah brings the sweater to her chest.

She lets her nose sink into the dyed wool. "Thanks."

"No prob," June says. "You look a little cold."

"Thanks," Leah says, with greater emphasis. "You don't even know what for yet, do you?"

June goes slack. She's mumbling, not quite processing what Leah means. Neither does Tara.

But both of them are taken by the wrist, Leah's new sweater slung under her armpit.

Before they go past the corner cafe, June digs her heels in. "Wait, wait!" she cries. "I'll go. I promise. I just," she says, putting up her hands. "I need a minute. We'll take my truck. It's better on the backroads. Wait here?"

Leah nods. She settles into one of the dining chairs, knocking her knees together. She's admiring a ficus beside the table. Tara can tell she's taking more deep breaths. Both sisters are prone to anxiety, but Tara can't fathom what Leah has speeding through her mind. Her first time out in public must be thrilling.

If overwhelming. Tara's feeling it, too. She leans against a support post.

"You want ice cream?" she asks Leah.

Leah looks up at her. "You didn't talk to her? All this time?" she asks.

Tara folds her arms. She looks away. What, didn't Leah see those letters in the car?

She had to have looked at June's first letter. They'd written so much between '08 and '09. June wrote this one much like she had in those previous years. Her words had been so casual, so ordinary. After everything, June had said she was fine. She'd spoken about Betty, about the nursery and Bonny, but nothing about camp. Nothing about that summer. Nothing about Leah.

Either she feared Betty would read it, or June had forgotten. Tara had never dared to open another letter to confirm which one it was.

It seems now it was neither.

June has disappeared into the backroom. She comes out carrying a backpack and a cooler. Her head jerks for them to come along.

No time to go back for those letters, then. If Tara goes to her car now, she'll lose her nerve.

Tara locks the Nissan with her keyfob. She'll have to make do with whatever's in her tote bag. They go through the backroom to a less congested side lot. On this one is Betty's decrepit Ford, a Prius, a Jeep, and a teal Chevy truck. June tosses her backpack into a tub bolted to the Chevy's bed.

Somehow, after ten years of growing, Tara is still the thinnest of their trio. June drives. Leah takes shotgun once more. This leaves Tara squished between the two, a leg on either side of the stick shift. Leah scootches toward the window, but Tara's side is still wedged against June's weight.

Thank god her face is as dark as it is. Blood rushing to her ears can't betray her so easily. She can feel June shiver through her boilersuit. Her fingers drum on the wheel, taking too long to adjust the dials and set the radio buzzing. Tara used to be so comfortable around June. Touching her had been natural when they were kids.

June had been her defender. Her confidant. Heat courses through Tara's body. She's only seeing now, in this cramped cab, that June might inspire other complicated and inconvenient feelings in her, too.

She lets out a rattled sigh. It's going to be a long drive.

55

6

June found the garden again without trouble. The creek she'd followed the night before ran right behind Madrone cabin, so all she had to do was trace it until she found the thicket. The hole had widened enough that she didn't get stuck. Instead of squeezing through the hedge this time, June just knocked on the gate.

No lizard arrived to meet her. The gate clattered open on its own, crackling dry vines to the pebble path.

June entered. The gate closed itself behind her.

Fairies peered from gaps in the bushes. One June had dubbed Cinnabon in her head, on account of all the hypericum buds, roped its way over the pebbles to follow her.

"You came back!" it cried.

"Back? Fool human," the tulip, Mary Kay in June's mental name scheme, scoffed.

"Weiss told me to come back," June said. The other fairies hesitated but eventually gathered around her feet. She stepped on tiptoe to avoid trampling anyone's roots. "Is he here?"

"The gardenkeeper is always here," croaked the stone fairy, Geodude. It struggled to keep up with her pace. She reached down and picked it up, letting its many roots latch onto her sweatshirt.

This must have been the cue the others were waiting for. More fairies tickled as they traveled up her body. She bit her lip to keep from squirming.

Cinnabon played in her hair. Geodude and Celeste the stargazer lily fairy grabbed each of her shoulders, another dozen clinging to her sweatshirt and shorts and even her shoes. Only Mary Kay kept her distance.

June slid into the sight of them like a warm bath on a cold day. She hadn't been dreaming. She hadn't made this place or its inhabitants in her imagination.

"Oh!" she remembered. Her hands patted her fanny pack. When she unzipped the pack, Geodude lassoed inside. June pulled him out, along with her Nintendo. "Weiss said I could entertain you guys. So I brought my DS, my colors, my beads…"

Her new friends oooed and aaaed. Even Mary Kay came closer to see the dual DS screens light up. June opened Pictochat for them to play with. She showed off her doodles. Celeste tapped at the top screen experimentally while June scribbled a face.

She drew the fairy looking at herself. Celeste cooed and twirled around, like the image would be her mirror. June drew as fast she could keep up. Three other fairies egged her on, led by a clover June had dubbed Honeybee. Honeybee usually had a bumblebee snuffling the flower on her head.

None of them seemed to understand how the pictures worked, but they all enjoyed the novelty. They liked her colors, too. A lupine used a stubby green pencil like a dance partner. Looping swirls were left in his wake. Honeybee tried the same with the DS stylus. The clover fairy's rooty face frowned so deeply when the stylus didn't leave any marks. Her cohorts, a coneflower and a daffodil, joined in Honeybee's disappointment.

June's camp necklace took their minds off it. Something about the plastic beads on a string of hemp fascinated Mary Kay, who finally crawled onto June's knee to study her.

June toured the tulip through her accomplishments. "I got this one for a bird watching competition, and this one's from when I made it off the ledge for the zipline. That one's missing for 3rd grade. Some girls were mean to my friend but I got in trouble instead of them. Still! Tara got hers, even if she was crying."

"You are very brave indeed," Celeste trilled. She joined Mary Kay on June's knee. They looped their roots around each other.

"My friend was brave, too! Real brave."

"You just said she was crying," Honeybee said.

June rested her chin on her fist. "We both jumped off eventually. Even if it was harder for her. What about you guys? What do you like to do?"

"We watch the master's garden," Mary Kay said.

"Tend the earth."

"Walk the grounds. Alert him when there are invaders."

"Well," June announced, "I'm here to take over your planet!" She made claws of her hands, speaking in a silly shriek tone.

Her maniacal laughter failed to impress the fairies.

She coughed. "I'm just glad I get to come back."

"Yes," Cinnabon said from June's hair. "Very strange."

"The gardenkeeper does not like visitors."

"Speaking of," grumbled Mary Kay.

June glanced around. She did hear footsteps, mingled with the thump of a tail against the dirt. From the ground, she couldn't tell which direction the sounds came from.

"So you came back."

Weiss loomed behind her. June pressed her lips in a line. His entrance had been mysterious the first time, but now his looming was getting kinda old. She looked up.

He stared down. "Well, sprout?"

"Hi!" she said. "I brought stuff to do like you asked."

"Did you?" he grunted.

June offered her Nintendo. Weiss squinted. "What on Earth is that?" he growled.

"It's my DS. You play games on it."

Weiss plucked the handheld between his thumb and forefinger, like he'd been handed a dead mouse. "I see."

He dropped it. June caught the device and stowed it away in her fanny pack, to the fairies' dismay. They tensed under Weiss's watch, though. If Weiss was the gardenkeeper, maybe that made him like their parent?

Carefully, June lifted the fairies back onto the path. Cinnabon rooted deeper into her curls, but her greens and whites gave her away among the orange. Weiss himself bent down and scooped her onto his moss cloak. "Come along, sprout," he said.

June dusted off her shorts. Weiss kept walking further into the garden. She sprang up to follow.

She jogged to keep up with his long stride. "Where we going?" she asked.

"I have work for you."

June pursed her mouth. Work? "As long as it's not boring," she groaned, taking up a stomp.

Weiss kept his back to her. "It will not be boring. I do not need more holes in my garden."

June stopped on the path. She snorted. "Not boring. Okay. What am I doing?"

"I have a pest problem. You are a pest. You should know how to get rid of them."

They came to a stop before a nerium shrub. June fawned over the pink flowers. Betty grew nerium shrubs for ornamental use, so June knew to look but not touch the poisonous oleander, as they were otherwise known.

On each leaf, she could see tiny black specks. "Oh! I got this," she said. "Leave it to me!"

Weiss's stone brow rose. June was already looking under nearby leaves. Her quarry could live just about anywhere. Her grandmother would often buy several bags of them at the nursery. Giant bags of wriggling, wiggling insects probably should have bothered her, but June actually thought it was funny that you could ship ladybugs around the country like packing peanuts.

She unzipped her fanny pack as she found red and orange ladybugs dotting the shrubbery. She had to look low. "Betcha the birds are eating the ladybugs. That's why you've got aphids," she said.

Weiss had already walked off. With great care, June collected ladybugs into her pack pocket. For good measure, she gave them a broad leaf and a stick to rest on.

Her pack dripping with collected bugs, she set them loose upon the nerium bushes.

She guarded them zealously. The fairies found her holding her arms out like a basketball player on defense.

"What in the world are you doing, child?" Mary Kay drawled, her roots crossed.

"Ladybugs," June said. "Birds keep eating them."

"Ladybirds?" Celeste asked.

"No, bugs," June told them. Then she gasped. "Can birds eat you guys?"

"They wouldn't dare," Mary Kay said.

"You're doing great," Cinnabon said, grasping June's ankle. The fairy scaled June's body to sit on her head again. Seemed to be the fairy's favorite perch. June grinned up at her.

Once she could see the ladybugs munching down on the aphids, their feelers writhing as the hungry predators went to town on their prey, June sat down to entertain the fairies. Weiss returned to June drawing them all, telling them she wasn't quite so good as her best friend. But that was fine! The fairies didn't mind.

Weiss leaned over the nerium.

"You are free to go," he decided.

"Oh," June said. She had arrived in the garden after dinner. The sun was now dipping out of view. "Sorry, guys."

The fairies lost interest. All of them extended their roots to Weiss's cloak.

June gathered her things. She waited.

Weiss just stared at her. He was scratching a claw at his chin, making a little tap that was audible since it was rock against rock.

"I'm coming back tomorrow, right? Please?" June asked. "I'll keep doing chores. For this one, though, you gotta get the birds to move. They'll eat your good bugs, so the bad bugs will eat your plants."

Weiss hummed. She was dismissed.

June only made it just on time for bedtime roll call. Tara had already rolled to face the wall, asleep. Britney told June to scrub the dirt off her knees before she got in bed. Otherwise, she'd gotten off scot-free.

Same for when she traipsed off the hiking trail the next day, then snuck away from the lake the day after that. She did get caught one morning and had to postpone her visit until evening. At least summer stretched out the daylight, but she was running out of opportunities to split from the group unnoticed.

Weiss's chores were all in the same vein as her first. He offered her a problem, with no obvious solution, and June used a combination of camp knowhow and tricks learned from Betty to solve it. First the nerium and the aphids. Then blossom rot, which she fixed by stealing a bucket of eggshells from the mess kitchen.

After a day she transplanted marigolds beneath the roses, to deter the rabbits attacking them, Weiss made himself scarce.

So she visited just to visit. Upon showing Weiss the predators who feasted on his plants, she found they were outcompeted by another species. A sort of bird moved into the trees that didn't prey on insects, these ones avocado green and thin as paper. June gushed when she realized their wings were monstera leaves, their beaks hazelnut shells that opened and closed when they sang to each other. A bunny she encountered had mossy fur, its toe beans pebbles from the path. They had the same beady black eyes as the fairies.

Weiss never mentioned them. He usually spent most of her visits in the greenhouse, which only formed doors when he asked it to.

As June wore into July, she didn't see much of him. The month of June, that was, not June herself. She'd had to hear that joke every day in Marydale's morning announcements that week. Maybe the director would stop since she scolded June for running off this very afternoon.

But she made it by sunset, anyways. Tonight June played her rhythm game for the fairies to see. She had gotten good at playing on mute in the cabin, but the fairies seemed to like listening to No Doubt. She caught Cinnabon humming along to Spiderwebs, entranced, while June tapped the buttons on beat. She'd gotten really, really quick. Betty had told her she should learn piano. It's just Guitar Hero, but more buttons!

It took a few songs before June realized there was a shadow overhead.

She didn't bother looking up. "Hey, Weiss."

Weiss was staring down at the DS. "What does that do?" he asked.

"It's for playing games. I told you!" June said.

Weiss lowered down, resting his elbows on his knees. His crystal eyes were glued to the screen.

"What do you do is," June said, "you press these buttons when they come up there. When you get it right enough in a row you get bonuses. That's gonna unlock stages and skins and stuff."

June showed him the last of the song. The peripheral made it so you held the DS vertically, strumming as you pressed the buttons on its side. She probably should have demonstrated how to play a game on her Nintendo normally for him to get the idea.

Not that the fairies minded, Weiss included. They were content to watch June for a half dozen songs more. Had any of them heard music like this before, she wondered? They didn't have electricity here, so radios and CDs were out of the question. Screens with moving pictures alone appeared a lot for them to process.

Eventually, Weiss held out a claw.

June cocked her head.

Weiss cleared his throat. All the fairies had taken perches at his head and shoulders. June smiled, but he indicated the DS. "Can I try?" he rasped.

June lined up his claws. Hopefully his obsidian talons wouldn't crack the screens.

He tapped at the lower one, his vine tongue blepping out. When he caught June watching, he slurped it in.

Weiss failed miserably. The concept of video games was new to him, to be fair. He got frustrated and fumbled the buttons.

Two more plays later, he was hitting notes. He put pizzazz into his tapping. His talons flourished when he finished a song with a mere thirty or so mistakes. He gave June a challenging smirk.

June snatched the game back. She played All the Small Things. She didn't miss a single note.

Weiss glowered. June just giggled. "You're good for your first time. I play a lot, though," she admitted.

He had his arms crossed. He hunched into his cloak.

June offered the DS. "Wanna go again?"

They passed the handheld back and forth. June was winning every round, but Weiss was improving. June liked seeing how excited he and the fairies got whenever input produced output. No wonder Betty thought these video games might be addictive.

It was difficult to tear the DS away. Weiss blinked the pixels from his eyes as June folded her Nintendo into its case. "It's gonna die," she explained. "Not die die, it just shuts off until it's charged again."

The fairies were curling their petals, rubbing their eyes. The sun was sinking.

"We're very like that toy of yours," yawned Celeste.

"You guys sleep?" June asked.

Each of the fairies with flowers closed them, roots slipping into the dirt. Even Geodude sank down and let his eyes close.

June's mouth quirked. "Sorry I came so late," she said. "They see when I leave. I'll try to be here in the morning when I come next time."

Done packing up, she stretched and yawned herself. It'd be a long walk to Madrone.

Weiss tapped her elbow.

She glanced over. He had reached into his cloak.

Between his claws was a blue flower, white and yellow in the middle. "Keep this in your pocket, sprout," he rasped. "It's scorpion grass. When you have it, the humans won't see you coming and going."

"Magic?" June said hopefully.

Weiss nodded into his palm. His eyes dazed, he reached over and ruffled June's hair.

June gasped, twirling the flower. She sniffed. Didn't smell especially magical. She'd find out if it worked soon, though. "Thanks," she said. "See you tomorrow?"

Weiss nodded again. June stuffed his gift in her pocket.

The radio crackles through channels. The Chevy's tinny speaker sounds the clearest on the county's pop station. Tara watches June hunt for the merge on 299, tapping in time on the steering wheel, left arm draped across the open window. She still has her gloves on, like a vintage dame on a day drive.

In shotgun Leah has her window rolled up, her forehead leaving an oily mark on the glass as she stares out.

It's about an hour from Bonny to Del Bosque Conservation Center, but the afternoon traffic tacks on another hour minimum. Tara scoots an inch more into shotgun, her butt half on her seat and half on Leah's.

Leah yelps. June and Tara jump.

"Do they not have Great Harvest anymore?" Leah cries.

Tara lets out a breath.

June inclines her head, paying her respects. "Nope," she says. "Gone under when I was in eighth grade. I miss the free bread and butter."

"Aw," Leah laments. "I missed bread and butter, period."

"You ate since you came back, right?" June asks.

Leah smirks. "Trust me, I ate." Before they got on the road, Tara had pilfered some freshly bought snacks from the Ayala apartment. Ginger ales, too. She should have grabbed something more exhilarating than chips and sandwich cookies, but Leah had torn into them like ambrosia on the drive to Bonny.

Tara has more in her tote bag, wedged against her leg on the floorboard. She scoots closer to June. Back to Leah. No matter how she distributes her ass, she's squashed between the two of them. For two hours, optimistically.

"It doesn't even look so different," Leah remarks. They pass fast food chain after fast food chain on the main thoroughfare, where the Great Harvest Bread Co. shop got replaced by a boba tea.

Tara hasn't been to Bonny much, but Leah had to drive out here for a volunteer gig at a nearby dairy. How she can visualize the town after a decade, Tara isn't certain.

Leah points to a corner. "It's the little stuff," she says. "This McDonalds had a play place, a super nasty one. There used to be a salon over here on 12th. Mom would drive all this way because they didn't fry her hair."

Tara lets her head rest against the cab's window. She nods.

"What else has changed?" Leah asks. "Anything major happen?"

Tara groans. June focuses on merging.

"Woman president?" Leah guesses.

Tara and June cringe in unison.

"Obama got another term," June says.

"Oh, cool. Who'd we get after?"

June's gunning it at 70. She brakes to a more reasonable 60. "Uh, we got gay marriage?"

Tara opens her eyes. What would it take for her to fade into the pleather interior?

Leah shoots June a finger gun. "Sweet," she says.

"Robin Williams died," Tara tries.

Leah frowns.

"Jeez, Tara," June says.

"What?" Tara cries. "That's a downer. Okay." She racks her brain. 2019 has been a shitshow. Honestly, Tara thinks it was a shitshow in 2009, and most eras before and after. But this adjustment could have been smoother if Leah had been dumped into the '09 world she's known, rather than this 2019 one that's visually about the same.

A big change, easy to show off… "Oh!" Tara says. "Everyone has computers in their pockets now."

"Seriously?" Leah asks.

Tara hands over her phone. The screen's busted, but she unlocks it and lets Leah examine the device. They'd had touch screens back in the oughts, didn't they? Leah taps experimentally, mind not especially blown.

"You can Google basically anything," Tara explains. "Plus it has music, TV shows, games. Lets you do all of them, basically."

Leah holds it by a corner, between her thumb and index. "It doesn't explode from all that in there?" she deadpans.

"They don't do that anymore," Tara says.

Leah chuckles. She hands the phone over. "Nice, I guess. You can still call and text and everything?"

"Pretty much," Tara says. "We can get one for you if you want."

"I'm good," Leah says. "What else?"

Huh. There's not much other future technology she can show off. No flying cars, no faster than light travel, just more solar panels and cannabis dispensaries than '09 ever had.

Well, what's the biggest thing with the least controversy to explain?

"They made a new Ghostbusters," June says.

"New Star Wars," Tara adds.

"New everything, really."

"People really, really like superhero movies. Like, a lot."

"Disney owns everything!" June chirps.

"Harry Potter's bad," Tara grumbles.

"It's kinda the same, like you said," June says with a shrug. "Just the little things are different."

She waits for Leah's reaction. Leah fell asleep while they were firing off future facts.

Tara taps on her sister's thigh. Leah startles. "Sorry," she says. "I'm awake."

"You're good," Tara says. "Are you okay?"

Leah's eyes hood. She snuggles into her new wool sweater. "Motion sick," she mutters. "I haven't been in a car for a while. I barfed on the way to Bosque."

"There's a bag in the glove box," June says. "Let me know if we need to pull over, okay?"

"Gonna try and not look outside, if that's okay. Thanks."

June drums the wheel again. That Post Malone song from the new Spiderman comes on the radio. Tara bops her head a little to the beat. The truck coasts, secure in its lane on the freeway for a good eighty or so miles.

Leah slumps against the passenger door.

June clears her throat. Leah doesn't startle.

"So," June asks. "You got a ride here?"

A small nod, eyes shut. Tara searches her sister's face. Leah looks exhausted.

"You got out of there," June says. "How?"

No reply. Leah's breaths have slowed. She's asleep again.

"Of course," Tara mumbles.

"Do you know?" June says, low. She dials down the radio.

Tara shakes her head. "She hasn't told me anything. I don't even know how she's her."

"But she came home."

"Yes."

"And it's just you who can-"

"It's just me, yeah," Tara snaps.

June tenses. Tara sighs. She scrubs her face with her hoodie cuff.

"I'm so sorry," June whispers.

Tara snorts. She digs her nails into her forehead, like she can tear out the part of her brain that makes her act like this. June, apologizing to her? Maybe she really did forget what happened.

June winces. "I am. If you'd called me, I would've…" She finds ten and two. "You could have come over. Had someone to talk to."

The glare on the horizon is giving Tara a headache. She can't help but chew her cheek, seeking any distraction from this cab. Out the window there's just grass and trees.

She looks at the dashboard instead. How does she even answer? What, she should have written and kept June shackled to her? That can't be what June wanted.

Tara had enough to bear on her own. June may not have forgotten like her family, like Tara feared. But she deserved a chance to be able to.

June sets her gloved hand on Tara's knee. Tara moves her leg, lowering June's hand onto the shift.

She stiffens against Tara's side. Tara squeezes her eyes shut, struggling to get air even with June's window rolled all the way down. June is rolling it up. Does she think Tara's shiver is from cold?

Tara looks up, about to ask her to leave it open. June's curls whip against her temple in the wind. There's a leaf in them.

She plucks it free from June's hair. June jolts. The truck jerks slightly.

The leaf is sucked out the window, along with any shot Tara can sustain this conversation.

June's eyes go to the road. Her hands tighten around the wheel.

Tara resigns herself to silence. It's what she's used to.

June and Weiss were playing by the pond again.

They played a lot of games, and not just the DS, either. They set up checkers with white and orange agates on the pond's shore, the board drawn out by an obsidian talon whenever they picked up a round. June had also taught him tic tac toe, chess, and a ton of card games once she stole them a deck.

Games could get heated in the beginning. For an apparent grownup, Weiss was not a good sport. He didn't have a poker face to save his stony hide. He pouted at losses, cackled at victory.

June taught him to play games. He had to come around to playing nice on his own.

How he cheated could get inventive, to say the least. June couldn't discern how exactly the fairies communicated with him, but he'd been able to consistently beat her at go fish for so many rounds that she grew suspicious. It was only once she took Cinnabon down from her hair that all the confidence fled his face and his guesses were appropriately hit or miss.

Now he didn't try such tricks. It was only fun knowing you could lose, he said, else why play?

June swished her hand in the lilies while Weiss considered his next move. "They're at the lake today," she said.

Weiss's brows were knit. Did they count as brows when they were just ridges of rock over his eyes?

He placed a white agate closer to her orange. He hummed acknowledgement.

"You ever been to the lake?" she asked. "It's got fish, too. They're just itty bitty." She splashed toward the carp in the pond. Like the birds and rabbits, they were green, though these ones were coated in slime rather than smooth leaves or fuzzy moss. Were they made of algae?

She took one of Weiss's white agates. He rumbled, scratching his head.

His next move won him one of her orange agates. He smirked. Winning, even just the battle and not the war, made him cocky. Even when he won War, which was more like pulling a lever on a lottery machine than a game of skill or strategy.

"Do you ever leave the garden?"

She moved into his home row and replaced her agate with a path pebble.

Weiss's frown became a smirk. "No, I do not," he said.

"Why not?" June asked. "Humans aren't so bad."

Weiss took another one of her orange agates, close to her home row. She filled the adjacent square to block him.

"You're still trouble," he hissed. "No offense."

"None taken," June said. She removed her shoes. She was gonna sweat through her socks at this rate. "Hey, can you even feel how hot it is? If you're, you know, made of rocks?"

He rasped a laugh. "I wilt a little," he allowed.

June smiled. Dork.

Weiss considered his next turn with care.

"Have you ever left?" June asked.

He'd been reaching for an agate, a grin on his face, before he saw her eyes fixed on it. Her staring made him hesitate.

He proceeded, anyway. "Why would I? Your lake is probably no more impressive than a puddle," he taunted.

"Yeah, yeah," June said. Before she made her move, she adjusted her sit on the pond's shore. When her toes made contact with the water, she shivered. Cold! Better than the heat of the cabins and pop-up canopies back at camp, definitely. July got so hot in Del Bosque, so most kids ran down to the lake.

Sure, June swam like a fish. But the lake involved getting gawked at for wearing her sopping shorts and t-shirt, instead of a bikini like Haylee Pierce and her entourage. It wasn't worth the sniggering or, worse, "concern".

She turned to the game. Her king took another white agate.

Weiss bit his talon, obsidian clinking on obsidian.

"Guess you wouldn't know for sure until you saw it," she said.

"And why is it you're here, instead of there?" he asked.

He took her king.

June brought her feet out of the water. She pushed her glasses up her nose, her knees drawn up to her belly. She leaned over them and let her hand hover over the pieces. How did she play this?

The scorpion grass did its job and then some. June didn't get any comments from Britney about spending sunrise to breakfast outside Madrone. Skipping mess or demonstrations raised no eyebrows. If she wandered the grounds on her own, not a single adult would demand to know where she was supposed to be. If they did see her, none of them would ever do more than wave like nothing was amiss.

She could move invisibly now. No more snide comments from campers about her weight, about her home in Bonny, about her bunkmate being a lunatic. Before, she'd had Tara to commiserate with. Now it was just miserable to be around other kids and feel Tara pointedly not looking at her.

Tara had been doing so long before June carried a *Don't Look At Me* spell in her pocket.

"It didn't used to be so bad," she said. "My best friend at camp, we used to play like this all the time. Even when we weren't supposed to. I don't know why she doesn't want to anymore."

She pushed the meat of her palm to her stinging eye.

June played her remaining pieces into a corner. "You win," she told him.

Weiss took the last of her orange agates. He lacked his usual satisfaction, cupping all her pieces in his claw. "We could play something else," he said.

June shrugged. The agates got jumbled as Weiss put them in a woven basket. She liked to imagine he'd threaded the reeds together himself, grunting in frustration when he made a mistake like Betty did crocheting. Cards nicked by his nails were bound in a stem among the stones.

His tail swept the board from the silt. Their games were put aside. "Are you alright, sprout?"

"Just the heat," she mumbled into her knee.

He tapped his talons together. "I see."

He gathered the basket and rose to his feet. June placed her palms on the shore, ready to join him and be escorted to the gate, but he put up a claw.

"If you must cool off," he said, "you are welcome here as long as you like."

June stared.

Weiss held his claw high a moment longer. Reached out. Returned his claw to his cloak.

He hurried away.

June sat alone on the shore. She untied her sweatshirt from her waist. She set her glasses atop the folded bundle.

A deep breath. Then June cannonballed in, holding her ankles.

The wobble of water drummed in her ears. Fish blurred by. Slimy scales skimmed against her hand, against her ankle. Lilies spun on the surface above, casting rounded shadows on the rocks below. She could see to the bottom, though she couldn't tell how far away it was. Floating gently, she let her limbs splay out, submerging a meter or so. She brushed a reed with her fingertips. She took hold of it.

Maybe she could just stay here, a little longer, before the inevitable.

Only her shoes were wet when she got back to Madrone. June washed the skimmers and pond scum down the drain. She returned to her room sleepy and soft, landing facedown in bed.

Above, Tara had out her sketchbook. Her flashlight was propped in the frame behind her head, illuminating her scribbles.

June lifted her face from the quilt. "Tara?"

Tara hmmed. June didn't get much more than a hmm from her these days.

She kept going, despite it. "Have you been hearing stuff at night?"

The scratch of Tara's pencil stilled. June arched off the edge of the bed. She looked up, but she couldn't see her friend's face through the flashlight beam.

"I just thought I heard someone outside. Late," June continued.

The flashlight clicked off. The sketchbook crunched shut, the pencil slipping off the bunk. June heard it hit the carpet. "It's probably a racoon," Tara said. "Don't worry about it."

"What if it's not?" June asked. What if Tara would tell her? She'd heard Tara climbing out of her bed at midnight dozens of times now. Tara had to have seen June slipping away before the scorpion grass. They were going to the same place. They were doing the same thing.

What if they could do it together?

The girl in the bunk above rolled over. "I don't know what you're talking about, June. Go to sleep."

9

As the Chevy veers onto the exit, the tarmac thins. Potholed country roads replace the freeway's flat, forward march. Sidewinding bends threaten to toss Tara into June or Leah depending on the direction they're banking. She's almost too late to brace the dashboard on more than one occasion. How did buses from Amarante Elementary take these corners without toppling?

Leah is immune to the hairpin turns. She even snores, sawing logs into the quiet cab. It'd take going off one of these cliffs to wake her up.

Thankfully, June's brakes are up to the challenge. She navigates curves at the bottom of the wheel, steadying her breaths and her hands.

Tara fights not to flop into her and throw them in a ditch.

Outside trash laden but moderately kept up highways, those ditches overflow with ferns and field bindweed. Ryegrass springs from the cracks in the cliffside, eating into the road wherever they can find purchase. Callas litter the hills above, white as snow.

The sign for Del Bosque Conservation Center is the last thing they see before Tara's phone loses service and the asphalt fully disintegrates to gravel. The center itself closed down due to budget cuts back in 2011, revived by donations to a graveyard crew in 2017. The crew clearly can't afford to maintain the land like they did when a profitable campground kept the lights on.

They can't afford to hire security, either, since June's Chevy thunders past the property without a single stop. Tara never thought to ask Betty if she's heard anything out of the ordinary from her old colleagues. Then again, most of the new staff must be grad students to commute so far from Del Bosque proper. Those theses on microbiology in temperate rainforests don't write themselves.

Maybe they know not to go looking for anything larger than a protozoa. These woods have been a conservation effort for ages, but not out of any sense of stewardship to the land.

Anyone who's dared to propagate a community here goes missing or goes running before the first foundations can be laid. There are rumors from towns on the Klamath, how intrepid frontiersmen and railroad workers walked into these woods and never came out.

But those tales are few and far between. Tara had to dig deep to find even these crumbs. How do you tell a story about a missing person if no one reports them missing? All Tara ever gleaned from the rumors: beware. Stay away. Don't go further than the creek, because no one who strolls past those boundaries returns with intel. If they return at all.

Tara makes out scratched signposts for Camp Cottonwood. She prays the founders will never know they've made a series of unsolvable cold cases, including perhaps their own.

June reaches across Tara to jostle Leah. "We're here," she says.

Leah yawns. She gives the signposts a bleary look, almost soothed back to sleep by the Chevy creeping along. They have to drive slow. The gravel, once weeded in the spring before the summer season, has been broken up by hens and chicks. The succulents crunch under the tires.

"Sorry about the mess," Leah says. "That's on us."

"Us?" June asks.

Leah points out the windshield. "Gate's up here."

The camp never reopened in 2010. June and Tara's final summer here is the last any child will spend riding its zipline, jumping into its lake, or talking late into the night in its cabins. At the time Tara just thanked the universe for closing it down. She never looked further into its demise. It had been enough, then, to know it couldn't claim anyone else.

The archway heralding Camp Cottonwood's entrance is creaked open. It's one creak away from collapsing to mulch. The grounds beyond are shrouded in untamed Himalayan blackberry. Swathes of stinging nettles jut up like spikes staked into the road.

Leah laughs sheepishly. "Pretty dramatic, huh?" she says.

Tara and June look at her. Leah presses her lips together.

June parks the Chevy a car length from the gate. "So," she says. "We just go in."

"There's no other humans for miles," Leah assures. "Well, other than, you know. You're not trespassing."

"We are, technically," Tara says.

Leah makes a vague motion with her hand. "Eh. No one's gone through as long as I've been here."

"Nobody?" June asks.

"Nope. Once we got the camp shut down, the big stuff moved out. Appliances, any assets they could sell off. There's a lot of junk lying around. Just no ovens," Leah says, rubbing her belly under her sweater. "Man, I regret not bringing bread."

June just idles. The Chevy quakes in place.

Leah's already hopping out. "Come on," she tells Tara. "We don't wanna keep them waiting."

"Not ominous," June notes. Tara heaves a sigh.

Then she's hopping out, too.

She joins Leah's side at the gate. She stands on her toes. There's not much she can see from here. If she didn't know better, she might have assumed the gate to be a vestigial structure. The last rotting tooth of a long decayed corpse, perhaps, rather than the mouth of anything alive anymore.

Metal jingles. Tara bends her knees, swiveling for the sound's source.

June holds up a chain of bells from the truck bed. She clips them onto her belt, along with a can of spray mace. She slings her backpack over one shoulder.

"What?" she asks.

Tara twists her mouth. "Is that for…"

"It's the middle of nowhere," June says. She catches up to the Ayalas, coming to a stop before the archway. "Might be bears. Cougars."

"Right," Tara says.

She doesn't want to be the first to cross the threshold.

Leah does, so naturally Tara follows. June is the last to step through the crack in the gate.

The road is no better on the other side. The gravel plunges into a thick copse of trees. Without landscapers, the formerly tidy rows of oaks and namesake cottonwoods are now walled in bramble. The inviting posts along the path are splintered, turkey tails overtaking their bases.

Worse still, more stinging nettles. Leah sidesteps, Tara at her heels. June brushes past them in her boilersuit.

"Sorry, again," Leah says. "It's a lot of precautions, but we had to be sure."

"You really need to explain the we thing," Tara says.

Leah ducks around a particularly prolific belladonna. She flaps a hand. "Me and the others," she says, like she's elaborating. "We moved in once the staff were gone. We just didn't want them getting back in once we did. Or, I guess, thinking it was worth the effort to get through. You can, people just see all this and don't try."

June keeps up behind, holding her backpack's straps. Her bells tinkle. Tara wants to fall back to ask what she thinks of this very telegraphed trap.

But Leah has taken Tara's hand to lead her in.

Dread cakes her like mud. It's not enough to make Tara turn back. Her sister's hand, firm in her own, feels too unreal. She lets the dreamlike quality of it all wash over her. This isn't a trap. This is a dream. And a dream can't get you.

June seems less inclined to this train of thought. She stops often, growing the distance, scanning the environment for hazards outside the obvious.

"What's that?" she calls.

"What?" Leah says.

Tara feels it, too. An uncanny vibration thrumming across the still earth. It's almost like the sound of June's fingers drumming on the steering wheel, a rhythmic *tickah*

tickah tickah of many digits making contact with a surface. No engine hums. Whatever this is, it's no tractor or mower.

"Leah?" Tara asks.

"Huh, that's weird," Leah says.

"What about this isn't weird?"

"The bells!" Leah exclaims.

June doesn't budge, the bells motionless. Her hand goes for her mace.

A massive shape charges through the bramble. No thorns or thicket hinder its pace. Tara tugs Leah's wrist, but Leah won't move.

June equips her mace. From a side pocket in her backpack she whips out a hatchet.

"Whoa," Leah says. "Put those down."

June does not. The shape is indistinct but larger than her Chevy just beyond the archway. They might not outpace this thing in the truck, forget on foot.

Tara lowers into the dream. This is a dream. Whatever approaches will wake her up in Del Bosque, not trample her.

June comes to the Ayalas' defense. Leah attempts to wrestle the hatchet from her. "Put it down!" she grunts, but June is stanced. Tara's arms are limp in her sleeves behind the pair of them.

Their attacker comes into view. A giant beetle has come careening from the forest. It stands higher than any human, its sickle-like legs cutting through brush like tissue paper. Striped shells armor its back, bisecting to reveal translucent wings. Those wings buzz as loud as a whole hive.

The beetle raises to pounce.

June held the beetle on her knuckle. One of its legs was missing, and it scrabbled at her hand to find its footing. It wouldn't get far if she didn't nurse it back to health, would it? She set it on a leaf and chose to carry it along to the garden.

"Don't you worry," she told the beetle as she tread the creek. "Weiss probably has a jar somewhere. I'll poke all the holes in the top and feed you. Wait, what do beetles eat again?"

The beetle said nothing. Fair enough. Not every creature June befriended in the woods needed to speak.

The garden gate swung open at her approach. Already the fairies were waiting in the roses and rhododendrons. "What've you got there?" Geodude croaked.

She knelt to show the assembled fairies her beetle.

"Poor guy," Geodude observed.

"Yeah," June said. "I dunno if I can put him in my pack. He might get hurt, so I'm just gonna hold him for now. Want to help me find a good home for him?"

Cinnabon crawled up to her hand. She examined their insect guest. "Looks like a ten-lined june beetle," she decided.

June oooed. The beetle must have known there was another June nearby to rescue him. She'd found him crawling on her bed frame this morning, about the size of a cough drop. Just as Cinnabon was describing how large these june beetles could grow, Weiss walked up.

He peered over. "What have you got there?" he asked.

June offered the beetle for his study. He blinked.

"It's got a hurt leg," she told him. "It won't eat any of your plants, promise!"

Weiss made a gimme of his claw. June handed the beetle up. With a delicate motion, Weiss's glassy talons tipped the beetle on his back. He kicked his five remaining legs.

June made a gimme gimme gesture back. Weiss set the beetle on her finger.

Cinnabon extended a root and petted the beetle on the wing. June did the same, even if her stubby finger could only graze against its wing without damaging it. "He's gonna need somewhere to live while his leg heals," she said. "You don't have any jars around, do you?"

Weiss hummed. He seemed to be thinking.

While the other fairies dispersed, Cinnabon continued her lesson on beetles. You could call this one a watermelon beetle, but June preferred knowing her beetle shared a piece of her name. This beetle could eat plants and act as a pest, though they only ever emerged during the summer.

June stroked the beetle's antennae, feathered like gaudy plastic eyelashes. The beetle hissed air between its shell and wings.

Weiss tapped her head. June looked up.

"Would you like to see what I do in the greenhouse?" he asked.

June's eyes grew huge. "Yes!"

Weiss smiled. He offered a claw. June took it, practically dragging him toward the frosted dome.

They passed the house. June was always struck by how empty it was. Lifeless, compared to the splendor of the garden. No wonder Weiss and the fairies stayed out whenever she visited. The house didn't seem built for living things, so she never explored it herself. Outside held more wonders by far, anyway.

Didn't mean she didn't leap at the chance to see inside of the greenhouse.

Weiss stopped at the edge of the dome. He glanced around, like someone might catch them in the act.

The lizard stooped down. "There are rules, sprout," he said. "The first is this: you mustn't touch anything. Anything at all."

June nodded. She squinted over his shoulder, trying to see through the misted glass.

He took her hands. His most thumb-like talons dented her palms, spreading her fingers. "This is very serious," he said. "Touch nothing. The second rule: do not ever do what is done here. This is for the masters of the house. It is not for humans."

June nodded more sternly this time. "Alright, alright," she said. "Cross my heart." And she did, the beetle on her index.

Satisfied, Weiss opened the door.

June's jaw dropped.

The greenhouse panels soared up and up like a dizzying skyscraper, lit by colossal sunflowers which cast light on the plants below. And what plants they were. Leaves glowed, the buds on flowers writhing with a sort of motion she might mistake for wind if not for the still breeze. Some branches had a look like the limbs of her fairy friends, like they might reach out and grasp her if she got too close. There were so many colors, arranged in a spiral like a living rainbow.

Weiss was right to caution her. June would have run through them, arms spread, trying to touch every texture she could. One of the vines had layered scales. Fur dotted another, soft as lamb's ear. Thick tufts came from seed pods, hanks of hairlike floss spilling through their shells.

She kept at Weiss's side as he navigated the spiral. He was collecting while they walked. A fallen shell here, some twigs there, a seed pod with short cropped fuzz. His obsidian claws trimmed off bits without fully touching them. Once shorn, they were placed in a fold of his moss cloak.

"This greenhouse," Weiss explained, "belonged to the masters. When they returned home, I stayed to guard their treasures."

A nearby hedge dripped with threads of silver and platinum. June wanted to run her fingers through the spools. Would they be hard and sharp? Or gossamer as they appeared, just barely visible in the sunflower light?

Weiss followed her stare. "Something more valuable than that," he chuckled.

"Like what?" June asked. Glittering diamonds, maybe? June didn't see any sticking out of the soil like grubby potatoes.

"Have you ever heard of mandrakes?" Weiss asked.

June followed him to the warmer colors of the greenhouse rainbow. Fluffed out pink dahlias the size of umbrellas swayed nine feet overhead.

She twisted her mouth, admiring them. "They're like little plant babies, right?" In Harry Potter, at least, they screamed. Otherwise they didn't show up in a lot of fairy stories. None June had read, anyways.

Weiss considered her answer. "They don't have them in this part of the human world. The closest, I believe, are mayapples. Native to the east of this land, if I'm correct. Only these mayapples," he said, "are a special variety."

Coral had amassed in sturdy walls, oranges and creams swirled together. She wondered what they'd look like underwater. Up here they were the fiery slopes of a canyon. Weiss lifted June through a gap in its mass.

Just beyond, at the center of the spiral, were the most ordinary plants she'd yet to see. Star shaped leaves, eight spokes each, and teensy white flowers. June might have made another joke about edelweiss, but edelweiss weren't this big. Edelweiss didn't morph from flower to a single yellow fruit, gritty and soft like a pear but small as a golf ball.

"May I see your beetle?" Weiss asked.

June handed the beetle over. Weiss bent down. "What are they for?" June asked.

"Watch before you ask," Weiss told her, but he smiled. June smiled, too. She rested her elbows on her knees, fists squished against her cheeks.

Weiss pruned the smallest fruit from a branch. He held the stem between his talons. From his other hand he produced the twigs, shell, and trimmings he'd collected on their walk. His talons moved deft but ginger, carefully prodding a hole in the dirt and placing the beetle inside.

Then his claw swirled to cover the hole.

"Whoa, don't bury him?" June cried. "He's not a worm."

"Mayapples bury themselves if you don't bury them," he said. "Don't worry, sprout. This won't be long."

June frowned. She didn't like to think of her beetle being smushed under the damp earth.

But sure enough, a green leaf punched out of the dirt. June let out a little oop and fumbled back. The leaf itself had eight spokes, the mayapple's in miniature.

She almost spoke before Weiss was pinching the stem and pulling the growth from its hole. He gave it a light shake.

Dirt tumbled off. Revealed was a grimy beetle, with helicopter seed wings and a knobbly nutshell head and beady black eyes. He'd gone from the size of a cough drop to that of a kitten. He bumbled up Weiss's claw, onto his wrist.

Weiss offered the beetle to June. She turned the altered bug in her hands. The beetle crawled atop her fingers, now too big to crawl between them. She brought him in front of her nose. The beetle's eyes were enormous now. He had more of a face than she could see before, displaying a tab just below the eyes like an upturned mouth.

"He's cute! But what happened?" June turned the beetle over. Along with a newly fuzzy belly, he had six twig legs wriggling. "He's got his leg back!"

Weiss stroked the beetle between the wings. The beetle hissed again, like a purr, wings humming against the outer striped shell protecting them.

"These mayapples are like no other," Weiss said. "When planted, they are restorative."

"Heals things," June said. "You healed a little bug."

"Yes. It can do more."

June leaned into his bubble, temple against his elbow. She frowned. "Why did the other stuff change, though? He's a wood bug now."

"The mayapple improves things. It grows things better, so they no longer need to eat."

"Ohhh. I guess that's better."

Weiss shifted his weight so she could see the beetle. She poked the beetle's antennae with her finger. The beetle nuzzled her. What a weird thing for a bug to do, but she couldn't deny it was adorable.

"Here," Weiss said.

He placed the beetle on her hair. She crossed her eyes trying to see. Sticky limbs clung to her orange curls and she fidgeted.

Weiss disentangled them. "It cannot die. You can take it with you."

June gasped. "What if Benson flies away?"

"What?"

"I named him already."

Weiss's chest shook with laughter. "Of course you have. Benson, do not fly away from your human," he commanded. "Is that better, sprout?"

"He listens to you?"

"Why do you think the creatures of this garden call me keeper?"

June brushed Benson's "lashes" against her knuckle. "Oh. That makes sense."

"The creatures you call fairies," he continued, "were made this way."

He tensed against her side. June brought Benson down from her hair. Now in her hands he nibbled toothlessly at her pinky.

"Why'd you do that?" she asked.

"To improve them."

"And to have friends, too?" June asked.

Weiss frowned. "I don't know. The thought did not occur when I planted them. Though I do not think they are going to replace my masters."

"What were they like?" June asked.

Weiss closed his eyes. A stillness overcame him.

Benson bumbled from her hand to Weiss's elbow. He pet the beetle, not meeting June's glance.

"The masters of this house made many mandrakes. Not as friends. As pets. They were pleased, for a time. But they were fickle. When they grew bored of this place, they sought somewhere else. I agreed to stay and tend the garden. I haven't seen them for a very long time."

June stood. Weiss looked at the mayapples.

He sounded so confused. Cast off, even if he didn't know why. "I'm sorry, Weiss."

"It is what it is," he said.

Weiss nodded. She offered her hand down. He took it.

He escorted her to the gate today. June had a feeling, especially with his cloak draped like a blanket around his shoulders, that she was the one doing the escorting. The fairies didn't seem to cheer him up, not that they ever did.

He flapped a claw for them to go. They scattered.

June pet Benson as they walked.

Then she handed him over.

"He's for you," Weiss said.

"I know," June said. "You probably need him more today, though. Just 'til I get back, okay?"

Weiss patted the beetle. "I will care for him."

June walked to the gate. She held her fanny pack close to her chest. She thought about her bunk below Tara. Hearing her leave in the night. How she seemed to hate June now, or at least didn't care to bother with her anymore. Was June really so annoying? Such a dumb baby kid, when they were supposed to be the oldest at camp and acting grown up?

She turned around. Weiss was still holding Benson. He waved.

June ran up and almost knocked him off his wooden leg, hugging tight. Hugging a rock wasn't exactly comfortable, but it was more than she'd gotten at camp.

Then she jumped back. Weiss and the fairies were all staring.

June's face burned. She ran through the gate.

Leah shoves in front of June, both hands raised. "Down, Benson," she soothes in baby talk.

The beetle's antennae tip tap at Leah's hair, pincers scissoring the air before her face.

The beetle lowers all six legs to the ground. A hum emanates from its wings, softer than the chainsaw buzz it made before. Its head butts Leah's stomach, rubbing against her. She spreads her arms to embrace it.

"Benson," June says.

"He's a lot bigger, huh?" Leah coos. "Arentcha, big guy? Did those bells scare you?"

June unclips her bear bells. They clatter to a pile in the gravel.

"This is your bug?" Tara cries. "Why is he huge?"

Benson approaches. His feelers dust the shape of June's face.

He chews her hair.

June replaces her hatchet. She spreads a hand between the beetle's eyes. He bucks. He shimmies in place, like a dog who's heard the word walk. His twig legs jitter to and fro.

Leah comes around to his left, patting his striped shell. "Yeah. It's them," she tells him. "Where's home, Benson? You gonna show us home?"

Benson tosses his head, antennae waggling. He runs a few circles before skittering down the road. His fuzzy belly flattens the nettles. The *tickah tickah tickah* of his tread sounds like a keyboard clacking.

"Good boy, Benson!" Leah calls after him. "He's so cute."

"Yeah," June breathes.

Tara inhales. She nods slowly, watching the beetle as he shatters a rotting signpost.

"Cute," she squeaks.

June hasn't moved from her pose, suspended for Benson's examination.

Leah takes the lead again. Tara follows Leah. June stows the bells in her backpack and jogs to catch up.

With the path carved out by Benson, they don't have much further to go. There's the curb where cars and buses used to pull up, concrete crumbling into the weeds. The mess hall stands to the west like a cardboard box left out in the rain. Condensation collects on the windows as autumn creeps closer. How much mold has formed on the rafters, the walls, the rows of dining tables and benches? Beside it are a series of equipment sheds. A door to one hangs loose on its hinges.

Benson has not cut a path toward the west, though. Instead he's knocked over picnic tables and tamped down grass on his way to the cabins.

There are voices. The closer they get, the more Tara strains to recognize a rasp among them, but no. Just a bunch of cadences she can't place, coming from the center of the green.

Leah's voice sticks out as she throws her arms wide. "Guess who's back?" she shouts.

They reach the first cabins. Tara staggers.

Conifers as tall as decades are splitting the Beech and Rowan cabins. Others, Maple and Oak and Alder, are overwrought with English ivy. Trillium acts as a second border around the campfire, lit to heat a checkered grate. Log benches bent and rotten encircle the pit.

There are people. Well, a person: a human man in his late twenties, early thirties. He has a green beard and shaggy green hair. He's growing moss, along with a few pebbles like zits lodged in his skin. He flips a kabob on the grate.

Like a parody of former campers, fairies have taken their seats on the bench behind him. Some of them are small as they were ten years ago, blending into the lichen and brackets. These ones range from common blue butterfly to Atlas moth in size. A larger pair cuddle together on their end of the bench, a lily tall enough to reach Tara's hip canoodling a tulip only reaching Tara's knee in height.

No one says anything. Leah's arms are still spread.

The moss man's mouth opens. Closes. The fairies murmur amongst themselves. The larger two, the stargazer lily and the tulip, begin exchanging whispers. A huddle of smaller ones, led by a clover, duck behind their log.

Leah's arms go slack. "Nice welcome, guys," she says.

"It worked," the man gets out.

"Kinda," Leah admits.

"That's," the man says, waving a spatula at Leah's company.

"Yeah," Leah says.

Tentatively, the stargazer fairy comes down from the bench. Her companion trails along behind her, their roots twined together. The fairies are more humanoid, less octopi, using four limbs instead of the numerous tangles they'd had when Tara last saw them.

The pair comes right up to June.

"Is it really you?" asks the stargazer.

June's pale face is almost green.

The stargazer wraps her roots around June's waist. "Our little girl," she says.

June's arms raise like she's controlling marionettes. She freezes there in the embrace.

Tara stays behind Leah. Not like her sister can conceal her, but she isn't interested in formally introducing herself to these people. She can't let her guard down. This still feels like a trap. But where is he?

The moss man inspects her. "Your sister's not so little," he remarks, itching his beard. He's wearing an old camp sweatshirt, this one dated for '05. Must have been in inventory somewhere. Where khaki shorts don't cover his legs is carpeted in moss, too. His nails are graphite gray, matte like cement's been painted on them.

"Mateo Valdez," he says. He offers his hand.

Tara takes it. His hand feels sandpaper rough. It's the same tired smile on his face, the one she saw on him before he vanished without a trace.

"Fuck, man," he mutters. He gives her hand a shake or two, just staring.

The stargazer prattles to June. "Why, I never thought you'd come back! You're all grown up! Look at her, Moe," she says to the tulip.

"Up and out, alright," the tulip drawls.

"Oh hush," the stargazer says. "Don't listen to her. She used to be just as big as you, you know. Now, we never properly introduced ourselves. I'm Selina."

"Celeste," June says.

Selina takes Moe by the torso and shakes her. "She remembers!" she sings.

"You were Mary Kay," June says to Moe.

"Ugh, what made you pick that?" Moe rolls her eyes. Instead of beady black, her eyes are brown. She grasps one of her petals, the pink feathered through with white like hair that's graying. "Tulips. Two lips. Oh, damnit."

The other fairies are rearing their heads. Any who aren't already around the fire are coming from under moldering eaves, through holes in wood panels. There's at least two dozen. Tara can't count them all with how quickly they assemble.

Mateo waves to June. "Hey, June Bug," he says.

"Geodude," June says. Her face goes red as a rose. "I can't believe I called an actual human person Geodude. Oh my god, I am so sorry."

His smile goes crooked. "You just had to name me after a Pokémon, huh? Least it wasn't Pikachu."

"Pikachu's adorable," Leah protests.

"I was not adorable," Mateo says.

Leah holds up her palms in surrender. "Fine, fine. You got food on?" she asks.

"What does it look like?" Mateo asks.

"Looks like it's burning," a lupine fairy says.

Mateo swears and returns to tending the grate, which appears to have been ripped off a golf cart. A stack of chipped ceramic plates gets distributed across the log. Walnut shells are balanced on one, for the smaller fairies who were here for dinner.

The others are here for June. There are several fairies scaling her body like tarantulas. June does her best not to squirm, biting her lip. Tara does not envy her.

"Well, would ya look at that?" says a clover, tugging a loop of June's hair.

"Get down this instant, Priscilla Ann!" scolds a fairy by June's boot, her head wrapped in a pasque petal like a bonnet.

"Ma!" the clover on June's boilersuit whines.

"Now!"

The clover, along with a coneflower and a daffodil, are climbing into June's pocket. "You let me play with her before," the clover protests.

A few others, a lupine and a valerian, perch on June's collar. "Let your girls have their fun, Winnifred Walsh," the lupine says. "Not like we get many new folks up here."

"Don't tell me how to raise my children, Frank," the pasque snaps.

"I'm Frank, this is Leon," Frank says.

"Hullo," Leon the valerian pipes up.

"That's the Walsh girls in your pocket there," Selina adds.

"Where's Dora?" asks Frank.

"Here," says a milkweed, lounging languidly on June's elbow. This flower looks like a cigarette should dangle in her root threads.

June's eye twitches. Her gloved fingers drum her thigh.

Moe begrudgingly comes to her rescue. Her radicles stretch far longer than fingers, extending several feet in length so she can pluck the fairies from June's boilersuit. "Get off the girl, she ain't a tree," she barks. "That means you, Frank. She better not be missing anything in those pockets."

"Guilty," he says, dropping the ring of keys he pilfered back where he found them.

The fairies pour off. Moe hands the Walsh girls over to Winnifred Walsh, who takes Priscilla Ann by the petal, her daughter yelping an indignant ow.

"You got the manners God gave a vulture," Winnifred huffs. "Except a vulture knows when to wait."

"Maaaaa," Priscilla Ann moans.

Tara takes a deep whiff of the kabobs. Even burned, the smell makes her stomach grumble. There's squash sliced up, sandwiched between mushrooms and rolled in herbs. A rosemary bush by the Alder cabin picks up in the breeze, its scent blown across the campfire and covering the smell of smoke.

She hasn't eaten anything other than chips today. But Tara steels her resolve. After all, this is fairy territory. You don't eat fairy food.

Does the rule still apply if Mateo's not completely fairy anymore?

Leah already has a steaming kabob in her hand. She glances at Mateo, who nods for her to go ahead.

She flops onto the log where Selina and Moe were sitting. "Anything exciting happen while I was gone?" she asks.

"You being gone was the exciting part," Mateo says. "So it worked?"

Leah pauses before a bite. "Not exactly."

"What do you mean?"

June has sat herself on the ground where she's been overwhelmed. The Walsh girls are at her feet, having broken away from their mother. "You're muuuuch bigger now," Priscilla Ann decides. "Do you still have the puppies?"

"The ones in the magic book," the daffodil trills.

"Please?" begs the coneflower.

June scoops the three fairies into her hands.

"She don't talk much no more," the daffodil observes.

"How old are you?" June asks.

"Twelve and a half," crows Priscilla Ann, folding her roots. "Ma says we been in one of them Tír na nÓgs. Stolen by the sidhe and such. Ciara's nine. Can't recall how old Maeve is. Then there's my brothers, and our ma, and our grandpa."

June crumples. She brings the little fairies to her chest, who yell but they're stuck under her forearms. She has a look on her face like she's holding baby birds with broken wings.

"Priscilla Ann!" says Winnifred, headed for the Alder cabin.

The Walsh girls escape June's grasp. They form a neat line and trail after their mother.

Tara hovers at Leah's side. She can't focus on either conversation before the other sucks her in. Does she go and comfort June? How would she even?

June chose to come here. She had to have known her playmates would be waiting, right?

To be fair, Tara would never have dreamt this up either. The creatures who evaded her in the garden, around the campfire like one's gonna whip out a guitar and start strumming Down By the Bay?

"What happened here?" she asks Leah.

Leah gnaws on a mushroom. "It's changed. Told you."

"How?" Tara asks.

"Ask yourself," Leah says, seeing something in front of Cottonwood cabin. "Weiss! Guess who I brought."

The *tickah tickah tickah* of Benson's steps begins anew, coming from the east.

Tara follows her sister's stare.

The silhouette that's been her boogeyman for the last ten years has emerged from the woods. A lizard on his hind legs, made of rock and timber, his tail lashing under a moss cloak.

Everything ended Sunday, August 12th, 2009, at a hole in a thicket.

"What are you doing here?" Tara asked.

"Nothing!" June cried, hiding Benson the beetle behind her back. The beetle climbed into her sweatshirt. June scrunched her face. His legs tickled. "What are you doing here?"

Tara scanned June up and down. Her eyes stayed on June's hair. June didn't have any of the mandrakes clinging to her, did she? Other than the one she was currently concealing. She did have some flowers in her hair, these ones inanimate. Cinnabon had knotted yellow hypericum blooms into her curls today.

June slapped at the blooms to get them loose. They fell and drifted down the creek at their feet. Tara had finally caught her. They'd both been coming earlier and earlier, longer and longer.

It was almost guaranteed they would intersect again.

Tara folded her arms, hands hidden in her baggy sleeves.

"Alright, fine, I'm going to the garden, too. Why do you keep going here?" June asked. "And why did you lie to me? I knew you were sneaking out this whole time! You could have just told me."

Benson crawled up June's neck. She squirmed. He was chomping on her hair again. She pried open his pincers and wedged him under her arm, letting his brown shell blend into her brown cotton sweatshirt.

Tara saw him. She stormed forward.

She snatched June's wrist and dragged her into the cottonwoods, stomping through the creek. June stumbled along. Her shoes splashed up, drenching her socks. Tara's brow was set, her mouth a hard line. Shadows darkened her eyes like soot.

June wrenched away.

"You're doing it again," she said. "Not talking to me. I'm not gonna stop going. I made friends."

"Those things aren't your friends," Tara spat. She grabbed for Benson, but June ducked. "They're monsters."

"They're nice to me!" June insisted. "I see them every day! Not like you noticed I was gone."

"I did notice, June! I just didn't think it was this," Tara said, waving to the hole in the thicket.

"What's wrong with this?" June stamped her foot. "I don't get it. You don't talk to me all summer. Our last summer, remember? We're in the same cabin and everything. It's not that hard to remember I exist, is it? But you act like you hate me and then get mad at me for making new friends."

"They're not your friends," Tara repeated.

"They are! They've been nicer to me than you," June said.

Tara's arms fell limp.

June hugged Benson. She didn't have much longer in the garden. She didn't have much longer with Tara either.

"I'm trying to keep you safe," Tara said. "That thing you're holding? It's dangerous. The gardenkeeper is dangerous."

"How?"

"You won't believe me," Tara said.

"I've been playing with fairies for weeks," June said, fist on her hip. "Try me."

Tara backed away. She was shaking her head. Both hands yanked on her ponytail, the flyaway strands catching on her nails.

"No. You won't. No one does. You didn't believe me last time."

June didn't move. "Last time?" she asked.

"When I asked you about Leah," Tara breathed. She lowered onto the gnarled base of a tree. She panted like she did before the zipline ladder. One foot after the other, on two by fours held together with electrical tape and wishful thinking. June wanted to hug her, just as she did then.

June stepped closer.

Tara's head snapped up. She glared.

"You don't believe me."

June squeezed her eyes shut. Benson kicked his legs at her belly.

She tried. "Leah," she said, testing.

Tara smeared her nose on the back of her hand. When June couldn't get to Tara, someone else could. Someone like Tara but taller, older, hair always in a knot at the back of her head. So serious, too. She had a shorter nose, but the same dark brown eyes. Lighter brown in complexion, more like their mom than their dad when they dropped Tara off, her brothers in the backseat.

This someone would stand at the curb. She'd embrace Tara once she stepped out of the car.

This someone had embraced June, too. "Your sister," June said.

Tara blinked. "Have you seen her?"

"No," June admitted. "Not since the first day."

"She's been gone," Tara said. "And in there is why. The gardenkeeper took her away. He made a deal with me. If I can find her, I get her back. If not…"

"No," June said. "That's not… That can't be…" She struggled to form a full sentence. All she could do was shake her head.

It couldn't be true. "But he's nice to me."

"Because he's probably gonna take you, too," Tara mumbled into her knees. "I don't know why he hasn't yet. Doesn't want to lose the game, I guess."

June sat on the ground beside Tara. She rubbed Benson between the wings.

Tara wouldn't look at her. "I can't believe you're friends with him."

June's eyes were hot. Even Benson's gentle buzz couldn't calm her.

She didn't want to fog her glasses, so she took them off.

"I didn't know," she said. "You didn't tell me."

"Yeah, well," Tara said. "He took my sister. And other people, too. You shouldn't go in there."

"No. He's my friend, too. If he did what you said, I wanna know."

"I knew you wouldn't believe me."

"Tara! You can't not tell me and be mad I don't know! I've been trying to ask you what's wrong all summer."

Tara scowled at her. "I shouldn't have to tell you. He's a monster, June. An actual monster!" Tara said. "Teeth, claws, everything! You couldn't even get Haylee Pierce to like you. Or did you forget that, too?"

June sniffed. She balled a fist in her eye. "She said she was my friend. Just because she lied don't make me stupid."

"You are if you're falling for it again," Tara muttered.

June stood. She drew shaky breaths to steady her voice. She didn't want to embarrass herself more than she already had.

Her voice still trembled, chest stifled, as she said it. "Maybe I am stupid. I mean, I thought you were my friend."

She didn't wait for Tara's reply. She began the walk to Madrone cabin.

Tara didn't follow her.

June couldn't go to sleep. She held Benson under the covers, stroking his fuzzy belly. His hissing made Britney accuse her of keeping a stray cat in her room. There were a couple roaming the grounds, after all. But Britney, Gabi, Vanessa, and Grace C were sound asleep in the other bedroom.

The bunk above her was empty. All the bunks around her were empty.

Tears welled in her eyes. She let them. There wasn't anyone to see.

When she was feeling empty, she got up. She looked in Tara's bed. Villain, Tara's stuffed rabbit. The map. The planner.

Tara's sketchbook. She'd never looked inside without asking.

But Tara hated her, anyway.

June spread the cover open. Pages and pages, filling every margin. A map of the garden, of the house within it, labeled hall after labeled hall. Sketches of the fairies, warped and contorted and all wrong. Tara had drawn one especially terrifying character. A reptile who spoke through obsidian shards, his eyes crystal and all-seeing. Questions surrounded him. What he wanted, what he could be doing in the forest, where the people he made forgettable were forgotten to.

June touched the pages reverently as she did when the monsters in Tara's imagination were imaginary. Those monsters had been kind. Frightening, maybe a little much to take in, but always kind.

She put the sketchbook where she found it. She climbed off the bed, throwing on her sweatshirt for the nighttime cold.

She set Benson on her pillow. "Stay here," she whispered. She pecked a kiss between his antennae. Benson's feelers tickled her tear-stained cheeks.

The gate didn't open at night for her. June waited for sunrise. She didn't rest, stooped in the hedge until her eyes were stale.

When the sun peeked out, and she'd watched Tara exit, June knocked on the iron bars.

Weiss opened the gate himself.

He smiled to see her. Then he cocked his brow. "What's the matter, sprout?" he asked.

"We gotta talk. Tara told me about why she comes over here."

June crossed her arms. She couldn't keep the pout from her face, even as she wanted to prove how serious this all was to her.

Weiss ushered her in. June stepped inside the gate.

He walked toward the greenhouse. He said nothing.

The frosted glass pane cleared. He stepped through, the door hanging open behind him. June followed. She watched Weiss pick a sprig of what looked like sage. Set it down. His claws were worrying at his cloak.

"She says you take people," June said. She'd wanted to talk out of earshot from the fairies, just to be safe. "That you make it so no one remembers them. Why would you do that?"

Weiss neared the rainbow spiral's outer ring. He dragged a claw along, searching the shrubs, before selecting a pair of wildflowers.

"Weiss?" June asked. She walked in his shadow. "Tara's my friend. Did you take her sister away? Because I can remember her a little now. Which is weird, 'cause I couldn't before. Her name's Leah. She's my friend, too."

He wouldn't say anything. June sniffed. She followed him into the blue, feeling stupid stupid stupid. Fighting for Tara's sister, who June couldn't remember beyond a face right now. A face, a hug, a braying laugh, nimble tan fingers braiding Tara's black hair. Mentions about her from Betty, proud the girl would go from babysitting to forestry if luck held out.

She could be making these phantoms up. But June trusted Tara. Tara had been so angry, so afraid at the thought of June choosing Weiss over her. Her drawings made him look so monstrous.

Among the pink dinner plate dahlias, spinning above like gears in a clock, he just looked sad. Far away.

"You're not even listening, are you?" she said.

June trailed after him. Orange and cream canyons curled them deeper into the spiral. Weiss plucked a fistful of California poppies. He was headed for the yellows, toward the weeds. What humans thought of as weeds, at least. He was crouching to gather some dandelions.

That's it. She prodded him in the arm. "Weiss! Say something!"

He hissed. He winced as soon as he did so.

His eyes shut. "What is it you want me to say, sprout?"

"Say you're sorry," June said. "Say you'll give Leah back."

Weiss bowed his head.

June slumped. "So you didn't take her?" she asked. Maybe they didn't have to stop being friends. Maybe this was all a misunderstanding.

He grasped June's arm. He stood.

"Maybe Tara can be your friend, too. But she thinks you took her sister away. If that's not true, you can just tell her."

Hope rose in June. That'd be perfect! Tara could stop being so sad and avoiding June. Weiss wouldn't be so lonely. Leah could come back, if they all worked together to find her.

Weiss had arrived at the spiral's center. June looked up at him, his claw still around her arm. "Hey?"

He wouldn't meet her eyes. He was staring down.

"Weiss? I just wanna help."

His stare didn't waver.

He was looking at the mayapples.

June shuddered. In the claw holding her arm was a round yellow mayapple. Only her sweatshirt sleeve kept the fruit from touching her skin, two talons pinched around the stem to keep it from touching the gardenkeeper's stone. In his other claw were all the flowers he had selected.

June tugged away. His claw was solid rock. She writhed in her sweatshirt, but the obsidian digging into her wrist just bit harder. "This isn't funny, Weiss," she said.

He didn't move. He didn't blink.

June scratched at his arm with her free hand. She kicked at his wooden leg, only smarting her toes for the effort. Of course she couldn't beat up a living statue. Of course she couldn't just force him to do whatever she demanded.

She needed to get out, like Tara said. She had to come up with something.

"Weiss!" she insisted. "You can't do this. If you don't let me go, I'm. I'm not gonna be your friend anymore. I can't be friends with somebody that hurts people. You took someone Tara cares about. She's my best friend. She's been my best friend ever since I got to camp. 'Cause I protect her from bullies."

He finally met her eyes.

June furrowed her brow. Her glasses had come askew.

"I'm serious. If you want to be a bully," she said, "I'm going to keep her safe from you."

He pressed the mayapple into the back of her hand.

It sank in. Her hand itched. Spiderwebs of roots spread below pale, freckled flesh.

Weiss released his grip. Gently, he placed the flowers into her palm. He folded her fingers to cover them.

"Sorry, sprout," he said.

The gardenkeeper has haunted Tara's nightmares from the moment they met. What he'd done to June only solidified his menace, placing crystalline eyes and obsidian teeth in every dark corner until she'd grown old enough to believe she might be safe from him.

Didn't mean she wouldn't wait for him to appear in the shared backyard behind her apartment complex. Didn't mean she fully let herself think he wouldn't slither in and spirit more of her family away.

And she's waltzed right into his lair.

The gardenkeeper stands with Benson at his back. The beetle must have gone to fetch its master.

Leah waves him over.

"What are you doing?" Tara bites out, taking her sister's forearm mid-wave.

Leah sighs. "This is why I put it off."

"You didn't tell me on purpose," Tara realizes.

"Do you really think you would have come here if you knew?" Leah says.

No. Never in a million, billion years. She dismissed it as paranoia. Why would Leah come back, human and herself, if the gardenkeeper hasn't been defeated?

Leah should know better than anyone. "Why? Why would you do that?"

Tara's sister tosses her kabob on the fire. Mateo cringes. His hands dither, like he wants to touch Tara. Selina does, taking Tara's elbow in a root as if to comfort her.

Tara flails. Moe growls but Selina caresses her tulip petals.

"We didn't know you would be coming," Selina says softly.

"Oh, good, we're talking about it," Moe says. "Great. Leah Ayala, did you go out there and lose your mind? What made you think this was a good idea?"

"What, I should have disappeared again?" Leah cries, throwing up her hands. "How do you think that would have gone? I go, 'oh, hey, it's me, your missing sister!' and just peace out?"

"It would have been honest," Moe snaps. The two foot tall tulip manages to make Leah avert her gaze. Moe's not having it and keeps on trucking. "And you never told us you were bringing anyone back with you. Did you think about any of us having to move when these two bring more humans with them? Who knows where they are right now? They're not going to get forgotten like we did. Someone's going to come looking."

"Moe," Selina says.

"I lost this camp once, damnit," Moe says. "We're not losing it again because you can't think before you act."

"Moe!" Selina shouts.

Everyone but Moe flinches, Mateo and Leah included. Moe's roots are bunched like fists, her petals flaring open and closed. Only Selina's frown keeps her from resuming her rant, or anyone else from interrupting.

"Excuse us," Selina says. "My wife and I founded this camp. It's very dear to us. We," she emphasizes, "are upset because Leah did not consult any of us on a plan to bring you here. If we'd have known, we might have been better prepared for you."

Tara digs her nails into her hairline. Yet again, she wants to rip a piece of her brain out. Preferably the part that's making her want to run up the gravel road in a panic, stinging nettles and mega insects be damned.

"I can't believe this," she says. "After everything he did to us. Everything he did to you. I didn't have a sister for ten years because of him."

"I know," Leah says.

"So why is he here? You were there. You saw what he did to June."

Leah sputters for an answer. The gardenkeeper begins walking toward the green. They need to get to the truck. Tara looks over, ready to see June hatchet drawn and mace unclipped.

June isn't there.

Tara rounds on Mateo, who puts up his hands. "Where did she go?" she demands.

"She ran that way," he says. His finger juts toward a crop of cabins.

Tara doesn't even look where he's pointing. She books it.

Leah calls after her, but Tara isn't waiting around. She passes her first cabin, Oak, smothered in ivy. Her second, Rowan, is split down the middle.

Their last, Madrone, rots in the middle of them all. Tara goes to the door, shut but recently opened by how the grime's been disturbed. There's a C scratched where the corner dragged through old pine needles and mud.

She grabs the knob. It won't turn. "June?" she calls.

"I'm fine," she hears.

Tara exhales. That's one mystery solved. "We need to go, June. Right now."

"It's fine," she hears. Tara presses her ear to the door. "I'm fine. It's going to be fine."

A crash inside. June's voice cracks. "Just go away!"

Tara cups her eyes and checks the windows. The glass is too dusty to see through, the common room obscured by grit. From the direction of her voice, that's got to be where June is.

There's movement on the other side of the door, though. Tara tries the knob again.

"I'm not leaving," Tara says.

"You already did."

Tara's lungs can't draw air. She can feel them heaving, but the ache in her chest won't subside.

She shuts her eyes.

So they're doing this now.

They don't have time for this. They've had ten years for this. "Fine! You know what? I didn't want this to be your life anymore," she says. "I have to remember. You don't."

Nothing.

Still that ache. Tara swallows and makes herself speak through it. "June. I don't know what you want from me. We shouldn't have come here. Leah lied to me. I should have left all of this alone."

No sound. Did June leave the cabin? The only other exits are the bedroom windows.

"Please," Tara says. She lets her forehead bonk against the wood, pounding her fist against the door.

The door crunches.

Tara flings out her hand, picking bits of rot from her nail. White mold eats through the wood grain. She takes her fist in her left hand, angles her elbow, and jabs. Once she blinks the sawdust from her eyes, she can see a hole.

Her hand plunges in and fumbles the lock, but what feels like thick rope has the knob so stuck it won't unbolt. How did June even get in?

Here's hoping Tara's Walmart sneakers can handle this. She staggers and kicks out her leg, readying her aim.

On three, she gives one good stomp to the door's lower half. The door folks like a disgusting lawn chair, fractured in the middle to half-decomposed mulch. Tara smashes the splintered remains. The door's top half collapses to the withered carpet.

Tara can't see what held it shut now that it's destroyed. What she can see is that June's not in the common area. Nothing is, no couches or tables or furniture that would have been worth something before the camp was abandoned.

She steps through the wreckage. She closes her eyes.

"I'm not leaving," Tara says. "I know I did. I know I'm why we're here."

She kicks a clump of moss. She lets out a bitter laugh.

"I thought I was making you happy. I thought you would hate me if I stayed in your life. I hurt you. And I got you hurt even more. I thought you might get to forget all this. If I didn't find out, I could just go on thinking you did. It would've been easier."

Silence. Tara gets nothing. She's run out of time. June's probably gone, en route to her Chevy. That's what Tara wanted. She wanted June to stay away from this.

So why does it make her want to sink to her knees on this decrepit carpet?

"I don't know why you kept trying," she says. "You kept sending letters. Trying to talk to me. I don't know why you would."

There's a chuckle.

Tara's head jerks up. She looks to the left. The left hand bedroom. Of course that's where she is.

"You really didn't read them, did you?" Tara hears. "You should leave."

"Not gonna happen," Tara says. One breath, two. The ache ebbs.

She can do this. She enters the bedroom.

Her breath seizes.

June is propped against a bunk. Her gloves are off.

"I tried to tell you," June says.

A trumpet played over the loudspeakers. Tara batted around for Villain, but he must have fallen to the floor in the night. She rolled to face the wall. She squeezed her eyes shut so hard stars sparked behind her eyes.

When she'd come in through the window from her nightly search, June was already up and out. That'd been about fifteen minutes ago.

Tara groaned.

"Rise and shine," Britney yawned, opening the bathroom door. The other girls were awake already. They were getting dressed, brushing teeth, and doing everything else Tara couldn't drum up the energy for.

Haylee Pierce told her to shower yesterday, pinching her nose and jeering. Mandy spread a rumor she was trying to get dreads, did Mexicans have dreads, she'd never heard of them getting dreads until Tara nodded off and missed whatever racist punchline the kid had to say.

Tyese flicked her in the ear to wake her. Tara fell out of her folding chair.

The instructor reprimanded Tara for sleeping during lessons. They weren't just here to swim and play, you know. They were here to learn.

Demonstrations didn't get graded, at least. Missing assignments or answering questions incorrect just meant you got fewer beads. Other kids already had ten or more by August. Tara had three. They'd been incidental, the default ones everyone got from activities everyone did. Tara didn't wear her necklace around at all anymore, lest she be pegged a lazy dumbass.

She had a feeling that if they weren't so late in the season, and if her parents hadn't already paid all her fees, they would have just sent her home. Tara was a zombie. She snapped at anyone who interfered in her zoning out, which was as close to dozing as she could get lately.

Day one, she'd been asking for people who weren't real. She only became more antisocial as the weeks wore on. The camp counselor, the one who actually acted as a therapist and advisor, asked her if anything was going on at home.

Like Tara had called her parents more than once this entire summer. That call had gone like this.

The morning Leah vanished, Tara phoned home. She had to use the phone in Marydale's office, which she got to when she claimed she was feeling sick. It wasn't a lie. Her stomach rolled as she dialed. Her parents would have to know what was going on, even if Tino and Marydale and all the Cottonwood adults didn't.

Tom Ayala picked up the phone. "What's up, buttercup?"

Tara wanted to complain what a baby she wasn't, that she didn't need pet names or soothing. But something was very wrong. She couldn't keep from smiling at his goofy tone, in spite of her fear.

"I want to ask something. It's gonna sound kind of weird. But did Leah go home?"

"Uh. Leah?"

Her heart dropped into her sneakers. She held the receiver away from her face. Her dad was racking his brain on the line, like Tara had mentioned the name of a pet or neighborhood playmate he couldn't place. Despite being Leah's stepdad, Tom and her got along. He would never act like he didn't adore Leah, much less act like he'd never heard of her at all.

Tara distracted him. Told him her stomach was feeling much better, actually. She would be fine. Sorry for the false alarm. He told her he loved her and to call again if she needed a ride or to talk to somebody. She said she would. She hung up.

The next few nights, Tara laid awake. June asked about the Leah thing, but Tara told June to drop it. She didn't need to humiliate herself further. Especially if June refused to remember like everyone else.

Leah had mentioned Mr. Valdez. How people didn't remember him.

When Britney was lounging in the common area, Tara searched the counselor's side table. But Leah's things were already out of the drawer, stuffed in a cardboard box under the bed.

From Leah's planner and her map, marked up by a sister who didn't exist, Tara found the garden.

She'd walked out the gate before dawn, the gardenkeeper's words reverberating in her ears. She had one summer. No more humans would be stolen, until she turned over every leaf, every stone, every petal and twig in his garden. Its gates were open to her each night. If she could answer him where Leah was, she was free to take her sister and leave.

Tara pointed out someone else was missing. Mr. Valdez, the guy Leah had come here looking for. The gardenkeeper amended the rules: any humans he had ever taken, then. If she found them, she could have them.

But only if she found them. Only if he kept his word, never taking another human captive so long as she was searching his home. She could only fix everything if she met the terms or he failed them.

She didn't see the gardenkeeper when she searched. His underlings, the creatures June called fairies, scattered at the sight of her. They always did. They never wanted to talk to her, if they weren't already asleep in the dirt before she arrived. Tara had dreamed of all this. Of a secret haven away from the world, full of fairies and monsters and magic. She'd pictured fairies a little less Spiderwick Chronicles and a little more Tinker Bell, but they'd been a welcome wonder when she first entered.

Of course June could befriend them. Of course Tara was too moody and spiky to get through to them. Of course Tara was mean enough to drive June off crying.

Tara clutched Villain under one arm. She glanced down. Villain laid sprawled on the carpet below.

The thing under her arm writhed. She held it up.

June's bug. Her wooden beetle with hazelnut shells for a head, its wings those whirly twirly seeds that spun when you tossed them. Its beady black eyes shone, its feelers fluttering against her chin, the long lashes of its antennae tickling her face.

Tara set the beetle on her belly. It nestled into the blankets like a cat.

Maybe she could take back what she said. Fix things with June.

Forget Leah existed, like everyone else had. Tara could never. She'd already failed so far. She couldn't stop now, not when she had mere days before August ended and Leah would be gone to the garden forever.

She would have to search even harder tonight. The pond, swimming with its slimy algae fish. The trees, which had filled with birds on leafy monstera wings weeks ago. The flowers and shrubs had never yielded any hints, so Tara had taken to perusing the house. It was so bare in those first halls, but the deeper she delved into the chambers the more she saw. One room was devoted to piles of old, rusty plate armor, layered in dust and grime. Another had a heap of tools, like pruning shears and a hand spade, arranged in the corner. She even spotted a few flashlights, but they ranged from faded orange plastic with a blocky Radio Shack logo to more modern Maglites and Evereadys.

These rooms made her uneasy. The house without furniture or decoration, just blank walls and junk placed carefully on some of its floors, was worse than any Haunted Mansion clone at the carnival.

She only found one space in the place she could stand. Well, not stand, given its narrow passage. Up a spiral staircase in the left tower, a cluster of white flowers trailed purple, always in the path of a moonbeam no matter what phase the moon was in. She could rely on its light to draw her clues by. She'd caught herself nodding off into the flowers themselves.

Maybe she could sneak a nap there tonight. She would have to earn such a luxury, though.

This thought gave her the oomph to climb down the ladder, tucking June's beetle under her pillow beside her sketchbook.

She walked to the bathroom. Still no June. "June must be at breakfast already," she murmured.

Britney put on a plastic, cheery tone, eyes wide as she applied her mascara. "Maybe. Are you going to play with June today?" she asked. Like the counselor was arranging a daycare playdate, not a program her parents footed a few hundred of the thousand dollar price tag for Tara to attend.

"Sure," Tara said. She plucked a thorn she'd missed from her pinky. Ugh, she'd torn up the knees on all her jeans checking those rose bushes. "Did anyone see her?"

Gabi shrugged. She paused in her flossing to stare at the ceiling. "June's not in our cabin, is she?" she said.

"I thought she was in Oak," Vanessa said through her toothbrush.

"No, that's Jenny," Grace C corrected. "Right, Tara?"

Tara looked at the three like they'd grown horns overnight.

"What are you saying?" she asked them.

Vanessa smirked. "You can't even remember who you've been sharing a room with all summer?"

"You do look like you need more sleep," Britney said.

Tara looked through her doorway. No June. Her bug wriggled under Tara's Pokémon blanket.

She looked at the girls in the bathroom, all returning to their routines. She looked in the mirror, at the shadows under her eyes and the snarls in her hair and her own stunned expression.

"Britney," she said. "June is in our cabin. You have her on the list for this cabin."

Britney said she'd go check. The other girls followed her to their room. Behind the door, they were muttering about Tara. First a fake sister, now a fake bunkmate? After getting so lucky to get a room to herself, too. Did she always have the room to herself?

Britney didn't tell them to stop. She just said "huh!" when she saw June Bug on her list.

Tara already had her shoes on, the bug under one arm. She scurried out the window before Britney returned.

Her steps splashed as she sprinted through the creek. The bug clung to her shoulder as she ran, struggling to grip her sweatshirt with its twiggy legs. When she found the hole in the thicket, she leapt through. Grass stuck to her jeans from the creek water. She didn't care. She needed to get to the garden.

Whatever June had been using to avoid attention, it hadn't been like this. She'd been able to ask someone where June was, and they might say the bathroom or the mess or talking to a staff member, but Tara would get something. June had never unexisted before.

The gate didn't open. Tara panted. Right, they only ever let her in at night.

She slipped through the bars, just as she'd done the first night she discovered this place. Tara set the bug on the ground. She scanned the shrubs. Would the beetle be able to sniff June out?

The bug drew near a rose bush. Tara heard a high whispering voice inside. "Benson?" it asked.

She froze. She saw a fairy bring itself out from the bush on its roots. They were so uncanny in how they moved,

like tentacles striding across the ocean floor. She hadn't
spoken to a fairy since the night she made the deal.

"This isn't yours," it said to Tara. "Where did you find
him?"

"He was outside. Just wandering," Tara lied.

"Hmm. That's not like her," the fairy observed.
"Thank you for returning him."

And the bug was being herded into the roses.

"Wait!" Tara cried.

But the two crawled out of sight. Tara got on her
knees. She peered into the tangle. Benson and the fairy were
there, hidden among a handful of other fairies unfurling as
they woke.

"Why can't you just tell me?" Tara begged. "I'll never
come back here again. If you tell me where Leah is, I'll go and
that's it. That's what you want, isn't it?"

The fairy on Benson's back, head adorned in
hypericum buds like miniature peaches, frowned. Its roots
reached out to her. It traced Tara's face.

"You're not supposed to be here," it whispered. "It's
not safe for you."

"I know," Tara said. "I need your help."

"I'll help you."

"What's going on?" asked some stones, rubbing its
eyes.

"Ignore her," a tulip drawled. "If she gets our help, that's cheating."

"Now we don't know about all that," a lily chided.

"We were told not to help her," the tulip said.

"You know June, don't you?"

The fairies stared at Tara blankly.

Tara tugged the roots from her face. "June Bug!" she said. "She's got big orange hair! Glasses! She comes here, I know she does. She says you're her friends. If you're really her friends, you're gonna help me find her."

"Well now," the lily said.

"That's," the stones croaked.

"That'll work," the hypericum said. "Keep down. I'll show you where she is."

Tara obeyed, letting the fairies join her mission. The hypericum's filament roots tickled her cheek. The fairy looped itself around Tara's ear like a secret service earpiece. The stones tucked into her sneaker laces. The lily and tulip clung to the hem of Tara's sweatshirt.

"She followed him into the greenhouse," the hypericum said.

Tara nodded. She drew closer to the iron bars and frosted glass. From the beginning, the greenhouse seemed connected to the disappeared people, but how to get in always stumped her. "I tried that," she said. "There's no door."

"Throw me," the stones said.

The other fairies and Tara looked down at the stones. It glared at the greenhouse from its spot on her sneaker's toe. "I thought it was magic," Tara said.

"It's only magic when he opens a door. Otherwise glass is just glass. Glass breaks."

"Is he in there?"

"No," the lily reported. "He's in the house. He's not gone in here since she didn't come out."

The words were so matter of fact. Tara's hands trembled.

The stones wound up her body, prying her hand open and placing itself in her palm. "Do it. You don't have a lot of time."

"She's already been in there long enough," the lily said. "Bring her out to us."

"He can't keep doing this. Not to you children," the tulip growled.

Tara steadied her aim. The lily and tulip let go of her sweatshirt. The stones gave a thumbs up made of its roots.

The hypericum grazed her cheek. "Good luck," it whispered.

It jumped off. Tara threw the stones.

A pane of glass at her height shattered. The stone fairy lassoed an iron bar, slinging itself outward to the dirt at the window's base. "Hurry," it said. "And don't touch anything. I mean anything, but especially not the yellow ones. Go!"

Tara climbed through the window. She cut her calf on the broken glass, but she couldn't do anything about the blood right now. Her pant leg stuck to the slash and she plugged through the pain. "June?" she called.

Her own voice echoed. The greenhouse dome was enormous, its ceiling lit with luminous sunflowers. She'd scoured the whole garden, but she had never been here, not even once. How was she supposed to see what was suspicious when some of these plants looked like they came from another planet?

Especially not the yellow ones, the stones had said. She trudged through the spiral of colors. Blue. Violet. Red. Pink. Orange.

At its center, a patch of plants bearing yellow fruits, their leaves shaped like stars, their flowers white. They were normal, mostly. She didn't understand. What was out of the ordinary here? What was she supposed to be looking for?

A lone dandelion sprouted from the soil at her feet. Tara watched as another four dandelions were trying to sprout, no leafy base around their stems.

Tara got down on her knees and dug. Dirt jammed under her nails. The stones told her not to touch anything, but it didn't understand. This had to be it. She had to. She couldn't leave her.

The five dandelions ended in a hand so pale it was almost green. Tara pulled it. Already dirt cloyed around her rescue, and for a second she feared that fatal tear that came when you missed a weed's root. The hand was so cold and clammy. Stems acting as its digits were stretched long and thin, limp and lifeless. They weren't gripping back.

"June!" Tara cried. "Come on, June, help me!"

Muffled words came from the dirt. Tara snagged on something in the soil around the hand. The muffled words turned into an "ow!"

Tara held a poppy between her fingers. Its petals were bright orange.

She dug with new urgency, even as she heard yelps from underneath her. Finally, she saw more vibrant slips of poppy.

"Stop pulling those!" she heard.

"Then help me get you out. Are you okay? Can you breathe?"

"Ow," the owner of the hand moaned. It certainly sounded like June.

Tara found the hand again and hauled back a few steps from the hole she'd made, when the arm attached came with it. Soon after, the head and shoulders of the thing that used to be June.

It wasn't a fairy, yet. It was still June-shaped, a girl with big eyes and big hair and baby fat that chose to stick around an extra decade. But her limbs were made up of those tapered stems, her hair a great big spray of California poppies, and her eyes were halfway to resembling desert wildflowers.

She scowled at her savior. "I was sleeping in there."

"June, please," Tara said, taking the girl by the shoulders. "It's me. It's Tara. We used to be friends, remember?"

June squinted. She didn't have her glasses. She had clothes, though. Her camp sweatshirt hung on her, the brown cotton dingy and damp. Her feet had split into fine threads, tying her down into the dirt.

Tara gave another tug. The roots loosened, and she held June up so they wouldn't worm into the ground again. "Come on, June," Tara tried. "You were my best friend before all this weird stuff started to happen. You like video games and swimming and. And being friends with people who don't like you. You're the nicest person I know."

"Tara." June tasted the word. "I know a Tara. I think. Who's this June, though?"

"June?"

"Yeah, June. I feel like I maybe know a June. I definitely know a Tara."

Tara stared at her. "June is you. You're June."

"Oh. Can I go back in the dirt now?"

"No, you can't go back in the dirt! What did he do to you?"

"Who? The gardenkeeper?"

"Yeah, him. I told you he was bad! He's hurting you."

June scrunched her face. "Yeah. Yeah, he is bad."

"Do you remember what he did to you?"

Tara held June at arm's length. June was no bigger than a baby doll. Her legs were unraveling to more roots, traveling to the ground. Tara bunched the roots into June's sweatshirt.

She whined, her belly flipping.

June blinked. "Nope. I know I'm mad at him. I don't like Weiss right now."

Tara didn't know who Weiss was. "I'm going to make you June again. I promise."

She wanted to laugh at how angry the half-fairy looked. When June got angry, she did it like a cartoon. A leaf stuck out of her mouth, her brows set and her mouth a grumpy frown.

It was her, but it was all wrong. Tara swept a clump of poppies from June's face.

Then it hit Tara. "I won."

"You won? Congratulations, Tara."

"You don't get it. I won our game. He said he wasn't going to steal any more people. He stole you. That means he loses. He has to change you back!"

"Whooooooo." June waved both arms, dandelions dancing.

Tara rose to her feet. She held June at arm's length and fixed those wildflower eyes with her own. "You can't go in the dirt again. Okay?"

June nodded. She wrapped her dandelion stems around Tara's neck, draping her like a scarf. Tara had her hands free to leave the spiral and climb out the window.

The stones were waiting. Its eyes caught on her and her bleeding leg, then on June. "Never seen one like that before," it said.

"Were you able to," the lily asked, and faltered. "Oh my."

"We're too late," the tulip said.

"No, we're not," Tara said. June crawled up her neck to sit on her shoulders. Her flowers curled into Tara's hair. "I made a deal with the gardenkeeper. He was going to give back the people he took if I found out where they were."

The fairies looked up at her. She looked down at them.

"You're all people," she said.

Somewhere, in this garden, Leah had been here the whole time. But which one? How had she never thought of it?

June's roots were spilling down Tara's shoulders, reaching for the dirt. Tara shuddered. June saw her tense and reeled the roots back into her clothes again. Tara hadn't let the theory form because it was too upsetting. Because the thought of her sister, transformed into something that couldn't remember and couldn't be remembered and not even given the comfort of her own body, made her feel like throwing up.

She had to focus. "Which one of you is Leah?"

The fairies said nothing.

"I've already won the game!" Tara said. "Why can't you tell me?"

A shadow cast over the fairies. Its caster loomed behind Tara.

June groaned. "Ugh, this again."

"What have you done?" the gardenkeeper rasped.

"Boo. Boooooo," June said. "You gotta stop that. It's not scary anymore."

Tara begged to differ. The gardenkeeper swept around to face her. He took one of June's dandelion stems between his talons. "What do you remember, sprout?"

"I remember you're a dirt clod," June said. "And a jerkface. And you're always a sore loser! You made my brain all foggy and I... I..."

Tara could feel June go limp. She scrambled to catch her before she could slip from Tara's shoulders. Her beady black eyes, ringed in desert wildflowers, were blank.

Tara's gut twisted. She glared at the gardenkeeper.

"You hurt her," she said.

"She isn't finished."

"You hurt her!" Tara snarled.

The gardenkeeper didn't deny it. Tara realized the fairies who'd helped her wore the same blank look June did now. "What happens when it's done? She'll be just like the other ones?"

The gardenkeeper turned away.

"Fix her," Tara said. "You did this to her. Undo it. Undo it to Leah. Undo it to Mr. Valdez. Everyone."

"I cannot."

Tara wound her hands in June's roots. Trying to keep the tendrils from the ground, but it was like juggling wet spaghetti. They slipped through her grasp. "No!" she cried. "We had a deal."

"That we did."

"You were the one who made the rules. You lost. You weren't supposed to take anybody else. Why did you take her?"

"I cannot undo what's been done. What's grown cannot be ungrown."

"Why did you take her?" Tara repeated.

The gardenkeeper didn't deign her with a response.

Tara fell to her knees. June in her arms had closed her eyes. Like she was sleeping. She was too small, and too forgotten, and she was all Tara had.

She clutched June to her chest. She hugged her like she hadn't since the first day of summer. When she stood beside Leah, and June liked her, and Tara hadn't ruined everything yet.

June's steps wrapped around her arms. Her chin found Tara's shoulder. "What's wrong?" she asked.

Everything. Everything was wrong. She'd held it together for so long, and everything only ever got worse. She'd hid and lied and run away. She'd made a deal with a monster for her sister, all alone. Now she wasn't going to get Leah or June back.

For the only time all summer, she wept. She hiccuped into June, who stilled. She gripped Tara tighter, pressing her weight closer, but it wasn't the same. It wasn't right. Soon she was going to belong to the garden and be gone, and Tara would go home empty-handed.

A dandelion brushed Tara's cheek. Tara sobbed as June tried to dry her tears.

The body against hers grew. Became more heavy, more substantial. Tara shoved her snotty face into June's sweatshirt. June's heft in her lap still didn't feel real. Her skin still had the too smooth finish of fresh bark. Her hair still clustered together in bunches of poppies.

Until the thumb under her eye pressed, really pressed. It lacked the light touch of a flower, now the cathartic tug of flesh on flesh.

Through tears Tara could see June. June held Tara's chin in both hands. She wadded her sleeve and dabbed Tara's eye with grimy, threadbare cotton.

"Better?" she asked.

Tara was holding June. Her June. She was covered in soil from being buried. But her feet were feet, and her hands were hands, and her eyes looking back were eyes and not blossoms.

The gardenkeeper watched. The fairies under his spell did, too. Tara didn't know which of them to take. All of them? But how many others were there, lost to the garden?

The gardenkeeper took a step toward them.

Tara summoned what strength she could to pick up June and run.

June remembers what came after. Trudging through the shore of the creek. Tara's leg bleeding, a long gash from shin to ankle, swirling the water pink. June still needed to lean on her, though. Her feet were numb, and she could walk on the bank barefoot, but if she stopped long enough in the grass she could feel herself sinking. The girls braced on each other until they finally reached Madrone.

Their families were called. They'd been in trouble before, but they'd never gotten injured. They'd never been covered in dirt and blood, tangled up tight in each other until the directors tore them apart. Tara disappeared with Tino into Cottonwood cabin.

June was dragged into Madrone, showered, dressed in fresh clothes, and sent to wait on the porch. Marydale stood guard over her. Betty would be there in an hour.

Police were brought in. There were questions. June didn't answer a single one. Betty told them to leave her granddaughter alone. If June didn't want to talk, she didn't have to talk. She threw June's suitcase and her wadded bedding into the Ford's bed.

June didn't even get to say goodbye. By the time Betty had her buckled in shotgun, insisting June didn't have to tell anyone anything before she was ready to, it was too late. June's toes wriggled in her socks the whole drive back to Bonny.

When she got home, she didn't have any appetite. She dropped onto her bed, in her room with its Goodwill paintings and coloring pages and Game Informer clippings taped all over the walls. She slept like the dead. Her suitcase lay unpacked on the scratched hardwood floor.

Betty would knock and check in on her. She'd been reading those books since June moved in, books about parenting even if she'd parented before, because June's grandmother confided she didn't feel she'd been much of a good parent the first time. If she had a second try, Betty wanted to do better.

She made sure to bring June food and water. June couldn't convince herself to eat the first. The second, she guzzled. She couldn't drink enough. She couldn't sleep enough. If allowed, she'd do nothing else.

But June could tell she was worrying Betty. She drafted a letter to Tara. They'd written dozens of letters to each other over the last two years. But what to say? June could ask how Tara's brothers were. How her mom had been enjoying her new clinic job. How her dad's surgery had gone.

How much she missed Leah, who June could recall in detail since her burial. How June could ever apologize. How she could ever make up for what they'd seen and done, all because June had been stupid enough to trust a monster.

Any attempt along these lines ended in a ball of paper under her desk. She filled a page with nothing instead. She gave it to Betty to mail off, to make her feel like she was helping.

As autumn arrived, though, June couldn't keep herself awake enough or warm enough. Sunset to sunrise, she bundled herself in quilts and chugged water bottles Betty put outside the door.

Betty drove her out to Mays Middle School. She registered June for the year. June walked from concrete to linoleum in a haze. Betty nudged her granddaughter. Did junior high make her excited? Nervous? It was perfectly okay to be nervous.

June shrugged her off. The moment they were home, she returned to her room.

Before the school year could begin, Betty knocked on June's door. June had been sleeping the day away again.

She woke up.

She saw petals on her pillow, orange poppies crushed under her head. Her limbs prickled pins and needles, fingers stretched to narrow stems, nails now yellow buds, toes splitting to roots and reaching for the floorboards.

June screamed. Betty begged to come in.

June hid under the bed. She fit underneath, among her shoes and lost stuffed animals. She just kept getting smaller. She'd changed back, hadn't she? She'd changed back. How could this be happening if she'd changed back?

Betty kept knocking. June whined.

Her grandmother finally entered. She knelt down to see June under the bed.

June wept milkfoam. Betty picked her up and hushed her, stoking back poppies. June murmured apologies. To Betty, to Tara, to Leah. Betty told her she didn't have anything to be sorry for, but she didn't know. So June told Betty everything.

As she talked the roots reeled in. Dandelions on her fingertips closed their blooms. Her wildflower eyes were groggy. Betty stood. She set June on the bed. She tucked June under a corner of comforter and gave her one more pet on the poppies.

When June woke again, there were no flowers. She was just June, human with no evidence of what had happened. She could believe she'd dreamed the night before, except Betty sat her down in the kitchen. She asked what June wanted to do. Did she want to go to Mays? Be homeschooled? Whatever June wanted, Betty would support her.

June studied her nails, yellowed at the whites like tobacco stains. She spread her thinning fingers across a school supply list, watching them twist into stems. At least Betty hadn't opened with a plan to storm the garden, but she could barely believe Betty remembered last night at all.

Maybe June would have pursued this, had she not been distracted. She'd been hearing things. Not quite a voice, not quite words, but insistent.

She's not done. She needs to go under. She needs to finish growing.

Here in the house, it was a whisper. Outside, it was a bellowing demand. June told Betty she'd rather try homeschool, please. She liked having friends, but her body acting like this made her anxious. Betty nodded. She let June pick the online curriculum they used. She gave any time she had left from the nursery to adjust June to her new schedule.

This made it so June could sleep when she needed to, which in winter was often. She could have her moments, her digits knotting into dandelions and head itching as poppies sprang from her scalp. She could pause her lessons when her ears pricked up and something spoke to her in its soundless speech.

The obvious source was the gardenkeeper. Under the earth she'd been able to feel him like an ache. A wave of his despair had crashed upon any under his thrall, even as his face stayed impassable stone. The sprout she'd been had drowned in it.

Then arms enveloped her. Warm as the sun, desperate as a drought. She sank into them. Tara. *Tara*. Her friend, trembling and terrified, and June in her embrace like her ratty stuffed rabbit.

No. This was not Weiss, hunched in on himself, lost in remorse and regret. That spring, she learned exactly what the soundless voice really was.

Betty didn't have a lawn. But the vegetables behind their house were displeased. There weren't enough worms. Wasn't enough water. Betty's attention had been too busy with June. She should do something. Couldn't she help them? They needed help.

Her roots kept tearing through shoes. She couldn't step off the porch without them wriggling in her socks to get free now. Seriously? June had built up rubber soles on this property's gravel and grit. She kicked off her third pair of ruined sneakers, about ready to call it quits.

But she couldn't focus if she didn't give the plants what they wanted. Huffing, she stepped onto the dirt.

Her foot plunged into the ground, now a thick bundle of roots seeking its neighbors.

She fell. Her head swam. She strained against the numbness, creeping from the mayapple embedded in her hand to her every extremity. Even without the numbness, there was no swimming in soil. Earth had frozen her in her fall. She couldn't move a muscle. Yet she could feel motion. She could feel a sting across her skin as it drank in the damp from the rain. So this was what Benson's transformation must have been like. Stuck in black amber, burrowing deeper and deeper until everything fell dark.

The other plants stopped their hollering. She could hear herself think again, at least She couldn't remember where she was, though. The garden? She must be in the garden.

"June?"

She didn't respond. Last time she was in the garden she'd been able to latch onto someone. Someone important. Who were they? She. They were a she. Her hair swayed long to her butt, black as night and prone to spiking like a hedgehog when loosened from its tie. She wore a great big cotton sweatshirt, baggy denim pants. Her skin like river silt, her eyes like fresh peat, her hands fine and precise as they sketched. Who? Who was this?

She was being yanked on. She did not like this. Her roots resisted, but loosened more and more with each tug.

June blinked. Betty was panicking. She bawled. She told June she'd been standing there, taking her granddaughter's arm in both hands, pulling her out and feeling herself forget the girl's face when she could see it right in front of her.

June gripped her grandmother for dear life. She'd almost forgotten. They both had.

They found June the thickest boots money could buy. Betty sourced them through a wholesaler. June wore garden gloves coated in rubber latex everywhere, from the grocery store to the bank to the nursery. Betty did not like June going to the nursery.

But June couldn't stay indoors forever. Yeah, the cacophony of soil had been a lot at first. The potted plants at the nursery weren't so loud, though. She could do those, couldn't she? Dirt in a pot couldn't root her, after all. Call it exposure therapy, she told Betty.

June could hear what the plants wanted better when she approached them one at a time. Diagnosing why a plant wilted or molded often fell to pH or fertilizer choice, but just as often they told her they wanted a song. They wanted to hear words. They wanted company.

If they were truly isolated she'd have to peel off a glove. Potted plants wailed when they were like this. To get any peace, she'd have to stick her finger in. The start's roots, cramped in their plastic cube, would tangle her dandelion. They had to split the stem to tiny hairs the plant could communicate with. Usually there was nothing to do but plant the starts who were this sad.

Betty let June do so along Dianthus Drive. June didn't plant according to any particular design. Flowers didn't care what their neighbors looked like, as long as they were far enough for their own space and close enough to share nutrients. They did develop a pattern anyway. She could plant a dozen at their requests, and they'd create loops and curls, unfurling down the length of highway.

June did fine. She finished middle school online, and high school, and a term of college courses before she determined they weren't for her. She liked getting her hands- well, her gloves- dirty.

And Betty had told her the nursery was hers if she ever asked. June told her she'd think about it. Betty's retirement made her anxious to consider.

Anxiety made her feet twitch in her boots. She staved it off by working full time. She took over crafting the yard decorations, dictated by Betty once her tremors made welding next to impossible.

June was happy. Everything was fine.

Until barkdust poured from a bag in a specific way, spitting dust up into her face. Until spring arrived, along with the seedlings shooting up all unawares and curious. They asked her lots of questions anytime she came in range. How could she hear them? How did she walk and talk as she did, when she listened like one of them?

She would set them up in a tray against their fellows and let the elder starts explain it.

Coworkers commented on her work ethic. They suggested mental health resources, like June could ever waltz into an office and confess magic existed without failing a psych eval. If she did actually prove it to a psychologist, doctors were another liability. So June had never told anyone but Betty about her transformation, and not even Betty knew about the not-voices.

But June had her own methods of staying grounded, in addition to her workaholic habits. When she'd confessed to Betty, her body had responded. The same came from writing to Tara.

Betty had sent the first one. June sent every other, more and more open in each update. Message by message, she told Tara everything, not-voices and all.

She remembers being so proud every time she managed to ship a letter off. They'd been hard to write, but what if this was the one? Whenever a handwritten envelope arrived in the mail, she was certain to scrutinize it for Tara Ayala's name and hand. She never got a reply.

Overall, it could have been worse. June had Betty. She had her coworkers, who weren't in on the secret but accepted her strangeness as the trade off for such a damned good grower.

She thought she'd be able to handle the place that strangeness stemmed from.

Apparently not. June's dandelions have stabbed through her gloves. Tara stands in the doorway to their old room in Madrone cabin, eyes glued to June on the floor.

June is cornered. She shakes out her hands. The gloves fall to scraps like a shed skin. June has another pair in her backpack, but she's going to have to wait until her fingers return to normal or they'll shred through again. The dandelion stems are surprisingly strong, capable of wrapping the doorknob and holding it shut.

Now they wrap themselves in June's poppies and pull. Tearing them out stings, but the stimulation fends off the pins and needles. Her boots usually keep her roots contained, but a few are creeping through the gaps in the laces. She should have worn her Wellingtons instead of these Bean boots. To think she's been doing so well lately.

Tara kneels down. June tucks her stems in her lap. She knows how she looks when she's like this. Her boilersuit loosening its fit doesn't help, the denim sagging as her body strains to stay person-sized. Betty still can't get used to June's stems stretching for out of reach items, and that's just her hands unraveling.

Unlike now, when all of her is succumbing. Fortunately her memory's only affected if she roots down. She can remember herself in here, with only carpet to dig into. She can accept looking like a monster. She'd be acting like one if she could accept forgetting.

June closes her eyes even so. She's not ready to see the horror on Tara's face again.

Then June hears wheezing. She blinks.

Tara's got her face puckered up, rubbing her eyes like there's sand in them. They're red and dry. "I can do it!" she says, seeing June's confusion.

"What are you doing?" June asks.

"Just wait, okay?" Tara sniffs. She snorts like she's trying to work up a loogie. Her eyes refuse to wet. "Shit. Shit! I can't do anything right."

"Are you trying to cry?" June asks.

"It worked last time!" Tara says. She growls through her teeth. "I knew this was going to be a trap! But she acted like Leah. She didn't sound mind-controlled."

June just squints. That's what Tara thinks? "You don't need to do that," she says. "It goes away on its own."

"Wait, this," Tara says, and waves to June, "just happens? Since when?"

"When do you think?" June says. She thinks about closing up. She thinks about night, when her buds shut and her roots cease their roaming. Nothing. Her dandelions dance in front of her face.

In front of Tara's face. Tara is staring.

"It's fine, really," says June.

"What?"

"I didn't need you to see this," June mutters. She plucks another poppy off her scalp. She throws it to the rotting carpet. The sheets on the bed behind her are threadbare, the foam mattress one breeze from blasting apart to chalky particulate.

Tara glances away. Her thick brows are set, she's so serious.

June smiles, eyes hooded. Tara actually fought her way in here. Tara really believed she could cry magic tears and make June human on command? The tears themselves didn't matter, insofar as they signaled to whatever had remained of June that Tara was upset.

Seeing Tara upset had revived something in her muddled mind. She didn't know who June was, but a spark ignited and she knew exactly what Junes did in such a scenario. She'd told Tara as much, committed to paper, confiding how she can cling to those instincts even now.

June reaches out. She brushes a dandelion under Tara's eye.

"Sorry. I didn't mean you can't look," June says. "I thought I gave you warning is all. It's not your fault you didn't get my letters."

Tara closes her eyes. "I got them."

June grows another poppy. She throws a frown up at it, but Tara isn't watching.

Tara's scrubbing a hand over her face. She heaves a sigh.

"You did?" June asks.

Tara nods.

"And you didn't-"

"Yeah, I didn't read them." Tara fondles her hoodie's drawstrings. "I read the first one. But then they kept coming, and I didn't know what to do."

Of course. No wonder Tara didn't answer, after opening that envelope of salt in her wound. Stupid June.

"Listen," she says. "It's okay. I get it. I'm okay in here. It's gonna take a second, but-"

"This would have been so much easier if you just hated me."

June looks at Tara. Tara looks at a root escaping through June's laces.

June flicks the root. The root retreats. June waits for Tara to go on.

Tara opens her mouth. Closes it.

"I'm fine," June says. "Really, I am. I just got overwhelmed out there. I only came back because of Leah. If she needs us, I didn't want to fuck it up again."

"Neither did I," Tara says. "But here I am fucking it up again. She's friends with *him*. The gardenkeeper."

"Weiss?" June says. She'd assessed the risk he'd be here when Leah showed up. Weighed how she'd handle the woods and having her brain cleaved in two, between all the shouting above and the shouting below. She braced herself for the worst headache of her life, basically.

To her surprise, the Del Bosque forest welcomes her. It's kind, letting her have room to think, but it's been waiting.

And the mandrakes. Maybe she didn't expect them to be angry, but she thought they'd at least resent her getting a life outside these woods while they've been trapped. Instead she's embraced, the prodigal plant returned. She's not the idiot kid too blinded by the magic to see where it grew from.

She wants to believe it's Weiss's doing. But she knows how mandrakes behave under his influence. She knows how it feels, and she isn't feeling it.

"I don't think it's him," June says. Tara arches a brow. June dithers her dandelions in the direction they came. "They were never like that before. They were always excited to see me, it's just... I could have saved them. Instead I was there playing my Nintendo. Getting buddy buddy with the guy who hurt them."

Tara cackles. It's so close to her old bray that June perks up, but there's no joy behind it.

She shakes her head. "You weren't the one who agreed to find them," Tara says, "and spent months looking under rocks when they were right there. If they should hate anyone, it's me."

"That's not fair," June says.

"What? It's true."

"You were ten."

"So were you," Tara says.

June folds her arms. "Touché."

Tara shifts on her knees. She glances at the shattered door. Right, they should be escaping, huh? June should be making a run for it, Tara over one shoulder like a bag of peat.

Instead they're sitting here. All that urgency and adrenaline, fueling June from Bonny to here, has drained out of her. She lets her neck settle against the bed frame.

Tara slouches on the carpet before her. "You had this going on," she says. "I'm such a dick."

June's mouth quirks at the corner. "Dunno about that."

"I am. I cut you off. And this was your life. I could have been there for you."

June shrugs, like she hasn't dreamed about this very thing for a decade.

"It's alright," she says. "No big deal."

"Let me apologize, will you?"

"Apology accepted. We're here now. 'Sides," June admits. "I might not have written all that stuff if I thought you were listening."

Tara's eyes go everywhere but June. She twists a drawstring around her thumb. "What stuff?"

"Too late, you have to live with the suspense," June says. Her dandelions flutter with mischief.

"I'm reading them as soon as I'm back to my car."

"They're in your car?"

Tara shuts up. She tucks her hair behind her ear.

A floorboard creaks.

"Someone's here," Tara says, jumping to her feet. She stands to block June.

June smiles. The gesture is sweet, until June's reminded of the panic Tara had shown up in. She can assume who might be following, though this thought doesn't make her as antsy as she guessed she'd be.

Then again, the mandrakes alone had overstimulated her to the limit of her human form. Will she be up for an encounter with their master?

Mateo, formerly Geodude, is who they spot in the main room. He sees Tara.

He sees June. He gapes. "Leaaaaah," he calls, unmoving.

Leah careens in after. Sweat beads at her temple, wisps of her bun slipping free.

"Oh. Um," she gets out.

June waves from behind Tara's knee. Tara squares her shoulders. Really? Tara's not gonna fight her own sister, is she? Despite how embarrassed she is, June does like seeing Leah and the other mandrakes with their true personalities. Before June got to know them, they echoed their keeper, an interchangeable greek chorus at his beck and call. Traits and tics emerged over time, but nothing so fleshed out as this. These mandrakes have too much to say for themselves to be coerced.

June wobbles on her feet. Even contained, the roots make standing up uncomfortable. She feels pinched up and too tight in her boots.

Mateo and Leah are stunned silent. Tara's grasping for a threat, for anything at all to say.

She flinches at the sound of heavy footfalls.

"They're in here?" rasps from the cabin's stoop.

Tara seethes. June measures her breaths. She grounds herself, steeled for Weiss's feelings and fears to finally paralyze her. Why haven't they? Maybe she's been outside his range, or it didn't take effect if he didn't sense her presence?

When Weiss arrives behind Mateo and Leah, June stifles a laugh.

Next to grownup humans, the looming stature she'd been convinced of as a child only reaches her shoulder. His posture dominates not at all. He hangs onto Leah like she might conceal him. Felted white flowers sprout from his stones.

Weiss meets June's eyes. He turns and walks out the door.

From the moment the children were beyond the garden's reach, Weiss the gardenkeeper wanted nothing more than to sink into the earth and let it claim him. He had made the same doom befall anyone else who entered his domain. Humans were a nuisance at best, a threat at worst. It was best practice when his masters were here that they were disposed of, exceptions made to extend their futures if they proved amusing.

When his masters returned to their home, he carried on this best practice.

First the explorers, boisterous and arrogant, attacking with metal and gloating how they would ravage this place in the name of a land Weiss had never heard of, much less seen. Weiss bided his time. Then he threw down his seeds, and their mandrakes joined the ranks of those his masters had spirited away.

He ordered them about. Because he'd planted them by his own claw, every mandrake in this garden followed his command. It was quite satisfying. These humans, they thought they could own soil that would chew them up and spit them out without a thought?

And somewhere, so deep he dared not look, he could feel the absence of his masters. They had plucked him from the ground. He did not understand them at first. They were roundabout, fickle, constantly bickering and outdoing each other. He was shared between them, a communal pet, hungry for purpose and praise.

If he could not be commanded, someone needed to give the commands. The gardenkeeper determined his time would be best spent caring for his masters' treasures. After all, what if they returned? What if they found his good work, commended it, realized their mistake and took him along to their home?

Of course, Weiss never considered these things consciously. Like weeds, they pushed up on their own, taking shade under shrubs and going unseen.

There were the miners, grubby humans who sought to claim the spoils of the earth's crust. He gave it to them. Settlers, too, they came to tame the wild. He made it so they had no need to. Mandrakes do not starve or die of sickness, after all. His last for a long while were a trio of criminals in search of amnesty. Technically, a thief none can remember cannot be caught.

He spoke to them. A facsimile of his masters, ranting about the day's highs and lows to something that could not listen or understand.

What was once satisfying was now dreadfully dull. How did these mandrakes lack the wherewithal he possessed? He had always been a bit different. It made him interesting enough for the masters to keep. He could speak words, think thoughts.

While there was a spark of sapience to his own mandrakes, they were missing that certain something to make them conversants. They obeyed without question. They did anything and everything he asked, before he asked it. What had he done wrong? What had the masters done to produce him that he had failed to replicate here?

Perhaps it was in the planting. Whenever his next human arrived, he did not select the seeds at random. He obviously combined mayapple and scorpion grass, in case the humans were sought out by their own. The last thing he needed was another army at his gate.

But nothing. He would harvest, only to find his work utterly in vain. The mandrakes would cling to his moss cloak. They spoke, but only to reflect his own ideas back to him. In time, these thoughts lingered and looped.

He concealed the garden. Any humans who drew near would not see it unless they looked, really looked.

It would be decades before two more stumbled in. A couple, clinging to each other, older than most humans Weiss had ever seen. They wrinkled like they had been overwatered. They were going to mold, if they kept it up.

They would not last. He let them look around the garden for a time. But eventually, inevitably, he led them into the greenhouse. He planted them.

Another few decades, and another human, this one alone. He spoke words in the same tongue as the explorers, so he was swiftly planted.

He waited, the mandrake of pebbles and moss coming out just like any other. Thank the stars these humans were getting so few and far between. Weiss did not think he could take much more disappointment.

Mere days passed. Then there was a human here, calling for the last. Weiss had an infestation on his claws. How did this one remember the other? She did not once she was planted, but it was curious.

So curious that when the night came in which Tara Ayala entered the garden, he made her a bargain. If she could tell him where to find this sister of hers, she could have her. She could be observed as she searched. Just maybe, Weiss could root out what he had so wrong about all this.

He had his doubts when she departed.

In minutes, the sprout arrived.

Weiss did not learn June Bug's name until she was already gone. Yet, somehow, she made one summer feel like an eternity.

First out of frustration. She pestered him to no end. She played with the mandrakes, drawing them out of themselves more than he had ever managed. He had never seen anything like it. Of course he had not, since he always kept the humans from discovering what the mandrakes truly were. June did not know the truth, but she always talked at them like humans talked at each other.

She talked at him like a human. While standing upright like one, he was very much not human. He begrudged it. He tolerated it. He liked it.

He didn't know what he would do without it.

He kept a mayapple in his cloak. Always, always deciding against what he knew would have to come. When Tara Ayala failed, and she would fail, Weiss would be free to plant the sprout and keep her. But would she be the same? Would this human ever again be just like this, a person who told silly jokes and played games and was so tantalizingly unpredictable?

He'd come around to another ploy. His sprout loved the garden. What would she say to staying here forever? He didn't know how to preserve her without his usual methods, but he would find one.

He was coming up with the words. How to phrase it? How to keep it from sounding as selfish as it was? She didn't just have him. But all he had was her, and the mockery of sentience any other mandrake barely scratched.

When she learned the truth, it was almost a relief. Finally, everything unraveled, uncomplicated, in one accusation. His options had whittled down to the same simple solution he had for every other human.

Taking her by the arm to the plot was like walking in a fog. He could feel his body threatening to betray him. His mouth was heavy, laden with excuses and explanations, so he kept it shut.

As soon as the mayapple took root, the fog dissipated. Humans always struggled. She just stared. The phantom of the mayapple curled in his claws. He couldn't take it back. He couldn't dig it out, condemning her to the soil even as horror soaked into his stone. He could not unplant what he had planted.

He hid himself away. He didn't know what to do. Had his masters ever regretted planting a seed? He didn't think so. He'd never heard them admit to remorse. Guilt. Tearing at him like termites, threatening to crumble his oaken leg and chest.

Tara did what he couldn't. She pulled June up. Weiss couldn't undo what he'd done, but this human child could.

He should have been furious. Challenged. He should have put them both under and won this wager once and for all.

All he could feel was numb. He might have failed. He might have made a huge mistake, but June didn't have to pay for it. Even if she hated him for the rest of her finite time in this realm, she wouldn't have to spend it as a hollow substitute for the real thing.

They fled. Weiss didn't stop them. They could go and tell the humans to come after him, but they wouldn't be believed. Scorpion grass made certain of it, unless there were more Taras out there. He avoided the greenhouse with its broken window.

He wallowed, letting himself drop to the bottom of the pond. He didn't want to exist anymore. Whatever he had been before his masters pulled him up by the stem, he would take it. He certainly deserved it.

His cloak floated up around him like seaweed waving in a current. Algae carp swam past his shoulders. He thought a carp swam into him when something jabbed him in the eye. He bared his teeth.

Unimpressed floated one of the couple, the feisty one. She'd managed to kick him before he'd planted her. She had a rooty finger extended, prepared to poke him again.

"You're moping," she spat. Her tulip flared out in the water. The words were clear through the murk.

Weiss didn't reply. He scowled.

She poked him again.

"Stop that!" he said. "I know."

He rubbed his nose. She kept assaulting his face, prodding through his talons with smaller and sharper filaments.

"I don't pretend to like you," she snapped. "But if you don't get back up there, I'll make this hole a living hell."

Weiss would endure it. He deserved to suffer.

Then he blinked. He spread a claw to block her, and she ceased.

"You're talking to me," he said.

"Yes, and stabbing you."

"No, that's," Weiss said, and trailed off. He studied the mandrake. She had a fierce frown on her face. He'd seen her make it at June, albeit softer. She could get annoyed sometimes, but only for show. She could talk, but never about anything. "What are you talking to me for?"

The mandrake rolled her beady eyes. "I dunno," she drawled. "Maybe because you're the only one bigger than a daisy around here? Maybe because this is all your fault?"

He took her into his claws, looking closer. "It is my fault," he agreed. When he said it aloud, his excitement waned. The mandrakes only told him things he already believed, though rarely with such venom as this one did.

Still, this didn't make her any less accurate. "You're right," he said.

"Damn right I am," she said. The mandrake crossed her roots. "Are you gonna keep stating the obvious or are you gonna get some air?"

"Neither of us need to breathe."

"If you say one more thing that's plain as day, I'll smack you."

Weiss closed his mouth. Yes, this was very new behavior.

He scaled the bowl of the pond, the mandrake holding onto the hem of his cloak. When he got to the top, three other mandrakes were gathered at its shore.

"Are you alright?" asked the stargazer lily. Weiss almost grunted a yes before he saw the question was directed at the tulip, who crawled up to join her.

"What are we going to do now?" creaked the stones.

"The garden's still safe, right?" the hypericum asked.

Weiss nodded. This was surreal. He'd never been particularly surprised by his garden's denizens before. He welcomed this over the usual simpering, but that didn't make it any less bizarre.

"If those girls go back and tell," the stargazer said.

"If another little one gets snapped up," the tulip sneered.

Weiss walked for the greenhouse. The mandrakes followed. They weren't talking to him. They were talking to each other. They were holding conversations that involved him tangentially, but not completely. How?

"Junebug won't be coming back," the stones sighed.

"I'll miss the dear," the stargazer cooed.

"I won't," the tulip barked. "I don't want to see another soul wrapped up in all this."

Weiss disagreed. How could that be? Was this really happening?

The hypericum stood on the back of his neck, facing her fellows. "If we want them to stay away, we need to get rid of the camp," she said.

Yes. Yes, they did. "How?" he rasped.

"You're the wizard, doofus," the hypericum said.

He turned. The hypericum on his neck clung on so she didn't get swept off. The others were walking in his wake, following his muddy footprints from the pond.

"You're all very invested in this," he observed.

"Why wouldn't we be?"

Because Weiss himself was? Perhaps. But he suspected something else. "I'll need to go outside," he said. "If I let you do so, will you?"

"Like we have a choice," the stones grumbled.

"You don't."

There it was. They froze up. The spark in their eyes dulled. Whatever was happening to them, it unhappened. "Yes, gardenkeeper," they chorused.

"Weiss," he said.

They didn't lose their daze.

Weiss pulled the hypericum from his collar. "Weiss," he said, looking her in the eyes. The daze failed to wear off. He sighed. "Come with me to the greenhouse."

They followed without a sound. They were normal again. He talked to them, hoping against hope the tulip would swat at him for it. He held her and the stargazer and placed them on his shoulder. The couple should be together. He scooped the stones to his other shoulder, the hypericum still balanced on his claw.

Then he entered the greenhouse. He was done talking to no one.

He'd spoke true to the girls. He had never attempted to ungrow what was grown. Once a seed cracked open, what's done was done. There would be no taking the resulting components apart.

But what if there was?

First, the camp. He assigned these four, given they were the closest to lucid, the task of venturing out. They were to bury scorpion grass along with non-magical plants to fend off returning humans. Stinging nettles, poison oak and ivy, his most vicious thorns and thickets all encroached on empty grounds. The facilities buckled under the floral onslaught, resistant to any herbicide the staff wheeled out.

He didn't know why he did it. It was an impossible task, for an impossible end. So what if he succeeded, anyway? It wouldn't matter. June would still hate him. Tara would still be out there, knowing a monster had stolen her flesh and blood. If the humans found out what had become of them, if they didn't know already, his mandrakes would riot. He was courting his own ruin for nothing.

Then one of them would snap at him. Crack a joke. Act like a person, and like maybe he was a person, too.

He hated how he craved that.

When spring came, the counselors didn't. The campers didn't. The mandrakes reported the camp had to close due to the new labor required to keep it. One of them mentioned a variable he didn't particularly understand. An eekah-no-mee? Whatever it was, it crashed last year. The camp stayed open one more summer, but the hypericum announced it would close for good according to its directors. Staff packed up. Anything that couldn't be salvaged was left behind.

With the announcement came one last task. Another round of scorpion grass encircled the property, and there would never be a revival of Camp Cottonwood. The business officially died.

Weiss had never tread outside the confines of his garden. Even the older mandrakes, those who showed no glimpses of awareness like those he'd sent out already, perked up at the prospect. No questions, just interest. They would wait here, he decided. Until it was safe.

Like he cared. When had he begun to? They were just a harvest. An odd crop, but they weren't people any longer.

They might be, though. And talking to him, also not a person, made him feel like one. If talking to something like a person might make it so, he'd at least humor the practice. His old practices never bore out any happiness for him.

"I'll be back," he said. "If it's safe, then. Then we might go out."

There were murmurs. Weiss took this as a good sign.

Crossing the threshold made him feel cold. He wrapped his cloak closer. Unlike his own mandrakes, he'd never been ordered to stay within the garden. He could go whenever he pleased.

But that didn't make it any less heretical to his masters. To himself.

Every step grew bolder. The creek he'd seen through the wall of thickets trickled across his feet. He didn't suddenly erupt in flames, or become ensnared in a trap, or any number of horrible things that swarmed his thoughts when he considered the other side of the fence.

He walked as far as he could see from the thicket. He returned.

The mandrakes huddled together. He waved to the gap.

This was how Weiss and his fleet of a few dozen mandrakes overtook Camp Cottonwood.

June's four, as he thought of them, thrived here. The couple claimed the largest cabin. They let Weiss work in the cabin's common areas, but not the bedrooms. The stones found abandoned machinery and described how they operated. The hypericum told him the names of the cabins and dug him out a tattered map. For being lord and master of all Del Bosque forest, Weiss was pitifully poor with directions.

Their invasion carried out, Weiss devoted himself to the second stage in his plan. He requested beetles. Benson rested under his claw while Weiss pondered. If planting a mayapple and other samples caused different effects, what would happen if you worked backward? What if you planted a former beetle with a current beetle? Would the components cancel each other out?

He buried Benson and a dead beetle together. He waited.

Benson crawled out from the dirt. Still Benson. Well, Benson and a dead beetle beside him.

He threw in other ingredients. What else had Benson been planted with? He listed them out to himself, examining Benson thoroughly to be sure. He procured the ingredients from his greenhouse. He planted them.

Nothing, again. Weiss let his forehead fall to the table he worked at, groaning.

"What are you trying to do?" asked the hypericum.

Weiss glared up. "I'm trying to fix this," he said.

"Fix what?"

He waved to her. This. Everything! "You know you aren't meant to look like this," he said. "Don't you?"

The hypericum frowned.

"You know I'm the one who made you this way," he tried.

No response. Just silence. Weiss growled.

The hypericum pet Benson on the antennae. "What did he used to be like?"

Weiss grunted. The hypericum patted Benson's wing. "Him? He had a broken leg. He was hers. I don't remember." He pointed to the dead beetle. "This, only alive."

"Is anything else missing?" she asked.

Weiss scratched his head. He'd been getting pollinated outside the garden. Buds were forming, and he trimmed them with his talons. "Something I'm not seeing," he muttered.

He walked the woods, to check his garden and gather supplies. Day after day, with no progress on his question. What was he missing? What was Benson missing? What was every mandrake he'd ever made missing that he somehow possessed?

His wanderings got him lost. Figured. He spent so much time out here and knew nothing at all. Compared to the humans who cultivated this camp, he was blind.

So he did not see the knobby white matter in the high grass as especially unusual, until bulbous puffballs were ballooning around him. By the time he saw the last pop up to surround him, he'd already inhaled.

Weiss woke in a ring of mushrooms. At their center, himself.

Himself and something else. He crawled back on all fours. His moss cloak got tangled.

The something else in the mushrooms was fleshy. Round and soft, creamy white aside from the patches of fungi formed across its belly and head. He'd mistake it for human if he didn't know better. Its misshapen limbs were spread, four of the gnarled appendages upturned to the sky.

Its eyes opened. It stared down.

Weiss hissed. "Who are you?" he demanded.

The fungi raised one arm. Its three fingers formed a doughy hand, waggling in a wave. A cloud hummed about it. Particles of indigo, moist and muggy, wetted the air. Then the strange something else disappeared, taking its mushrooms with it.

Weiss retraced his steps back to camp. He didn't know what this thing he'd encountered was, but it had given him an idea.

He brought Benson to the greenhouse. He let the beetle down on the ground among the mayapples.

Benson only took interest in them when ordered to. When he touched his feeler to the yellow skin, the mayapple fused with the insect. Weiss tossed his other ingredients into the hole that soon formed.

He waited. No leaf popped out.

No viney leg did either. Weiss had to unearth Benson himself.

The beetle hobbled out of the dirt on five legs. Benson was small as an acorn. He was chitin and elytra, an animal. He was no longer a mandrake.

Weiss brought Benson under his eyes. He got the urge to put the beetle in his mouth. He suppressed this urge. The vision, courtesy of the being in the mushrooms, might have scrambled his instincts a bit.

But it had gifted him a revelation. He planted, replanted, planted again over and over. If Benson touched the mayapple on the vine or on the ground, the same conclusion.

The only time Benson did not return to fauna from flora was if Weiss picked the mayapple himself. If he planted Benson, it didn't work. If Benson planted himself, it did.

By the time Weiss assured himself of his success, Benson was very large indeed. Large mayapples made large mandrakes, small mayapples making small mandrakes. Benson was tiny as a seed one germination, too mammoth to walk out the greenhouse doors when Weiss brought him up last in mandrake form.

"Come on," he called. Benson perked up to follow. The beetle did not act like a mindless insect, and nothing like a dazed mandrake who followed the gardenkeeper's whims, either. He ignored Weiss if he wanted, running off to chew a pine branch, but when Weiss caught his attention he might nod or shake or twitch his antennae in response.

At camp the mandrakes panicked with the gargantuan beetle's arrival. Weiss caught up to Benson tapping inquisitively at the hypericum with his feelers. She pet his head. Bensone nuzzled her, before scurrying to rest on the roof of Oak cabin.

"What does this mean?" asked the stones.

"What did you do to Benson?" the tulip said, clutching her stargazer. "He's going to demolish what's left of this dump!"

Weiss scooped the hypiercum onto his claw. She would be first.

"Where the hell are you going?" the tulip shouted after him. The other mandrakes watched him splash through the creek. It would be their turn soon enough. He found himself looking forward to it.

"Seriously, where are we going?" asked the hypericum in his grasp. He had her cupped to his chest, running on two legs even as his brain kept badgering him to four.

"The greenhouse," he told her. "You're about to loathe me."

The hypericum froze. She didn't seem to process this information anymore than she could process being human at one time.

Weiss set her down in the center of the spiral, as he had Benson. He waited. She stood there.

Ah, still awaiting orders. "Hold this," he said, handing her a sprig of scorpion grass. "And touch one."

The hypericum did as bid.

The hole ate her.

Weiss waited. He waited longer. Humans did take more time than beetles to grow, he supposed. Still he tapped his obsidian talons at his knee. He bit his knuckle. What if it didn't work?

A leaf with eight spokes popped from the soil. He'd been nodding off into his claw when he startled awake. He got down so his eye could be level with the ground.

"Shit!" he heard.

Weiss's glee evaporated. Oh. That.

"Holy shit. No, no, no, no…"

The cries were muffled. Weiss inched out two talons and pulled the mandrake free. She held her face. She touched her buds. She looked up.

She screamed.

"What is your name?" he asked over the wail.

"Who are you? Wait. You. You!"

She wrestled around his claw to try and get at his face. "You!" she shrieked.

"You're Leah, aren't you?"

"Where's Tara?" she yelled. "If you hurt her, I'll-"

"Long gone," he said. "If she's hurt, I had nothing to do with it."

This did not make her calm. Hmm. Probably not the right thing for him to say.

"I'll put you down," he said, and did so. She wobbled on her roots. Awareness came with a certain clumsiness, he noted. She wrapped her limbs around her central bulb. Her eyes squeezed shut.

"Leah?" he asked. "Leah Ayala?"

She looked up. She nodded.

"I order you to," Weiss said, only to scowl. What should he order her to do that wouldn't end in further upset? "To stand."

She snorted. "Give me legs and I'll think about it."

Weiss laughed. "That is fair. How do you feel?"

"Like I've been hit by a truck," Leah moaned. "Like I'm going to scream and throw up. Is that enough for you?"

"I don't know what throwing up is," he said.

"Well, yeah, you're a rock. And a San Joaquin Fence. Those don't throw up."

"A what?"

"Forest reptile," Leah mumbled. She gripped her head. "Might be an alligator lizard. My book at home, it has- Ugh. This is a lot at once. It's like having a migraine."

"It hurts?" Weiss asked. He reached out and rubbed between her eyes.

She slapped at his talon. "Metaphorically!" she said. "Sorry, I'm thinking. I think I remember a lot. It's too much right now. Don't ask me things."

Weiss nodded. He stared.

He grinned. Leah glowered. He struggled to fight his joy down to a more reasonable level.

No luck. He kept fidgeting. "It worked," he rasped. "It really worked. Do you remember everything?"

"I remember Tara. I remember camp. David and Alex. College. I'm going to go to CR. Soon. But I have to finish summer. Mateo's gone. I found a..."

She fixed her eyes on him.

"I found a garden. You did this to me," she said.

"Yes!" Weiss hissed in triumph. "I did!"

"You're a monster."

"I am," Weiss agreed. He'd been waiting for so long to hear it.

Her glare fell into a squint. More and more information must have been returning to her.

He let her absorb it. All the while, he sat with his legs folded, claws digging into his ankles. She was still small. She was still a plant. But she was thinking, feeling, having impulses of her own that didn't stop when he intervened. She'd continue to do so as he worked to reverse what remained.

With Weiss's exit, the mandrakes are upon June once more. Selina rushes forward to take June's dandelions in careful roots. Moe clings to the skirt-like petals about Selina's waist. Winnifred Walsh grapples her flock of children down from June's poppies, and others June never got the names for cover her so quickly she can't even make them out by species. They fuss and fret and June's too tired to reassure them, only appreciative that Mateo and Leah are staying in the door frame instead of joining their smaller kin.

Tara tries to calm the rest down. She gives enough explanation to get across this is not a new development. June's been like this the whole time.

Which invites even more questions June doesn't have the energy to answer. At least now she isn't spending so much effort on staying human. She can set that everyday burden down as long as she isn't where she might break ground.

This doesn't mean she's up for a detailed description of the last decade, though.

The setting sun is what saves her. She sees the light fading through the grimy cabin windows.

All but the Ayala sisters stretch their leaden limbs. Some yawn.

"Answers can wait for morning," Leah suggests.

June nods. The mandrakes pour off and filter into the common area.

Tara stays leaned against the bunk, playing tough bouncer as June readies herself. Her spare gloves, plain red compared to the blue bees she's torn to tatters, slip over her rewound fingers. Night tends to reverse the less convenient parts of her transformation, so her feet are solid in her boots once more.

As everyone departs Madrone, the Walshes leave for Alder. Frank and Leon and Dora skitter up the eaves of Maple like spiders, several more taking nooks and crannies elsewhere in similar fashion. Mateo has gone over to douse the fire before they lose daylight completely. Then, after a hug for Leah, he heads off to a hammock hung between Beech and Cedar.

Leaving the three newcomers alone next to the pit.

"We're gonna stay the night, huh?" Tara mumbles.

"Unless you want to drive back to Bosque," Leah says.

June stretches. No chance she'll be up for driving those snaking turns in the dark, and by Tara's grimace she won't be either. "Any of the beds in good shape?" June asks Leah.

Leah makes a face.

"Great."

"I mean," Leah says, "everyone who needs them already has them. Mine's in Cottonwood. I could see if we have any more hammocks?"

Contingency plan it is. "I'm good," June says. She jabs a thumb toward the road. "My truck has a setup. You okay sharing a mattress, Tara?"

Tara nods. Then stills. "Uh."

"If you're not, it's cool." June can sleep in the cab. Maybe should sleep in the cab, based on Tara's deer in the headlights reaction.

"No, you're good! We can do that," Tara says. "Yeah, let's go."

"Guess I'll see you in the morning," Leah says.

Tara gives this a grunt. She walks for the gravel road. Seems like the sisters got into an argument after June ran off. Fair enough, if they had. June herself should be more grumpy at Leah for the lack of preparation, but she hadn't exactly been forthcoming with the facts either.

Still, she glances back at the elder Ayala. Every time she's reminded Leah is here, that she's real and herself and human, June fights the urge to run up and tackle her in a hug again.

Leah smiles. She waves.

June waves back, before following Tara to the road.

They make the trek to June's truck in the dying light. The dense overgrowth takes particular care to traverse now. Where Benson's belly had flattened them, the nettles have reset, springing high to protect the sleeping mandrakes.

June will be among their number if she doesn't hurry up. She can't have Tara trying to carry her if she passes out past sunset.

So she'll risk it. She rips off a glove. As soon as she does, the ground picks up its wordless speech. She speaks a little too loudly when she asks, "Can you, uh?"

Tara glances up from a blackberry bush that's snagged on her jeans.

June offers her bare hand to Tara.

Tara takes it.

June bites the bottom of her other glove and peels it off. Glove in her mouth, she bends down. She lets her fingers graze the gravel, letting them hover just inches above the road. Threads wisp from her pale skin, the tiniest tendrils sinking between the rocks. She's been asked to do a lot by the plants she hears. Sometimes, it's worth convincing them to return the favor.

The connections seal, and June grips Tara's hand tight. Even drowsy, the plants under their feet are undeniable. Their queries are almost as overwhelming as the mandrakes' were, but June presses her thumb into Tara's palm, feeling her life line.

She thinks about her truck, and how she'd like to reach it, and how she prefers not to damage any life underfoot as she had when she'd entered through the gate, please.

The nettles part. They arch over, bending toward the road's shoulder like a book spilling its pages open.

June tugs her hand up. The threads tear like velcro.

She replaces her glove. "Thanks," she says.

Tara stares. She looks like she's about to say something, but decides against it.

June keeps walking, Tara's hand firm in hers. She relishes the sensation, a soft brush of flesh against flesh. They'd been touchy as kids. Girls can get away with PDA easier when they're young. More than boys can, anyway. This should be natural. Casual.

Instead June's scalp prickles with new poppies. She lets go when the teal truck comes into view, stuffing her hand in her pocket before it turns too floral.

June pulls her keys from her belt loop and approaches the rig. "I'll get it set up," she says.

Tara follows her through the gate. She nods.

June can feel Tara's eyes on her back while she unpacks her emergency tub. Her electric pump howls as the air mattress inflates to fill the truck bed. The blankets are a little stale from being folded in a plastic bin so long, but the smell clears once June flings them out.

"Do you go camping a lot?" Tara asks.

Ha. June drapes an old quilt over the mattress. "I have a pack just in case."

She tosses out a pillow. A rolled up doormat. Last but not least, a lantern. Tara turns it on and sets it against the wheel well. "That's nice," she says.

Gnats dance in the lantern's glow. The bulb shines bright, the batteries full. June put the box together back in high school, for the same sort of exposure therapy working at the nursery provided. Why didn't she ease into nature again, at her own pace? First an experiment in the driveway.

Come morning she'd awakened in the front seat, her roots creeping through the gap in the driver's side door, curling against the tire, reaching for pavement cracks to sneak through. June hasn't so much as touched these supplies since.

Hopefully she'll do better tonight. "Yeah," she lies. "It is nice."

Tara takes the rolled up doormat from June's fumbling hands and lays it out on the tailgate. She climbs in. She kicks off her sneakers.

June hops up and begins to unlace. Her fingers slip on the triple knots in the new dark. Before she can fully remove her boots, she closes the tailgate. Just in case. Then she kicks her boots onto the doormat.

Just normal feet in holey socks. June lies back, relieved.

Tara sits against the cab beside her. Already it's getting chilly, and she pulls a throw blanket onto her lap. She looks up through the canopy. Stars poke through the branches above, breaking up the purple and black.

"It's so quiet," she says.

June begs to differ. Night is better than the day's cacophony, but dirt is dirt and dirt has not-voices even if they dim when the sun goes down. There's an ambient hum to it now, like a refrigerator buzzing in the background of life.

Not to mention the cricketsong, chirping away in the darkness. "Yeah?" she yawns.

Tara shrugs. She closes her eyes, and June names the stars to herself. Cottonwood campers had to know Cynus, Casseopia, Orion. Got you a bead, back in the day. She hasn't had much use for constellations since.

Tara hunches into her hoodie. "It's cool you can still do this stuff," she says.

June traces Betelgeuse to Bellatrix in the air with her index. The sky's stunning. It's almost stunning enough for her to ignore the world underneath this truck. Almost. The tremor of ants tunneling just below the topsoil, the forest quaking with near silent motion, the ground itself vibrating across miles and miles of individual organisms, a sprawling web she's missed under the asphalt and cement that comprise her usual haunts.

It takes her breath away. Her lungs go still, like earth has packed them full all over again.

She's dozing off when Tara slides down to lay beside her. That wakes June right up.

"I probably could have gotten out more. It's just," Tara says, and pauses. Her face scrunches up. "Leah was the one who did stuff like this. So it all looks like her. Then when the boys were going to outdoor school? I fought my mom and dad on it. They weren't even coming here, just to Eureka, but-"

"I'm sorry," June says.

"Don't be," says Tara. "You didn't do anything."

June flushes. Their faces are close enough to feel Tara's breath, June's lack thereof.

Those letters. How much easier would today have been if Tara had read and responded? If June had bothered to drive down the hour, instead of throwing bottles in the ocean and resenting no reply? Maybe Tara wouldn't have understood everything in them. Not how June can feel the earth spinning, shifting, shaking itself into new forms as seeds lodge in and life grows out.

But the feeling of being alone, cast off into a normal where their experience is nothing more than a bad fairy tale?

Tara takes a loose poppy from June's hair. June trembles. Tara's ring finger brushes June's temple.

June can't do this. She just can't. Tara had been her best friend, but the Tara she'd known had lived in a world where the sister she loved no longer existed, even in anyone's memory, for ten years. June may have spent that same time in a body that never stopped reminding her what happened, but she deserves this.

Tara doesn't. She shivers in her emerald U of O hoodie. They're going their separate ways once they help Leah, the real thing they're both here for. June can't let this reunion be anything else. Tara will go to Oregon, and June will return to Bonny, and nothing else will bind them together except for the summer that tore them apart.

And this, Tara reaching out between them. Her hand lingers. June had spent so long believing when she reached out, Tara would rise to meet her.

June curls her arm around Tara's. Their fingers thread.

June yawns. "Sorry," she says.

"I'm sorry," Tara echoes. "If I'd known you were still… I could have…"

"You could've what?" June says. "Come and watered me? C'mon. It's not the worst thing in the world. It's not my whole life either. I'm not just a plant. I'm gay!"

Tara laughs. God, hearing her bray like a damned donkey puts a little grin on June's lips.

"How did Betty take it?" Tara gets out.

June groans dramatically. Her other arm falls to cover her eyes. "She thinks I need a girlfriend. If someone comes in with, like, any hair color that's not natural, she thinks it's time to play matchmaker. It's a lot."

Tara rubs her eyes. "I bet," she says. "Sounds better than how my parents reacted."

Hope. June's high on hope. Is this a dream? "Knew it."

"Laugh it up," Tara says.

"No, like," June says, gesturing vaguely. "You were always doing the whole 'gender is dumb' thing. Never cared about boys. Never did the 'ew cooties' phase, either. Also, vibes. You were putting out the vibes."

"Fine," Tara says.

They lay there, hand in hand.

They say nothing.

Tara's the one to set it off. It's like lighting a fuse, a snort that sparks off into laughter that quakes the whole truck, sending roosting birds overhead to scatter. June can feel giggles bubbling up from somewhere dusty and disused. And there it is. So long, alone, and then something clicks together. They sprawl there, sliding into the same grooves they'd worn over mere months. Those hours of jostling each other just to get a smile, whispering secrets after stealing away to the other's cabin in the night, were short. But not as shallow as June had feared.

June should probably be ashamed of how much she wants to believe they can do this again. Shouldn't it have been too long? Too much? The Tara she'd written her letters to was not the person she lays next to now. But she thinks about getting to know this new person, and she can't resist the relief rolling through her in a wave, her hand stretching out to grasp Tara's entire arm. She wants to be wrapped up in her, to make up for lost and wasted time.

Tara picks at a dandelion twining her elbow. "June?" she asks.

June stiffens. She releases her hold, stems splaying. There are more than five of them, all longer than fingers or even June's forearm ought to be, growing from where her elbow bends.

She lets out a final, frightened laugh. "Uh. That happens sometimes."

"Are you okay?"

Very okay. June's ecstatic. Her mandrake side reveals itself in any great emotion, just the bad. She runs her flesh hand through her hair and shakes out poppy petals. Normally June can't keep herself awake past dusk, and here she is with blooms bursting out at night.

She thinks about closing. She can't.

Not while Tara examines her arm, still unspooled to those near-translucent fibers. They gently plait together into something resembling a human radius and ulna. Skin weaves to cover muscle red as a peeled beet, limiting the transformation to where metacarpal meets phalange and beyond.

Tara sees this. She draws a fingertip along the length of the dandelion stem.

June's face burns. "It's okay."

"It is?"

No. June has unraveled more today than she has in months, if not years. She understood coming out here might be the end. She should be terrified, and she is, but. "Just missed you," she blurts.

And here. This forest. How? How can she? But she did. If she steps on the ground, her feet bare as they are now, she's gone forever. Betty would forget. June would forget.

Tara wouldn't.

Neither would Leah. "And her," June says. It's not a lie. She did miss Leah. She's always wondered which of her fairy friends Tara's sister had been. She wonders what might have happened if she had figured it out sooner.

Tara furrows her brow. "Yeah."

They're here for Leah. June manages to get her hand looking more like a hand and less like green pasta attacking her friend. She rolls over, bunching into a ball.

Tara says nothing. June squeezes her eyes shut. Why did there have to be just one bed? Why had she asked Tara to share it with her, like tweens at a sleepover?

There's no shift in the mattress beside her. Poppies threaten and she scratches at her pomp, crushing them before they can surface. June begs silently that she can get away with what just happened, no questions asked.

Tara turns over. June's racing heartbeat slows.

They just have to get through tomorrow.

18

"Good morning, sunshine!"

The sung greeting stirs Tara from sleep. Sun does indeed shine over the air mattress in the truck's bed. She wallows into the musty quilts and tries to block it out.

Then Tara bolts up. She's in a truck bed, in the middle of Del Bosque forest. Their wake up call comes from two flower fairies astride a beetle bigger than this Chevy. From behind the gate, Selina waves. Moe is seated behind her, the pair perched where Benson's head meets his wings.

June is rubbing her bleary eyes, squinting without her glasses. She sits up and stretches her arms, very much just flesh and freckles, over her head.

Selina and Moe share a look.

Tara's eyes go wide. She looks at June, who shrugged halfway out of her boilersuit in the night. She wears a yellow tank top underneath. Under her armpits are clumps of orange petals. She scratches them and yawns.

Both fairies grin at the sight, Moe more visibly amused than Selina. Tara fluffs her hair and pats around for her rubber band, but she can't find it in the nest of blankets. Her hair's come loose from its tight, tiny ponytail. It sticks out over her head like a thistle.

Nothing happened last night. Does Tara wish something did?

Does June? June's tugging on her boots while Tara briefly buffers. Gloves on, she opens the tailgate and clamors out. Tara slips on her sneakers and lets June help her down, deliberately not noticing that June's left her boilersuit unbuttoned.

After shutting up the truck for the day, they wedge through the gate and come to Benson's side. June pats his shell. He almost bucks the fairies off, running circles like a bunny in his joy. He clicks and hisses and June coos at him like an oversized mastiff.

"He missed you so much," Selina says. Moe clings to her like a flagpole in a hurricane, her roots wrapped around Selina's stargazer a dozen times over.

June tickles Benson's feelers. "Missed you, too, little guy," she says.

Tara keeps her distance. The fairies hold tight as Benson rears up, grasping at June's lapels with his forelegs.

"He's a lot faster than walking," Moe mutters, by way of explanation.

"Yes, we don't usually have to travel so far so early!" Selina says. "Down now, Benson. We were asked to come and fetch you. Leah's closed herself up in Cottonwood since dawn. Benson!" The beetle is chewing on June's hair again. He lets go when Moe taps his eye.

"There we are," Selina says, shaking her head fondly. "Yes! Leah said she may have some idea of how to make herself memorable again."

"She's plenty memorable," June jokes. Tara stuffs her hands in her hoodie pouch and kicks a rock from the gravel. If only.

She trails alongside June and Benson. June has a gloved hand spread on the beetle's shell. He vibrates it against his wings, buzzing his content. The walk isn't long enough. Tara dreads getting to the end of the gravel, given her blowup yesterday.

The nettles bend out as they approach, folding inward once they've passed. Tara stares at June. The feel of her hand, warm and alive even as her fingers stretch to stems, dances over Tara's own. Tara smooths the pad of her thumb across her palm.

"How'd you do that last night?" she asks.

June glances over her shoulder. "Just asked nicely," she replies.

"Do what? Are you doing that?" Moe barks down.

"Oh, I did it when we were walking yesterday," June says. "I didn't wanna trample them, but we didn't really have time to get stung going in and out. That's okay, right? They said it was fine."

Moe and Selina murmur to each other. June's cheeks go red.

"Do you guys not do that?" Tara asks.

"Hell no," Moe says.

"Can you, like… hear them?" June says.

"Hear the plants," Moe deadpans.

"Well, when we hear each other," Selina laughs. She dances her roots in Moe's petals. Moe rolls her eyes. "Get it? But you must mean the ones who aren't us. We don't hear those."

June hunches her shoulders, stuffing her gloves in her pockets. "Oh."

The Rathbones don't get to ask further. Benson runs up ahead, taking the fairies with him.

Tara picks up her stride. She nudges June with her hip. "You can hear plants? How do they sound?"

June looks at her boots. "It's not like words. Just thoughts. Feelings, I guess."

"Vibes," Tara teases, waggling her fingers. "Have you been hearing them this whole time?"

June nods. "They're quiet right now. Waking up. These are probably doing that on muscle memory," she says, indicating the nettles at their backs.

Tara wants to ask more. Yet again she kicks herself for not reading those letters. But they're caught up to their guides. They arrive to see Mateo around the campfire again, this time unlit. He's eating a pomegranate as he looks over some baskets lined up on a log bench.

Mateo tosses a pomegranate Tara's way. She fumbles to catch it.

The choice of fruit is a bit on the nose for fae food. Her stomach rumbles anyway.

She hands it to June, who winces. "I don't have to eat," she admits.

"Don't you want to, though?" Mateo asks. "First thing I did when I could was eat. Mornin', by the way. There's persimmons and figs here, too. Or apples, if you're boring."

"Yeah?" Tara asks. She sees those and more stacked in the baskets. Lemons and limes, clusters of grapes that she sees the lupine Frank rifling through, even vegetables like the squash they'd been treated to last night. There's a lot of variety to choose from for the middle of nowhere.

"We've been farming them," Mateo says. "Keeps us busy, me and the Union."

It's too early for Tara to ask about a union. She selects another pomegranate. June tries to give her the other one back, but Tara dodges her. She holds up her index. "Breakfast," she insists.

"I don't need it," June says.

"Eating is important," Selina declares. She and Moe have dismounted Benson, the beetle investigating Mateo's bounty. The stargazer fairy chooses a fruit of her own, breaking the rind of an orange on a nearby rock. "Even when you don't need it! It's quite grounding for the senses."

June rolls her eyes a little. Selina's watching the two of them expectantly.

Tara lets Mateo break open the pomegranate rind. The fact he can do this with his bare hands is not lost on her, nor is the fact juice is now going to be all over her hands. She takes a bite of a pomegranate seed. The seed's squishy aril bursts between her teeth, sweet and refreshing and she's devouring all but the bitter flesh the seeds are housed in.

She wipes her sticky hands on her hoodie. She didn't even realize how hungry she was.

Mateo shoves a basket into her arms. "Try to get Leah to eat, will you?" he says. "Since she's the only one of us who actually has to around here."

Tara juggles the offering but manages to balance the basket in the crook of her elbow. Inside the basket are apples of every shade and size.

Mateo ruffles her stuck up black hair, his knuckles rough like a piece of pumice. Tara's been thoroughly noogied. "Thanks," she manages.

He salutes. "Good luck," he says. "Don't let them freak you out."

"What do you mean?"

Mateo does not elaborate, grabbing a basket with straps like a backpack. He's gathering items for whatever his morning routine entails. Tara sees shears and a trowel but a few bottles and a sleeve of dirty cards poking from the pack, too. He slings it over his shoulder and jogs off, Frank latching onto Mateo's wrist as he departs.

Selina and Moe have their arms looped like a pair of promenading belles. "We'll be around, don't worry," Selina says.

"What did he mean by that?" Tara asks.

"See you, ladies," Moe says, giving June's knee a pat.

And she and Selina are off strolling toward the creek. It's just Tara and June.

Benson prods their butts toward Cottonwood cabin.

June smears her glove on her thigh, dripping juice down the rubber coating. She licks a seed off her lip. Tara is staring. Tara has got to stop staring at this woman.

They ascend the steps. Tara braces on the railing, her calf throbbing slightly. She feels the line drawn from shin to ankle flare up. It's scarred, a white dart of lightning seared into her skin. It never pains her, but the last time she climbed these stairs, she'd been bleeding into the wood.

From the porch, she can hear Leah's voice echo through the cabin. "I know you don't want to, but I think it's a good idea."

"Are you sure that's what we need at this moment?" rasps another voice. The gardenkeeper.

No, Weiss. Tara takes the title off the lizard. He's not her boogeyman anymore. At least, according to Leah and everyone else he's stolen.

Through the doors is no longer an office with a scratchy old couch and the desks where Tino Medina and Marydale Barlowe filed their paperwork. There's desks, yes, but pushed to the walls to accommodate endless glass jars, ceramic pots, and aluminum cans filled with dirt. Drying branches hang from the ceiling, clipped to an old length of fishing line.

"I just think we should consider them," Leah says. She's sitting at one of those plastic fold-out tables formerly used for demonstrations, now a cluttered workbench that includes a book made of peeled birch bark pages, bound in vines. A grimy tackle box full of seeds lays open across her lap.

Weiss hisses. He paces the room, claws tapping with a *clink clink clink* of obsidian. "I don't see why you want to bring them into this. They probably already know. There's very little they don't know," he says.

"That's exactly my point," Leah says.

Weiss straightens up. He sees the girls before Leah, who swivels her stool and waves.

"Morning," she tells them.

Tara steps deeper into the apothecary. She sets the basket down beside Leah's book. "Who are we talking about?" she prompts.

June skirts Weiss to stand by the Ayalas. The lizard turns around, trailing his talons over a branch of rosemary hung to dry. His tail tucks under his moss cloak.

Leah digs through the basket for a honeycrisp. She tosses it from hand to hand. "I think I have an idea for how we can make people remember us," she says. "There's someone we can ask for an answer. They're a little weird."

"Like we aren't," June says.

Weiss doesn't turn around. He seems fully engaged with some basil in a sand pail. "Not too many details, please," he tells Leah.

Leah purses her lips. "They're, like," she says, thinking. "Indirect. They don't talk. But they communicate? They're hard to describe like this. What they might do is give us insight on how to ungrow the part of us that makes scorpion grass affect humans."

"Ungrow?" June asks. She comes closer to the workbench.

Leah spreads her arms. "It's how I'm me. This me, anyway. Wait, did I tell you which one I was?"

Tara shakes her head. June snaps her fingers.

"Cinnabon," she says. "The buns! How did I not put that together?"

Tara can see it. The little fairy with the hypericum buds. The one who helped her. "You're how I found June," she realizes.

Leah nods, hands on her knees. Her bun's been slept on, about ready to unbind. Tara aches. Her sister had been there, right there on her shoulder, talking into her ear. She'd befriended June twice, without either of them knowing who the other really was.

June glances at Weiss, who is busying himself trimming ivy grown from a hole in the wall.

"So you ungrew yourself?" June asks, still watching him. "How?"

Leah pulls an eight-spoked leaf from her box. "The mayapples," she says. "I don't have any here. They only fruit in the greenhouse."

"Mayapples?" Tara asks.

"They're what makes a mandrake. If a living thing touches one, off its stem, it plants them," Leah explains. She says mandrake like Tara should know what it means. June leans over Leah's notes like she very much does. "Whoever picks it controls what comes up. So if we plant ourselves…"

"The mandrake can think on its own," June says. She blinks at Leah. "That's how everyone's changed. You planted everyone again?"

"They planted themselves," Leah corrects. She hops down from her stool. "You could, too, if you wanted."

"But the mayapples make people forget you," June says.

"Nope," Leah says. Another dried sprig comes from her box. She matches it to a sketch in her book: a blue flower, white at its center, its pistil a golden yellow. "That's the scorpion grass. Forget-me-nots, ironically. It's this and the mayapples together that makes you and everyone else forget."

Weiss's tail twitches. He stills in his trimming.

Leah continues her lecture. Tara feels like she and June should be sitting criss-cross applesauce for the lesson.

"Ungrowing something is just what we call negating part of what you're planted with. If you go under again with another piece of the same plant, it sort of cancels out. It's a lot of trial and error. I mean, why do you think it took ten years to get to human me?" Leah says. "Mateo's second closest. We thought since I have a human body without any mandrake in me, people on the outside would remember. They don't."

"Betty does," Tara says.

"Yeah. I don't know why that is," Leah says. She scribbles something down in her book. "When I called before, it didn't work. I'm gonna bring that up when we talk to our, uh, consultant."

"When you called before?" Tara's lost. If calling this 'consultant' last time didn't work, why would it now?

"I still don't think we should," Weiss says.

"They helped you," Leah calls over. She scribbles something else, then smiles for the girls. She claps her hands together, lesson complete. "They're the one who gave Weiss the idea that it's planting yourself, not anyone else planting you. They have a good track record."

So whoever this consultant is, they made Weiss change? That seems off to Tara. As does Leah blazing past her question, again. She folds her arms and settles back, for her sister's sake. It's too much of a novelty to see her sister nerding out after so long.

"This consultant doesn't talk, though?" June says. "Can they hear?"

Leah shrugs. "They don't have to, really."

Having replaced her book and box, she moves for the door.

"They see into your mind," Leah says. "Give you a vision of what you're looking for, it sounds like. I've never done it, but I hear it's less like giving you an answer, more like giving you the right questions to ask. Right now, I'm all out of good questions."

"How?" Tara says. She keeps an eye on Weiss but follows Leah down the stairs.

"Spores," Leah says, giving jazz hands.

"Spores," Tara echoes.

Weiss walks toward them. "We aren't ready yet," he rasps.

"They're a mushroom person," Leah says. "We've been calling them Musten. They're pretty much always around, you just have to get their attention."

There's a commotion by the campfire. Benson, curled by the logs, buzzes in surprise and books it.

A rather large circle of white puffballs has sprung up, mirroring the fire pit to its left. At the center, there's a humanoid shape.

Weiss has a talon raised. He lowers it. "They'll hear you," he warns, too late.

"Hi!" Leah shouts. She jumps the steps two at a time, stomping onto the grass with both feet. "Everyone, meet Musten."

Tara and June come up behind her. Weiss keeps at their heels.

Musten smiles, eyes closed in a round face. They're the doughy color of a mushroom stalk, speckled here and there with brackets like skin tags across their thick torso. Their ears are knots of truffles, their head adorned in a crown of amanita muscaria in reds and oranges and yellows. They have their stumpy legs folded atop the biggest toadstool Tara or probably anyone on Earth has ever seen. Their four arms, more like tentacles ending in three bulbous digits, are upraised to the sky.

They open their eyes. They appraise the group. They give an inclination of their head to Weiss.

Weiss sweeps his tail. He waves a claw. "Hello again," he says.

"Musten, meet everyone," Leah says.

Musten studies her down their nose. Their smile is so serene, if amused by Leah's salutations.

"Well, for real, I guess," she says. "They keep an eye on our forest."

They wink, chest trembling with a silent chuckle.

"I don't think this is wise," Weiss rasps to Leah. He has a claw bunched in her sweater sleeve. "You've never done this before."

"What else are we supposed to do?"

Weiss frowns. "You could get hurt, Leah," he says.

"Like I've never taken risks before. C'mon, it's not like all the ungrowing did anything to hurt me. Even when I came up the last time, I didn't have any injuries."

"I don't like it," Weiss says, hunched into his cloak. He makes himself look so small next to Leah, even if they're about the same height now. "Musten is a being I don't fully understand. I can take their visions, but you're human now."

Leah shrugs. "I gotta try, bud," she says.

She rubs her hands together. Before Tara can interject, Leah makes her request.

"Let's do this. Musten, I'd like a vision, if that's okay."

Musten inclines their head. They take a long, deep breath.

They exhale. Within the confines of their puffballs, the air moistens. Bluish dust creates a dome around the mushperson, thick as snowflakes in a globe. Their eyes hood, then close once more.

"You're really about to do shrooms for this," Tara says.

"I'll go in," June says.

"Hang on," Tara says.

June comes to the edge of the circle. "I'd like to help her," she tells Musten.

Musten opens their eyes, lids heavy.

"I'm not human," June says. "It might work for me, if it doesn't for her."

The mushperson nods. Their lower two appendages grasp each other, as if in prayer.

June takes Leah's hand. Musten nods again.

"Wait," Tara protests.

They step over the ring's border, into the dome.

As soon as they've crossed inside, the two go limp. They drop like ragdolls. Puffballs spring from the grass to break their fall.

Spores flood June's lungs, and the ground below her feet morphs. Fescue around her ankles rises, growing to brush against her knees. When the world stops swaying, a fine white grass surrounds her on all sides.

She stumbles. These visions don't take long to kick in, then. She inhales, exhales. A puff swirls through the cracks in her fingers, off and away like humid indigo smoke.

It stands out against the whites and grays and drab cream of the world around her. The most she can compare the space to is the meadow outside the garden, but in place of bee balm and bluestem, she sees enokitake, thin stalked mushrooms ending in caps like dull pearls.

A wave of oyster mushrooms flows out in a vast, impenetrable wall behind her. Ahead she sees what look like the Redwoods-sized birches she once traveled through, but the dark eyes on their peeling bark are solid white, the stalks of featureless foam cut off a hundred feet high by flowers of black and dripping gills. Shaggy mane, she thinks, or inky cap? She only just began spawning mushrooms for the nursery last year, so it's her best guess on any of these fungi she hasn't seen in a grocery store.

Okay. She's outside the garden, sort of. She breathes deep. Spores tickle down her airways.

"I'm here," she says. "What do you want me to see?"

No reply. Right. Musten can't, or doesn't, speak. She won't be getting any verbal answers here.

The dense wall of ashy, silver caps leaves no room to climb through. The shaggy mane soaring up above forms a maze much more tightly packed than the garden's grove, but it's the only path that lies before her. She takes a step forward. Below her boots, through the enoki, she can see a glow pulse out in a ripple. It's like a stone skipping out ahead, lit up like synapses sparking between neurons, spaced out unevenly.

Footprints. Another step, another ripple, this time going deeper into the shaggy mane.

She calls toward it. "Hello?"

It must be Leah. Is meeting up in the vision their first step?

A giggle echoes from behind the stalks. June stills. So do the ripples.

"Um," she tries. "You can come out," she says.

The light twinkles tentatively. She squints. A colorful blur darts among the dust and cream, leaving the footprints in its wake. June struggles to glimpse it in full. She makes out two arms, two legs, a baggy chocolate brown sweatshirt, and a bright bush of carrot orange hair.

Little June's footprints retreat. Her path glows through the grove.

June gives chase. She has to. She can't let it happen again, not if she can prevent it. Enokitake clings to her legs, swatting at denim and sticking like burs. The stalks thicken as she nears, as if to block her, but she extends her stems until her gloves burst and she props the trunks apart. If she can just catch up to little June, it won't matter what state her gloves are in. If she can keep the kid from getting to the garden, she can nip this in the bud.

What would that even be like? Would she still have been friends with Tara, for all that there would be a sprig of scorpion grass keeping Leah from her mind? Her body would be her own again otherwise, unmarred by the mayapple. If she can just get ahead and stop the kid before she reaches what lies at the center of this grove-

She makes it just in time to see the garden gate clatter shut. The hedges within aren't hedges. Instead turkey tails in layered fans stretch behind the iron.

"Wait," she calls. The gate won't budge, and she's too big to slip through the bars anymore. She climbs over the top, snagging her boilersuit's belt loop on the gate's spikes.

Past the turkey tail hedge, the rose and rhododendron shrubs have become amanita muscaria, salted white over yellow and pink and peach. No mandrakes emerge to meet her. No Weiss, either. But where's little June?

A crunch. June whips around.

Where the pebble path forks, there's little June. She says nothing. There are no poppies in her hair. Her skin is pale, but absent any shade of green.

If she's going to keep it that way, they have to move quickly. "We have to go," she tells little June.

Already her feet in her boots are unbinding, tunneling through socks and into soles. She staggers. She just has to hold it together a little longer. Maybe that's what this vision is all about. A do over. If she can just stop the seed, if she can get out unscathed with little June intact, then they won't need to hunt down some magic macguffin to be remembered.

But the second she steps for little June, she trips. The boots keep the hole from opening below, but her missing gloves leave her hands exposed to dive down between the pebbles and stick. She rips them up. The stems tear, rapidly regenerating to reach for the ground again.

Little June cocks her head.

Her bare hand reaches down. Little June's fingers are stubby and nail-bitten.

June can't think of anything else. She takes it.

She means to stand up, using their joined hands as an anchor. But she's already standing, and there's no one else before her.

"Whoa," she says, hearing the word come out much too high. She examines her hands. Stubby, nail-bitten, a little dirty. She touches her face. She runs her fingers through her wild mane of orange curls.

Roots are not eating through her grimy tennis shoes.

The gate behind her isn't blocked off. But she frowns at it. This garden isn't the garden she knows. The rose bushes aren't thorned but powdered, sanded down to caps and stalks. Hundreds of truffles like balls of peppercorn cover the ground where fern and bracken used to lurk. Where was once nerium are morels and chantrelles.

This can't be the same place that made her life so lonely. Not when she feels like she does, feels as she did when the garden first opened itself to her wondering eyes. She's awed, amazed. *Elated!* That's the word. She wants to do laps around this place. Touch everything, talk to anyone she can find. There's no one here, though. Is this altered garden abandoned? Mycorrhizal fungi of every sort and shade are here. She sees the pond, now dry but alive with shiitake and spawn. She looks into the house, where the archways are almost smothered in pretty pink coral fungus.

Her exploration stalls in front of the greenhouse. Like the gate, like the stone of the house, it's unchanged, just glass and metal and memory.

Elation fades. The toadstools around her spin like flowers seeking the sun. They all bend to face the broken pane at her own height.

Didn't she come in here looking for someone?

June trembles. Movement from the entrance, light rippling down the broken pane and over the path she's come. Sparkles of it glitter into the underbrush. Is someone else in the truffles? The morels? The shiitake? Who else is in here with her?

There has to be someone else. Someone she's not seeing.

She follows the trail. She creeps closer, using the fly agarics for cover.

At the entrance are those turkey tails again, framing a gate that's now propped open. On the iron bars are impossibly tight swathes of cobwebs, a bundle of cotton candy collected on a cone. June struggles to make out its shape, obscured by the glow of a many headed mass, cast in the same light that's illuminated her path here.

Whatever it is- or they are, as the mass seems to have two distinct heads and three growths about its lower half- it is silent and determined, dragging along the webbing.

"No!" she hears. "Not yet! I worked too hard, please, I-"

"Leah?" June asks.

The swathes slack, then tense to regain their grasp. The mass seems to be hauling her from the garden. "June?"

That's who she's here for! June barges forward, balling her fist in a clump of cottony filaments. "Let her go!" she tells the mass of light. "Now!"

The mass evaporates. Luminous particles run like quicksilver, slipping into the earth once more.

The swathe slumps in a heap. Like a taut rubber band let go, the threads collapse to a familiar form. Little Leah is much, much smaller than her own little June. This Leah is absolutely miniscule, no bigger than a monarch butterfly. She's made up of roots and radicles, hypericum buds dotted across her head.

Leah looks at June.

"What's going on?" she asks. "What happened to you?"

A vision. A very visceral vision. June got lost, and it's taking effort to keep from getting swept into those emotions and sensations threatening to overtake her. She can feel her fingertips rubbing together, her steps colliding with the soil's surface, her lungs expanding and contracting in her chest. She sighs out another indigo cloud. This feels real. Maybe more than real.

She offers her hand down.

Leah climbs on, taking a perch on June's head. "Sorry you saw that," she says. "Have you seen anything to make me memorable?"

Right. This isn't about June. She shakes her head.

Whatever will help Leah has to be in the garden, if Musten has gone to the trouble of rebuilding it and railroading them inside. How did she forget Leah? Again? Stupid!

"I don't know what to look for," she admits. Her voice in her ears sounds so strange. She wants to say something else. "Fuck!" she cries. "Ha! That's cute."

"Focus, June," Leah says.

This isn't about June. But she giggles. She can't help it. Little June's baby kid voice saying swears is adorable. She wants to say more. Do more. She wants to enjoy this.

She starts undoing her laces.

Leah coils her roots in June's hair. "What are you doing?"

Shoes are off. Socks next. June kicks them into a pile.

Roots don't form from her feet.

She twitches her toes, worming them into the damp dirt. She pats her freckled face. She laughs. This. This is something else.

"Thank you, Musten," she crows.

Leah scrambles off her head as June lets herself flop onto her back. She makes dirt angels. She hasn't been free to enjoy the earth in so long. Hasn't been able to feel clods of it tumble through her fingers without those fingers turning to stems, sprouting delicate root hairs, searching for a place to sink in.

Leah taps her forehead. June crosses her eyes. Leah's talking to her.

June can't hear her. She does hear something, though.

It's the same soundless whispers she gets from flora. Instead of their hungers and thirsts and loneliness, she hears another want. Her grandmother, yanking her from the ground. Sobbing. Betty had almost forgotten. June had almost forgotten.

Her bare toes unspool.

"Shit!" she squeaks.

She claws at the dirt, digging into loam. Her fingers don't pull like taffy into stems. Her mop of curls doesn't bloom into poppies. Her eyes shut, but they don't go beady and blank.

Instead her skin cracks, her lips dry and chapped. Yellowed like ancient paper, hair wilting on her scalp. It's numb. It's nothing. She's a clipped cutting, decaying and dying. The only parts she can feel are the ones diving down.

Stems wrap around her wrist. June dares to peek.

"Tara?"

Little Tara. Her Tara, the one she shared a bunk with. Shared stories and sketches with. The one she dries the eyes of, whenever and however she can.

She wears her camp sweatshirt, matching June's own. Said sweatshirt is beginning to grow baggy and sheer on June. Like her skin the cotton thins. She'll be a husk if she stays up here.

Tara tugs. "June, you have to listen to me," she bites out.

Tara is saving her again. She shouldn't be. She shouldn't have to. June's caused her enough misery as it is. She's already forgetting. She might as well let herself be forgotten. Ripples of light reverberate through the hole she's dug herself into.

Betty's voice fills her ears in the same wordless way, just as the light from the dirt fills her eyes.

Is this what she wants? Wholly and truly?

Little Tara goes limp. She glances around herself, as if hearing something June can't. The moment leaves June slipping, gripping tighter, sliding deeper down all the same. That's not quite right. She feels tugged not directly down but out, dragged in the direction of the greenhouse.

Little Tara looks down at June. "No," she says. "I'm not letting you have her."

June's withered hands have vanished. In a glow of white light, they're not stems. They're not her own pale, stubby little June hands either. They're slender, brown. They're Tara's.

Leah above her, human and eighteen, keeps pulling. "You can't have my sister!" she says.

She's not Tara. Leah's not Tara, as much as they both cry out her name. They're saving each other, taking Tara's hand and yanking her along. Leah flickers to Tara. Betty. June herself, twenty and taking little June out of the hole where she's been for a decade. Little June, little Tara, little Leah.

Who is she? Stuck above and below, on the surface and under the earth? Bound up in each other like this, will either of them ever know?

Tara paces around the fairy ring.

The spores hum slightly in the dome like television static. Every so often Musten tilts their head this way, that, reacting to whatever information they receive from the bodies below. Tara walks. Watches. Waits.

Already she's worn a moat around the mushrooms, stomping a rut as she guards her sister and friend.

"Walking will not make it go any faster," Weiss says, seated to mirror Musten. His knees are brought to his chest, far from the calm crossed legs and upraised tendrils of the mushperson.

Tara growls and continues pacing. What else should she do? Sit and stare? She should be the one in there. She should be taking care of this, not some stranger Leah has summoned by speaking their name. This is her second chance to solve the mystery that eluded her, and she's been cut clean from the investigation.

June's eyes flutter beneath their lids. Tara takes a step toward the puffballs.

Weiss's claw catches her sleeve.

Tara hisses.

Weiss lets his grip go, his shoulders slack. "We don't know what would happen to you," he reminds her. "You shouldn't inhale the spores."

"Who cares?" Tara rubs her wrist. She scowls. "If either of them get hurt-"

Weiss raises his claws, tail lashing under his cloak. "I will step in," he snaps. "Now sit down."

"Make me, dickhead," Tara says.

Weiss sighs. He scratches his flowers and says, "Very well. I'm only as nervous as you are. Leah has never done this before, even when she was still a mandrake. It might be upsetting, if it does work as intended."

"What did you see?"

Weiss smiles. "Oh?"

Tara crosses her arms and returns to stomping the ring. What good will talking to him do? She can't trust him, for all Leah seems to. Which she still can't entirely believe. The gardenkeeper turned over a new leaf? Right now, Weiss rests a talon at his temple, annoyed with her.

But he's not doing anything about it. His eyes are locked on Leah. He looks at Leah like Alex watched Tara pack up her Nissan.

If he's acting, it's one hell of an act. Does she prefer it being real? Leah thinking Weiss is her friend, rather than her tormentor for the ten years Tara abandoned her?

Tara stops her stomping. "So you really think this'll work?" she huffs.

"I'm not certain, but there's a good chance," he replies. "Musten is… kind. As kind as they can be."

"What's that supposed to mean?"

Weiss takes a blade of grass in his shining black talons. "They see all. They know all. They're not very good at communicating. Having so much knowledge, it can blind you to how it feels." He taps at his knee. His obsidian clinks on the stone. "If they believe helping Leah and… well, if they believe helping us is in their best interest, they will try."

"How was helping you in their best interest?"

Weiss smirks. "I do protect these woods, you know," he says. "For as long as I've existed. That's what my masters used to do. Not that they ever incorporated more than themselves in that duty."

Tara jerks her chin.

He digs a hole near a puffball. "This Musten, the fruiting body they use to express, needs the entire woods from soil to sky content. It knows my power over humans has kept its webs from being broken up."

"Power you're not supposed to be using," Tara fires back.

Weiss rolls his crystal eyes. "I can still use it on humanity at large. Humans on the whole are not welcome here anymore. That's not for me to decide. I'm only going to remove them," he says, searching for the word, "ethically now. I no longer plant them without consent."

Tara looks to June. To Leah, now human after everything. "I still don't believe it," she mutters.

"That's only right. You were not here," Weiss says.

Tara glares at him.

Weiss flinches. He runs back over his words.

"I wasn't here," she says, "because I was too scared of you to come back. And you said you didn't know how to fix this."

"I didn't," he says. "I got help. I…"

He trails off. He fiddles with a hole in his cloak.

"I want to protect your sister. All of the mandrakes. I should have protected them before. And you, and her," he says, glancing at his lap.

Tara snorts. "That actually happened," she says. "She actually made friends with you. While you were still screwing me over."

"I didn't plan that," Weiss says. He shrinks into his cloak. "We had a bargain. My masters did not break bargains.

So I had to wait until you had lost. She wanted to be friends, not me."

Tara closes her eyes.

She sits down beside him.

They sit there in silence. June's gloves wriggle. Leah's nose wrinkles.

Tara wants to do something. Anything. She's so useless right now. Beyond useless. So is Weiss, who caused all of this.

Tara mimics her sister's slow, measured breaths. Maybe she can convince herself Leah is sleeping peacefully.

"I'm happy you won, if that means anything."

Tara looks at Weiss. He looks at June.

"Letting go of Leah," he says. "I had warning. But I thought of you both when your sister left. You and June Bug."

He utters her name like a spell. Tara thinks of the other thing he called June.

Sprout. Just a seed, not a person. People were incomplete to him, an ingredient, a component in the magic he made behind wrought iron and frosted glass.

Tara kicks herself. She can't forget what he did, even if she wants to.

Without any words between them, she has no distraction. She watches June fidget with more frequency. Leah's slow, measured breaths quicken. Indigo motes darken around the two, somehow thick as fog. Their joined hands begin to twitch and tremble.

Tara stands up.

"Don't," Weiss says.

She rolls up her hoodie sleeves.

"She's going to kill me if you get hurt."

She steps into the dome of spores, breath held long enough to place a hand on both Leah and June. Her ankle catches on a mushroom before she can pull them free.

"Tara?"

Her leg aches. Blood soaks into her denim, caking her pant leg in mud. Quick drags of blue billow from her lips.

She kneels in the garden. She sees two shapes on the soil, screaming for her. Grappling her legs with threadbare roots, each entrapped by their own monster. She hardly registers the flora turned fungi before she's on her knees and exhuming them. A mandrake of hypericum, the other of poppies and dandelions, each being jerked in opposite directions. The first to the gate, the second to the greenhouse.

They see her and freeze.

Taking their attention makes the masses of light that entangle them dissipate. The two mandrakes go quiet, glancing at each other.

Tara takes them into her arms, their bodies nestled in the crook of her elbows. She has to save them. It's her job to save them.

Even as the mandrakes writhe against her. "Tara?" Leah cries. "You shouldn't be here!"

"You need to get out," June shrieks. Her voice is airy, the same whisper the hypericum fairy had. Has.

Tara's small. She's scared. But they're smaller. They have more to be scared of. Her heart pounds, reverberating out of her ribs and pounding into her ears. This isn't the garden Tara knows. But the walls closing in are the same.

She ducks toward the exit, only to swerve. Turkey tails have jut up to block her, shuddering with the same manic fervor she feels. The two mandrakes coiled around her arms squirm to get free. They beg her to let them go, to let them help her. They can't help her. Tara has to do this herself. She has to do it for them.

They need to let her.

The mushrooms have blocked off the gate. The greenhouse. The pond. Tara never found much there, anyway. It was the house she'd pored over, wanting to believe the seamless stone would protect her from the gardenkeeper.

She makes it inside just in time for the coral fungus to barricade the doorway. There are no doors here. No bedrooms, no bathrooms, the whole building bare and sterile even with the overgrowth threatening to sneak through its blocky windows and sloping arches. She lays on the other side of the fungus, panting. The hall is filling with blue.

Leah and June take this chance to get loose. They tangle her hands in their roots and tug.

"Let us help you," Leah insists, dragging as hard as she can. The most she does is pop Tara's knuckle. Doesn't she see the light looming behind them? The many headed mass, six humanoid figures sloughed together into their dual monsters?

Tara shakes her head. No. No, they don't understand.

A turkey tail erupts from the stone floor. Another few fans follow. Tara shoots up to her feet.

Mandrakes twisted in her hands, she takes up a sprint. She passes the room full of armor, glimmering below an onslaught of white button mushrooms. The tools are heaped against a wall, now devoured by portabella. The bottom step of the stairs is the only path she sees without the glow.

The tower it is. "I'm going to save you," she says. "Just let me do this."

The walls graze her shoulders as she runs up the spiral staircase. Under her feet the steps crack. Each one changes from glowing rock to golden chicken-of-the-woods. Slats of them clip at her heels. She makes it to the landing before fungus consumes the stairwell.

In the tower, a moonbeam casts across the floor. She's been here before. Under the window are the flowers, the only ones she's seen in this entire reimagined garden. The only ones she ever saw in this horrible house.

She's shoved into them, the turkey tails and chicken-of-the-woods springing through the archway. They shoot from the ground and up like stalagmites. The flowers break her fall. Her head swims. She squints up through the foliage.

Purple blossoms plucked down, white flowers stretched up. Yellow pistils, ten petals alternating in a pinwheel. She admired them. They were the closest to peace she'd ever experienced here.

"Tara?" June asks. "Tara, are you alright?"

"Stay with us," Leah says.

June takes Tara's cheeks in her roots. Hands. She's little June, smudged with dirt. Leah, flesh and blood, hovers over her injured leg. It aches so much Tara can feel it pulse in her ears. She slaps a hand over it. She has to apply pressure, staunch the bleeding.

The flowers fluff around her. Tara pushes against her sister, her friend.

"I have to get up," she says.

June hushes her. She's drawing a thumb across Tara's temple. The flowers have become plush as down. The sweet scent of them makes her drowsy. No. No! She has to get up.

Her eyes hood just as she sees the claws outstretched. Her monster has finally arrived. It's not here for her. It looms just over June and Leah's shoulders, lurking there curved and cruel and jagged as black glass. They seem to crinkle under the shadow. Their images like petals creased in a book, fading and fleeting and all she wants to do is keep them here, just as they are.

"No," she murmurs. "You have to let me do this."

The claws do not fall on their backs or grab their collars. Instead, a lizard no longer than pencil scurries up to Tara's chest.

She swats at it, feebly. It licks her chin.

Then it scatters to indigo spores. The two girls bent over Tara dissolve with it.

Tara isn't alone, though. Her monster is still here, glowing a white so bright she shields her eyes. She scarcely has the energy to press against the wall, crushing the flowers beneath her, straining to escape whatever terror has captured the only people she cares about in this place.

Her eyes squeeze shut. If she can't see it, maybe it can't see her.

A flash. She hears a shift across the stone floor, breaking stems in its trod.

And then she's tucked against someone, someone green and topped off spiky black. The person holding her, wrapped in flimsy purple flowers, does not look like a monster. Tara's never seen her before. She's seen her every day.

The person being held is small. She's failed to save Leah. She's failed to save June.

But doesn't this person deserve to be saved? However spiky and sharp, angry and afraid?

Tara sags into her own embrace. She's being held. She's holding.

21

June surfaces. Musten watches from their toadstool, but she isn't lying in their puffballs anymore. She's sprawled outside the dome. Leah lays tossed beside her. She spits up spores. Tara. Where's Tara? Last she saw, a little Tara had been in the vision. Or she'd been Tara, or Leah had been.

But, no, June reaches out to find grownup, present day Tara unconscious in the grass. Leah rolls over and groans, curled into a fetal position.

Between the three girls and the dome, a lizard hisses on all fours, tail lashing. His cloak drapes off him like so much Spanish moss.

Musten smiles at him. It does not reach their eyes, which weep black dribbles of ink.

Then they draw a deep breath, and every spore they've exhaled sucks inward. Up into gills, into teeth, before their form caves in and they're gone. Puffballs shrink from basketball to golf ball to nothing as they slurp back into the soil, leaving upturned hunks of fescue behind.

A final fly agaric is all that remains, dead in the circle's center.

Weiss breathes heavily. She'd forgotten he could breathe. He fixes June, Leah, and Tara with a single crystal eye.

He coughs up blue and falls over.

Leah unclenches. She makes the effort to roll back and look at June. Weiss must have dragged them from the circle. Him, or the two mandrakes now dithering over them. Selina's roots are smoothing June's hair, Moe climbing onto Tara's chest. Tara isn't stirring.

Moe checks Tara's pulse. Selina hovers to her wife's left, leaves creeping down June's arm like kudzu in her worry. June doesn't have the heart to shrug her off. Leah shakes Weiss's shoulder to wake him.

June takes Tara's hand. Gently, she nudges Tara onto her lap, pressing two fingers to her wrist. The pulse is steady, if slow. Her breaths are the same. She could be sleeping, if it weren't for the indigo escaping her lips.

"She's alive," Moe says. Her voice stays low, more soothing than June has ever heard it to be.

Weiss has sat up. "You were in there too long," he rasps. "Longer than I've ever been. I thought you weren't... that you wouldn't..."

Leah pats his arm, staring at Tara. "I'm back, bud," she says. "She shouldn't have gone in there."

"Why did she?" June asks. As if she can't guess. Tara's chest rises and sinks against June's knee. The motion might be the only thing keeping June from panicked laughter. She could tell they were upset. Of course she'd want to save them from it.

Weiss stands. "I'm sorry, Leah," he says, tugging his cloak about himself. "I didn't reach her in time."

"What?" Leah cries.

"She's not-" June says, voice cracking.

"I already said she's alive, idiot," Moe barks. "Lord, Weiss. That's enough melodrama. Get her in the house."

They all stare at the tulip mandrake.

Selina ahems. She wraps a root around Moe's bicep. "You all heard the lady. This girl will need food, water, and somewhere to lie down. Let's get her up," she says.

Before Leah's on her feet, June has lifted Tara bridal style. "Where do I take her?" she asks Selina.

Selina leads the way. They're headed for Cottonwood cabin. June carries Tara up the steps, letting her roots through her laces to grip the boards. She's out of it herself, so she can use the extra support climbing the porch.

Leah follows behind her. "Get her to my bed," she says.

June does so. Selina brings her to Marydale Barlowe's old room. June has never been inside, but the wallpaper is discolored where Marydale's horseshoes and ribbons for equestrian championships used to hang. When the camp closed, did she go back to riding horses? The only other trace of her is the twin bed, a saddle blanket carefully folded over the somewhat dusty mattress.

Tara mumbles against June's tank top. It's taking everything June has not to bend her wrist and stroke the back of Tara's head, where her hair's sheared short and bristly, to comfort her.

Instead June lays her out on the scratchy wool.

"What now?" she says.

"She's still tripping," Moe diagnoses. She's broken off from Selina to stand on the bed, hands on her hips. "Might be a few hours. If she's anything like I was, she'll need to be watched."

Leah raises her hand. "I'll do it." June cocks a brow, about to protest, but she's pushed aside. Leah shakes her head. "She's my sister. She needs me," she says.

She parks it on an ottoman by the bed, beginning her vigil. June stands there behind. Her roots slither between her laces, a loose end. She can't take her eyes off Tara. How her face strains, then goes placid, then returns to a wince and she tightens up. All June can do is watch as Leah draws another blanket over her sister, taking a canteen from a bedside drawer.

There's a touch on June's arm. She startles.

It's just Selina. "You can take it in turns," she says. "It's going to be a while."

"I can't just leave her," June says.

"You aren't any good to her right now," Moe snaps. "Get yourself some air and clear your head. It's going to be a lot quicker for you, since you're not all human."

The Rathbones share a look, glancing at Leah, and June sees their reasoning.

So she trudges to the porch. She slumps into the swing bolted to its rafters, the chains swaying with her impact.

Nope, too much movement. She stomps to stop the swing's sway. She puts her face in her hands, elbows propped on her knees. Ugh. Her stomach lurches. She will not throw up. She refuses to throw up.

Weiss enters the house past her. He said they'd been in the vision a long time, but it didn't feel like it. It was seconds. It was forever. It was so much. It was not enough to feel so worked up about. Tara needs help right now, not her.

No. That's not what the vision had told her. But the vision told her something impossible. Something she can't sit in without feeling like the earth is spinning so fast it'll fling her off its crust.

What else is new? She smears her gloved fingers over her eyes.

She has too much to mull over. The vision still swims under her eyelids.

The whole porch buzzes. June grips the chain, feeling the vibration in her bones. Her lignin? She's never gotten the courage enough to find what her body actually contains under the veneer, physiologically speaking. What would putting herself under the microscope do?

Benson has crawled up the side of the porch. His compound eyes peer through the railing, antennae fluttering against the topmost one. June brings her knuckles over his feelers. His buzz loses its intensity. Instead he seems to purr.

"What are we gonna do, big guy?" she chuckles. The buzz does feel good. Rattles her teeth, sure, but his drone brings her down from orbit. She pets under his chin.

His pincers gnaw her glove, love biting. "You're a good boy," she says. "I'm sorry I pulled an ax on you."

Benson chitters. He slouches against the house, only barely quaking the cabin with his weight.

Inside, June hears conversation. "How is she?" Weiss asks.

"Fine, Moe says," Leah replies. There's a pause. "Thanks for pulling us out."

"She wanted to help you, you know."

June rocks in the swing. Leah sighs on the other side of the wall.

"And how are you? What did you see?" Weiss rasps.

"Gonna be honest with you, I'm not ready to go into it."

A beat, enough for a nod or a claw on Leah's shoulder. "As long as you're alright. Make sure you're taking care of yourself."

"Thanks, bud."

Silence. Heavy footfalls. Lingering, in the main room just beyond the door.

Then Weiss steps out. He leans against the window into the cabin, eyes shut. Seems he needs to recover, too. June had tasted some of his emotions, along with Leah and Tara's. When Tara entered, the pair had gotten swept up and June's sweet relief, Leah's resignation, soured to white-hot fear. All those wants, desires, phobias swirled together into a soup of three people who did not need to be sharing a mindscape.

Four, when she caught whiff of Weiss's old despair and insecurity. Something new came with it, but she hadn't had much time to study it closely.

She slows the swing. She caresses the spot between Benson's eyes, making the beetle butt her hand for more.

Weiss's eyes open. He looks over at June.

He marches for the stairs.

"Hey," June says.

He's petrified, becoming a statue on the landing.

"You wanna talk?" she asks.

Not a twitch. He's frozen in her sights.

Then he turns. His cloak hangs off him, his claws clicking and clacking and stimming. He arches over, craning around the swing to see her.

He opens his mouth, sharp teeth exposed. Closes it.

"We might as well talk this out, 'stead of avoiding each other," June says.

Weiss steps up. He sucks in a breath. He clasps his claws in front of him, like he's about to pray.

Or beg. "I'm so sorry," he rasps. "I never should have done what I did."

"I know," June says.

Weiss's whole body stiffens.

"Ah," he says.

"I haven't forgiven you," she says. "Dunno if I ever will. I just want to talk."

Weiss scratches at his blooms. The flowers have the look of a craft project, like felt strips and cotton balls hot-glued together for Mother's Day. Soft sage-like leaves frill him like scales, dappled down his neck where his cloak meets his stone shoulders.

June pats the seat beside her.

His eyes gleam. His tail swings behind him. He can't seem to move otherwise.

June rocks. She lets her heel tip her back and forth, forming a rhythm to match Benson's.

Weiss nears her. He looks at the seat.

June nods. He has to calculate his sit, threading his tail through the space under the armrest. His tail thumps against the chain. He keeps his mouth shut tight.

"So," she says.

"I thought about seeing you again," he rasps. "What I'd say to you."

"Same," June admits. She'd pictured more of a confrontation, to be frank. A final fight with her archnemesis, a villain worthy of her suffering and sorrow.

But June just slouches into a swing. Maybe that's what she would have gotten in 2009. As she's grown older she's reflected. Processed. Weiss struck her less as someone who did things out of any malicious intent. Had a superiority complex, yeah, acted unaffected and uninterested. Then as soon as he'd warmed to her, he was so easy to please it was almost sad.

"How do you feel?" he asks.

She lets her eyes close. "Overwhelmed."

"I'm sorry."

June shrugs. "It's just a lot. Thought I might be over it by now."

"I understand if you aren't. I gave you a terrible burden."

June feels her roots wriggle, perforating her socks to swiss. "Wanna see something?" she asks.

He stares.

She peels off her glove. Stems already stick out, so this is an extended effort. She lets her fingers lengthen to thin green stems, blooming dandelions at their ends. She waggles them.

His face falls.

She smiles. "Pretty cool, huh?"

"Does it hurt you?" he asks.

"Not really. I've scared my grandma with it. And Tara. Oh, and Leah. Mateo. You," she says, tapping each dandelion.

"I'm… I didn't want to think… I should have," Weiss stammers. Didn't have a big speech prepared for this outcome, did he? Seeing him struggle for words feels just like their games in the garden. He never did have a poker face.

Or maybe he had. Maybe June just hadn't known what to look for.

"It's not so bad," she says. Her stems extend to stroke Benson. Benson bites a flower off. It stings a little, like pulling her poppies out, but it regenerates within seconds.

She offers it for Weiss to inspect. His claw is ginger, trailing a talon across the stem as Tara had.

"Before I learned better," he says. "Before the others, I thought I would make it up to you," he hisses through obsidian teeth. His crystal eyes fall to the floorboards.

"Yeah?"

"I," he says. He falters. "I don't want to convince you of anything. I just want to undo some of the damage I've done."

June lets her stems spool up to fingers. She flexes them. Her hand is freckled and fleshy again. "I don't think we can be friends," she says.

Weiss nods.

"I don't think I want to be enemies, though," she continues. "You're trying. So. That's cool. Good. I want you to keep it up. It's just. It's not my job to…"

"I understand. It's not your lot in life to make sure I don't do any more harm," he says. He glances into the cabin. "It's not hers either. She's been kinder to me than I deserve about all this. They all have."

June follows his gaze to the green. Mateo has emerged from between Beech and Cedar, a procession of other mandrakes laughing and nudging along behind him. He's got a basket of summer squash, where the Walsh girls are nestled and chatting his ear off. Their mother frets at his heels. She prods the fly agaric Musten marked their departure with. An older, knobbly bulb like an onion shouts for her to get back from it. She yanks her limb back as if burned, then frowns at her fellow.

Frank and Leon, Theodora on Frank's arm, sashay over to see the hubbub. Selina exits the cabin to mingle among them. It's decaying here, decrepit and destroyed by time.

It's full of life, who talk and think and have a community grown up around this campfire.

"Can I tell you something?" she asks Weiss.

He straightens to attention.

"There was something in the vision," she says.

"Yes."

"I'm not finished," she says. "Growing. You said so."

Weiss flusters. "You weren't finished, no," he says. "Not like the others. I still don't know how. But I'm happy you weren't. If I'd taken away what made you… you. Taken your you-ness. I would never have set foot outside my greenhouse again."

She crosses her arms. She bobs her head. She taps her toe at the porch, roots leaking through the laces.

"I'm sorry," he blurts. "No, I- you aren't responsible for-" He covers his face with his claws. "That's not your burden. This shouldn't be either."

"What if I finish it?"

"What?" Weiss hisses.

"In the vision I got to be me again. Me before the mayapple. I've been wound up ever since. I've never been able to just… rest. Let my guard down. I just slip up, one time, and I'm gone forever."

Weiss says nothing. June squeezes her eyes shut.

Cool stone claws graze her fingers, guide her hands to Benson's muzzle. Is it a muzzle if there's no nose or snout?

Between his eyes and mouth, then. Benson's buzz strikes her like a tuning fork.

She opens her eyes.

Weiss is tensed, waiting for her to snatch away. She sighs. He brings his claws to his lap.

"It's selfish." She shakes her head. Benson's hum grounds her, but it's not enough to keep the truth from coming. "I can't do it."

Not to Betty. Not to the Ayalas in the cabin behind her. Not to herself. She can't forget. She can't let herself be forgotten. But what if Musten's onto something? She has no clue who she is without the mayapple threatening to bury her, without her mandrake nature a secret she keeps so it won't burden someone else with worry.

And, yet, she's removing her other glove. She feels so heavy she could sink into the soil, rest her weary roots, and sleep until she's finally done. Until she's through running and holding herself so rigid, for what? A lonely summer had already become a lonely decade. Why keep it up for a lonely rest of her life?

"I don't think it's selfish," Weiss says.

"Do you?"

"No, June."

She laughs. "That's the first time you've ever called me by my name," she says.

He cringes. "You didn't tell me. Tara did."

"It's so weird to hear you say our names," she says. "To be fair, Tara didn't call you Weiss until, what, literally yesterday? And we've all known each other how many years?"

Weiss wears a sheepish little smile. "Thank you," he says.

"For?"

"For talking to me. I was so afraid of you. I'm very afraid of her."

"Tara?"

He gestures toward the agaric. "She wanted to protect you. That's why I stepped in. She saw you and Leah distressed."

"That's familiar," June mutters. She gives Benson another scritch, resting her chin on her fist, her elbow on her knee.

"It is," Weiss agrees. "You might not have much to fear. Finishing it, as you say. Did you see anything in the vision? Anything to answer our question?"

June shrugs, though her face burns red. "Honestly? Not much. I kept getting pushed to the greenhouse, but I never actually made it inside. Maybe Tara saw something. I feel like Musten was herding us around."

"Yes," Weiss says. "They do that."

June looks over. She finally puts her finger on what she'd seen flicker through the end of the vision, the perspective of something small scurrying under a leafy bush weighed down with yellow fruit. She smirks.

"You were that little lizard."

A few flowers pop into existence on his head and neck. He steeples his claws in front of his face. "Yes. It's the first thing they showed me. That I'm not created."

"What do you mean?"

"I'm a mandrake, like you are. Like I did to everyone, other than Leah's sister. I thought I was doing what my masters wanted, what they would do. If they made me, I owed them as much. But I'm not. I'm not made for any purpose. I was just an animal. I ate a mayapple. And I'm this, now."

"You're a lizard a plant gave thoughts to."

Weiss makes a vague wave of his claw. "A lizard who ate the ability to have thoughts from a plant. It's very disconcerting." He hugs himself, gripping his biceps under his cloak.

"It's cool," June says. "Makes sense you were bad at being a person. No one told you how."

"It's no excuse," Weiss hisses.

"Yeah. Just explains a lot. You were, uh. What's the word?"

"Inexperienced?"

"Sure," June says.

"Our neighbor's visions are mostly like those," he admits. "Flashes of memory. Insights. I've had a few more since. But they're indirect. They prod you toward what you already know, force you to become intimate with it. This one was much more elaborate than I've seen, but. If their vision suggests you plant yourself, I will do everything I can to help you."

"Only if I can be remembered," she says. It's not fair otherwise. Even if she wants to let go, she can't make herself another mystery to resolve.

"We'll see if Leah saw anything that might make it so," Weiss replies.

22

Fieldnotes of Leah Ayala
regarding encounters with unknown
Podophyllum peltatum *variant*

Encounter #1, 6/7/2009:

Mateo Valdez did not disappear without a trace. There were plenty of traces. A nametag, attached to a leather jacket in the equipment shed. Paperwork under his name, a birthdate, an address, even his SSN in Tino's desk. There had been a phone number, but the woman on the other end of the line didn't recognize Camp Cottonwood as her nephew's place of employment. Was this a scam? One of those tricks to get her to give away her credit card info?

The best lead had been a missing lawnmower. Leah Ayala volunteered to search for it. She discovered the mower abandoned in the northeast corner of the map, where no trials led. The camp counselor investigated the scene further. Still a key in the ignition, but no sign of a struggle. Just a hole in a nearby thicket, lying at the end of the creek that bisected the campus.

Leah spent hours poring over her maps. Three seasons in the Del Bosque forest gave her an intimate understanding of its ins and outs, and yet she never got a detailed layout of the northeast. Why was that? No one fenced it off, but she'd never been guided through it during counselor orientation. No one mentioned it, not enough to make it somewhere consciously avoided. It simply didn't exist.

Like Mateo. If she asked any other landscapers or groundskeepers, they never had a Mateo. Did she mean Martine? Leah asked the camp directors. No dice. This man worked here for over five years. He'd been one of the first staff to approach Leah, razzing her for being a nature geek whenever they chatted on the green. He encouraged her to sign up for College of the Redwoods last summer, despite her own reservations.

Mateo and her hadn't been close, per say. Leah couldn't say they were best friends. They were acquaintances at best. But the fact he'd dropped off the face of the earth, no one to recall he ever lived at all, kept her awake at night. Was this a cover up? Did they have a Jason Voorhees in their midst, axing horny teenagers and innocent gardeners?

Someone had to search for him. Someone had to mourn him, if he couldn't be found. If Leah didn't do it, no one would.

Story of her life, really. Her mother joked if Leah didn't do it, it didn't get done.

She asked Tara and June about Mateo. Tara confirmed her fears. Leah wasn't crazy, was she? This man had once walked, talked, worked among these very cottonwoods. Someone else had witnessed him.

And Leah would find him. She gathered her gear after putting the girls to bed. Vanessa Schmidt sat up in her bunk, slapping a palm over her eye. "Ms. Leah?" she mumbled.

"Lights out," Leah hushed her.

"What are you doing?"

Leah couldn't say. She couldn't risk it. What if this was some conspiracy? What if she was about to get iced by whoever iced Mateo?

She shook her head. What if she found a body and a kid trailed after her, only to be traumatized for life? No. Leah sighed. "I'll be back. Just getting more TP," she said.

If Vanessa thought it strange Leah had on her backpack and hiking boots for a mere supply run, she didn't say anything. She tucked back under the covers. Leah slipped out.

She walked the creek. The woods in Del Bosque were another world at night. Moonlight streamed through the branches, forming spiderweb shadows over the water. She watched it dance silver down and down and down, until it deposited where she'd seen the mower.

No other leads were here, now that the mower had been hauled back to its shed. She didn't see bootprints to indicate Mateo's path. Only the hole in the thicket.

Into the thicket it was. Leah managed to climb through. One hand at her backpack strap, the other firmly around a Maglite. She casts its beam into the darkness, stepped as if barefoot, her boots making no sound on the bee balm and bluestem.

Neither were native to this part of the Pacific Northwest. "What?" she muttered. She took a hot pink bud between her thumb and index. These bergamots shouldn't be here, should they? Not if this area of the grounds sat untouched by human hands?

She kept walking. Did someone live out here? She saw a house in the distance, through birches as big as the Trees of Mystery. Christ, what if she found a sasquatch had snatched up her friend?

Beam slashing through the shadow, back straight, bun sensibly knotted tight at the back of her head, she shoved the thought from her head. A logical explanation would reveal itself. Why wouldn't one?

Even as she approached the iron gate. Even as she could see how the towers spiraled up, more like a castle than a McMansion hidden beyond the camp. Even as she clattered the gate open to see a lush garden, where she could hear murmurs among the plants.

The first creature made her freeze. She stared at it. An animal?

No. A tangle of roots, skittering over the pebbles, with eyes and a mouth and a flower sprouting off its head.

She stayed still. Did these things track movement? Or were their eyes like certain insects, only capable of sensing changes in light? Others were emerging from the foliage. Leah staggered, only to see more at her heels. They were small as songbirds. She had never seen anything like them.

She slowly bent down for a better look. They weren't equipped with claws, fangs, or even thorns.

One approached her hand, a cluster of stones threaded together. How? When all the others were floral, it seemed odd a living thing would be made of nonliving material? She let her finger graze its rocky appendage.

"Are you lithop?" she asked, testing the give of the rock. "No, that's ridiculous. Those are from Africa. Why would there be lithop here?"

The little creature frowned at her. It certainly did feel like rock. "Is that really your first concern?" it asked.

Leah flinched. Oh. Talking. These things talked.

She bolted up. She needed a moment to process this information.

"I believe you have more pressing problems to worry about," rasped a voice at her back.

Instinct kicked in. Mace first, questions later.

Only the thing she maced just glared through the phenacyl chloride. Its eyes were opalescent gems, its face hard granite gneiss. It stood at about her height. Leah's brain reached for the sort of lizard it best matched, perhaps genus *elgaria*, before it rumbled a low growl.

"You talk," she got out.

"Obviously," the lizard said, rolling crystalline eyes. It didn't even wipe the dripping pepper spray off on its moss cloak. So mace didn't affect it? She had a knife, but what would it do against this bipedal dinosaur person?

What had she gotten herself into? "Sorry," she breathed.

"What is your business here?" it hissed.

"Uh." Leah struggled for words. Obvious questions were going to piss this thing off, weren't they? On top of her attacking it, when she was the one in its territory.

She'd come here for one thing. "Mateo Valdez. I'm looking for Mateo Valdez."

Didn't seem to ring a bell for the lizard, nor for its underlings. It arched a brow.

"Another human. Which I am," Leah said.

"That I can see," the lizard drawled. "And are there any other humans searching for this Mateo Valdez?"

Leah shook her head, then thought better of it. Maybe not her best idea. "I get a question now," she asked. "Who are you?"

"You want answers, do you?" the lizard asked. Its underlings scaled up its moss cloak, taking grasp on the pseudo fabric. Whoa. She wanted one of those. How could you weave moss into living cloth?

She reached out to touch it, and the lizard snarled.

Another bad idea. No getting her hand bitten off by the obsidian-toothed monster. "Yeah," she squeaked.

"I am the gardenkeeper," the lizard announced. "And this is my garden."

"It's really anachronistic," Leah blurted.

The lizard frowned.

"It's nice," she corrected.

The gardenkeeper huffed. "I don't have time for this. Goodbye, you who seek Mateo Valdez."

Before Leah could inquire further, something brushed the top of her bun. She blinked.

The earth swallowed her up.

Encounter #2, 4/15/2011:

She laid there splayed across the soil, memory smearing by like a car going ninety. Focusing on any of the images too long made her want to be sick. Plants cannot be sick. She could not reconcile these facts without screaming.

The facts were these:

Leah Ayala had spent every second since her birth justifying it. Her mother, having had her through a rebound boyfriend just out of high school, kept her even if said rebound had decided not to stick around.

Rebecca had been in school at the time. She'd finished a degree with a toddler on her lap at graduation. Rebecca had sacrificed boyfriends, partying, traveling the world, any of the things a reckless twenty something in college would want to do. She had done so much to keep Leah around.

So Leah did what she could to make those sacrifices worth it. Her room stayed pristine and spotless. Her homework from kindergarten onward would only be perfect A's, only getting glowing reviews in parent teacher conferences. When her mother wore out, she'd be there sweeping the kitchen or attempting to fold laundry into passable lumps of fabric, crammed into any drawer that would contain it. It didn't have to look good. It just had to be done.

One day her mother wanted her to meet someone. He smelled like cigarettes and had tattoos. His name was Tom, and Rebecca asked Leah if she liked him. She liked how happy her mother was around Tom, plus he'd brought her and her mother flowers. For her mother, a pot of roses. For Leah, a cutting of wisteria in a vase.

She put the wisteria on her bedside table. Rebecca married Tom when Leah was eight. Nine months later, Leah had a baby sister.

Tara was fussy. She cried a lot. She liked to be held. She broke Leah's toys. Leah had been an only child for a long time.

But she got used to it, because Tara thought the world of her. By the time Tara could toddle she thought Leah made the sun rise and sink in the sky. She wanted to do anything Leah did, watch anything Leah watched, and always wanted to be near her.

She hated it, sometimes. But sometimes she didn't. Tara could be a whiny pain who couldn't keep up. She also drew Leah pictures, which Leah tacked around her desk while she did equations and wrote up essays

Then Tom got sick. He'd been a high paid mechanic. Rebecca had been on leave, pregnant with David. Tom broke his back. He'd be in the hospital just as Rebecca gave birth to her third kid.

When Leah was thirteen, her mother returned to work. Tara started school. Leah alternated caring for David, their dad, and her own mounting pile of homework. There were parties. Dances. Tailgates. She called in an excused absence from classes at least once a week. Her mother needed her. Otherwise, why was she here?

And Tara needed her. Small, unaware David needed changing and fed and bathed and put to bed. Rebecca got pregnant again, this time delivering Alex who had pneumonia right out the womb and required another hospital stay.

Then Leah saw a corkboard that a camp an hour out of Del Bosque hired teens as young as fifteen.

She applied. Her grades and references got her in. She also earned another benefit.

It'd been a hard couple of years. They were not only able to get Leah free room and board, on top of a few thousand dollars for her labor, but a discounted program for Tara. Wouldn't it be nice, she said, for them to have the two girls out of the house for the summer? Her parents waffled a while. They needed the extra hands for David and Alex.

But Leah could see it, when she got too busy to take on the load herself. Tara heating up mac and cheese on the stove for David. Tara cleaning spit up formula from Alex's slobbery cheek. Tara's own chores accumulated as their mother worked and their father recovered.

Their aunts agreed to watch the boys when the girls were gone. Leah and Tara were dropped off before Cottonwood cabin on the same day. Leah would be at orientation while Tara explored. Being a camp counselor compared much to being at home, though with far fewer hospital visits.

Leah hated hospitals, she decided. She hated sterility. The feeling of death behind closed doors, never spoken but thick in the air, sprayed away under disinfectant and antiseptic. The forests she had hiked with her parents had none of those things. They were alive. When death happened in the forest, the decay formed new flora and fauna and fed into a larger story always ongoing.

She planned on a degree in environmental science, on track to join the NPS. Her parents' income or lack thereof netted her a Pell Grant worth two years' tuition at a university, longer still at a community college. When she graduated college and did her last summer at Camp Cottonwood, she'd finally be in dorms and on her own.

Her reputation made getting Tara in her cabin a snap. She had to fight a bit for both her and June, given the ruckus they were known to cause, but Tino and Marydale believed she could keep them in check.

She'd have the perfect final summer. The best goodbye she could possibly offer Tara, even as guilt wracked her deep down.

Leah's burdens wouldn't disappear when she moved to Eureka. They'd just be hoisted onto Tara. Her mother continued working full-time at the clinic. Their father had yet to be able to work again, other than his hobbies. Baking. Glassblowing. He had a business coach in vocational rehab. He was considering his options.

Leah considered her own. What if she just commuted the hour and a half to College of the Redwoods, every day? Rebecca assured they would be alright without her, only for Leah to hear her muttering about money in bed with Tom through the wall.

She couldn't do it. She just couldn't. It made her a horrible person. She would make it up, though. She could make Tara's last summer, free of those burdens, the happiest she had ever and would ever have.

(See Encounter #1)

Being a mandrake, much like being a camp counselor, had been a lot like a skewed version of home. Following orders, acting without question, taking on expectations unspoken but clearer than the thoughts in her own mind.

Until the scorpion grass had ungrown, and the dreamlike blur of Weiss's control fell away.

She returned to camp to bring back Mateo Valdez, Moe and Selina Rathbone, Frank Donato and Leon Ellis and Theodora Dirk, the eight Walshes, every former railroad worker or former miner that would make up what they called the Union. She was always the first in the dirt, the first to test a theory or experiment.

It only made sense she'd be the first to reach out. If Leah didn't do it, it wouldn't get done. She caught a ride on Weiss close enough to the conservation center, sneaking in as a staff member arrived for their morning shift.

Then Leah was alone. She traveled up the leg of an office chair, onto a countertop where a blocky black phone waited, light blinking. As the phone rang, she checked over the papers for familiar names. She'd known some of these staff in passing. None of these people matched any she'd interviewed before her college application.

The ringing ended. A voice picked up. "Hello?"

Leah froze. Beside one name, and a date. May 2011.

The voice on the other end didn't sound like two years had passed. It sounded like her mother.

Leah didn't sound like Leah. Didn't look like Leah. She couldn't slot back into her life like the last two years hadn't happened.

"I'm going to hang up…"

"Wait."

A rattle, the phone being readjusted against her ear. "Yes? Sorry, I'm still listening, just give me a second." Alex crying. David yelling he didn't do anything, don't listen to Alex!

"Boys?" she said.

"Yeah, I just gotta- wait, you sound familiar. How did you get this number? Are you one of Tara's friends? Oh, hold on! Tara!"

Leah couldn't do it. She just couldn't. She hung up.

Encounter #618, 8/22/2019:

Leah could pinpoint the exact second flesh lurched from under her lignin, like a fruit breaking and skin oozing out of her mandrake form. There was a burst, and the dirt around her fell suddenly silent. She reached out, but her fingers stayed mere inches long. She couldn't stretch them any further, no matter how much her knuckles cracked and her nails scratched at the soil she was stuck in.

She gasped. Her chest filled and emptied, barely. She needed air. Air! Her body couldn't drink in the moisture pressing against her, respirating as a root might. She writhed. She cried out.

Above heavy footsteps were drawing near. How near? How deep below the surface was she? She could no longer tell. She couldn't hear, couldn't see.

She could feel something grasp her wrist and tug. A hard pull, so hard her shoulder popped. Sharp shards dug into her forearm. Her nerves warmed at the pain. Rivulets of blood were soaking into the earth around the wound.

"I'm sorry!" missed a muffled voice above. "Leah?"

Muffled, until it was clear. Her head broke topsoil and she gasped in a lungful of air.

"Leah!" Weiss had a hold of her shoulders, shaking her gently. His crystalline eyes were panicked. Leah squinted. He looked so small, and so did Mateo. All of the mandrakes who had gathered in the greenhouse for what she had theorized her final time going under, they too were small. Right. They looked small, because she was larger. Larger than she'd been in years.

She hacked up dirt.

"Leah?" Mateo asked.

"It worked," she said.

Weiss's claw was slick with blood. Before, she'd only ever drawn milkfoam. Papercuts bubbled up white and frothed. Now she bled red as peeling madrone bark where he'd pierced her. She licked the blood from her wrist, salt and metal tinged with earth.

He was already placing his moss cloak over the wound. "We shouldn't have worried," he said, a little to himself.

"How do you feel?" Mateo asked.

Leah tasted the blood on her tongue. Taste. That had been late stage, like the soft flesh she now found herself wrapped in. She prodded her bicep. The dermis gave, rising up like dough from the pressure. Fine hair sprouted down her arms, and everywhere else, but numbed without connection.

"I'm alright," she said. Her voice hummed through her throat, and she slapped a hand to her naked chest. Ow. Boobs. Those hurt to slap.

The others watched her face. She smiled. She couldn't tell if anyone bought it, but Selina had the stack of clothes she'd requested. Right now, she wanted coverage. She was so vulnerable, half her senses cut off and new ones grafted on.

But everyone was more than happy to help, as they had been for as long she'd been building to the culmination of her work. She'd been seeking this end after the day she'd returned to report her findings: she had not been remembered. She would have to become herself, as she was when she disappeared, to do so.

Those years were spent in study. She learned what the earth had to teach, everything she could about each and every member of their newfound community.

She learned that if she didn't eat, Mateo would send along food. If she had been cooped up inside the cabin too long, Moe or Selina would take her by the root, later arm, to walk the grounds. If she fell asleep at the workbench, she'd wake with a moss cloak draped across shoulders that got progressively larger and more human with each replanting.

"It worked," Weiss echoed. Perhaps aside from Mateo he'd been most invested in her progress, carrying her samples in his basket from the greenhouse, offering insights on their functions and purposes. His investment in her research had paid off.

All of them had put time and care into her for this result.

She nodded. She forced herself to smile, stilling the shake in her hands. "Sure did, bud."

23

Tara is awake. Probably. She's no longer in the tower with the flowers, at least. But she can't say she feels fully out of the vision, her eyes bleary and her brain struggling to settle on the sizes of things in her new surroundings. The bed's either too massive to ever scale down from, or the floor's so close it could be just inches away. Why not just roll off the side to get down?

"How lucid are you?" drawls a voice to her right.

She glances over. The tulip mandrake, Moe, perches on a fraying ottoman. Hadn't Leah just been sitting there? Maybe Tara's too out of it to rely on her recall just yet, but she could swear her sister had been slumped over the blanket she lays beneath now.

She shimmies up on the pillow. To Moe's question, Tara shrugs. "It's like," she says, swaying, "normal. But with those 3D glasses on. Not the good ones. The shitty paper ones that give you a headache."

"Sounds about right," Moe says, veiny roots crossed. She offers one up. "Come on. You don't want to be inside for this. Your first time, right?"

Tara can't quite parse what Moe means, but she grabs the root. It's warmer than she expects, and stronger. She feels five fingers, calloused and rough, rubbing at her knuckles in a comforting rhythm. Thin filaments aren't enveloping her hand. It's human, light peach, a pastel shade of the tulip's pink petals.

Except there are no petals. Moe has been replaced with a butch, stocky woman in a stained tee with its sleeves ripped away. Her belly peeks out from above the waistband of denim cutoff shorts. Strawberry blonde hair layers her scalp in greasy tuffets. Her sure grip on Tara winds her wrist and holds firm as Tara lowers her feet to the floor, socks scratching the boards, splinters catching but unable to break through the thick cotton.

The cabin unfolds beyond the bed and its itchy wool blanket. It ceases to be anything else but this room, with this woman as her nursemaid, the walls decorated not with faded crescent moons and shooting stars but yellowed maps and bleached Polaroid photos. She bunches her fist in the sheets. Not threadbare linen, but hardy flannel. Something about the altered texture feels too much and too little, too big and too small.

Tara lets the woman lead her down the hall to the back door. The cabin walls on the way aren't pockmarked with decades of tacks and nails, but are freshly built and fill the air with the scent of chopped pine and sap. She inhales deep. The scent of dried herbs from her sister's workbench suffuses the air, too, mingling what she sees now with what she remembers.

Not just from this morning, but from a decade before. Funny, she recognizes all of these rooms. When she'd come out of the creek, hair spilled loose, blood crusted in her shoe from dripping down her calf, she'd been brought here. She sees Tino as they exit to the back porch. She sees herself sat on the stoop, away from prying camper eyes, even if it didn't do much for their perceptions of her.

She hadn't cared at the time. Torn from June's embrace, the girl on the step sobs into her elbow, arms around her knees. What else is she supposed to do? Return to June? Find the garden, perhaps Leah? Which of those little monsters, the ones to give her friend back, was her sister?

Tino had left her there, having spent hours trying to talk her down. Tara didn't speak a word of what happened. Where they'd been, what they'd done, why June had no shoes and Tara was covered in blood. Telling the truth hadn't worked before, and it never would again.

The girl on the stoop shimmers away as Tara gets closer, like a mirage. Tara misgauges the distance between steps without her, slipping onto her ass somewhere in the middle of the stairs.

The woman grapples for her. "Just stay put," she orders.

Tara rubs her eye. Yeah. Wait here, to go home and for everything to be the way it was, even if it never would. Instead, she'd be a laughingstock in Del Bosque. Her sketchbooks would be snatched from her hands, the drawings of her nightmares jeered at by Haylee Pierce and her ilk for all of junior high. They couldn't remember Leah, but they remembered Tara believed in her. There would be counselors she wouldn't dare step into an office with, because what could she tell them that wouldn't be gone the second they were out of earshot? She didn't need her peers' bullying, and she didn't need grownups' pity. It was enough for Tara to stop drawing, to stop talking, to try and disappear herself.

In the lingering afternoon sun, the trees shine. Beams of sunlight look solid, tangible, chock full of dust and pollen and seedlings trapped in poffs as they dance through the air. Had they looked like this the night she returned home? Couldn't have. It'd been too late in the summer then, and it's too late in autumn now.

Tara leans toward them and spreads her fingers. The cottonwood seeds bob and weave, just out of reach.

The woman catches her before she can tumble forward. In her free hand she's got a blunt, the cherry end aglow in the shadow of the cabin. "What did I just say?" she barks.

Tara almost demands to know who the woman is. Before she sees the woman's gaze go to the treeline. Shuttering like a film reel, another mirage coalesces. Another woman. This one slender, bespectacled, her sundress spinning as she turns to face a class of eager children in matching t-shirts. The woman glances over at the stoop.

She winks at Tara's butch.

At Tara's side, Moe Rathbone takes another toke. She sighs out smoke through her nostrils, flushing.

"What?" she asks.

Tara's been staring. Musten's spores swirl in her bloodstream, metabolizing to psilocin. She wants to be angry. What makes their fungal friend's effect any different from Weiss's? She scrabbles at her rage, at being incapacitated when June and Leah need her. It slides off her hands like a soap bar in the shower, until her anger's just suds swept down the drain.

The emotion just can't find purchase. The cottonwoods here rise like the birches outside the garden, but there's none of the foreboding. They don't foretell the misfortune that awaits past the meadow and the grove, nor do they watch her failures with those black, unblinking eyes and pass judgment.

They just are. They don't ask whether they're heard when they fall, because they know the answer. The mycelium will mourn them no matter what, shortly, before setting to its work.

And what work it is. She can see the mold that let her into Madrone yesterday. Its lattice under wood boards, like nerves webbing through tissue.

"You wanna be outside," Moe says. "Can't stay like this forever. But me and Selina, we always liked how vivid it gets. All the details nature hands you when you're tuned to listen."

Tara's eyes hood. She slouches against the steps. "Exhausting, though," she mutters.

"Sure as shit, kid," Moe says. "You're not meant to feel this much all the time. More than a dose here and there, you're too wired. Winds you up."

Tara hums. She wouldn't describe this feeling in those words. It's not like she's been zapped full of energy with nowhere to go, bouncing around in search of release.

It's like she's cleared her airways after nothing but breathing smoke, and the effort still aches. She's waiting for the smoke to come streaming in. Bracing and bracing for pain that doesn't come, but she's still open. Still raw.

It hurts. But she can breathe again, even as oxygen scrapes down her sinuses.

"We wanted to carry that part," Moe goes on. She anchors to Tara's arm. A swathe of roots bands her elbow like a net. Or is it a hand, wrinkled and scabbed, spotted with age? "Sometimes it's good for you. Gives you a change of perspective."

Tara nods. She can certainly see how a view like this might make you want to live in the woods and never leave, dragging any campers and counselors who seek the same along with you.

Still, watching Selina, she has to ask. "You founded the camp. Is this why?"

Moe smirks. Gray streaks her strawberry blonde, her posture crumpled. "Just fell in love with the forest," she says. "Someone had to tend it. I didn't think I'd get this long to do it, but no one tells you how long you've got to stick around for.

Lucky, Selina thinks. Dunno if I'd go that far. But I love her, and we love this place."

"And you don't want to go back out there? To the real world?"

She spreads her fingers. Roots curl off to better cradle the blunt. Tara blinks and the woman's gone, a tulip mandrake blazing instead.

"What makes this unreal to you?" Moe asks.

Tara frowns. Moe rolls her eyes, flickered to a middle-aged human again.

"Fine. I thought about it a while. Maybe doing what Leah did, getting myself dolled up in skin and bones. For what? Everyone I knew who worked at this camp is dead, or they lost their marbles like I did. The center's all fresh meat. It's like that old… oh, what is it? If you take a ship and replace all the parts, is it the same ship? I'm not the captain anymore. That's what matters."

Tara nods. Theseus, she thinks dimly. While the ship of Theseus gets thrown around a lot, she finds it ironic he's remembered for seafaring, when his main claim to fame is running underground in the labyrinth. She closes her eyes and wonders if such a labyrinth exists below her feet.

She tips her head back. She closes her eyes. Is this anything like what June experiences, when plants speak to her? She can't hear any words. But the language must not be entirely unlike how she can feel the thoughts bouncing across near invisible fibers, empowered by threads these trees and grasses can't fathom or fully see apart from itself.

"Anyways," Moe coughs. "I made my peace with the outside world a long time ago. I would have liked the choice to make up with my kid, but I could have done that long before me and Selina got put on ice."

"You have a kid?"

Moe sniffs. "What, she'd be sixty? She was just outta high school in '79." She strokes her chin. "Hard to recall. I wanted her to meet Selina someday. Never really turned out how I wanted. You don't get a lot of chances to pick what happens."

She sighs. Tara looks into those black and brown eyes. She sees more of the mandrake now. Creases on her central bulb like wrinkles framing her face, patterned in variegations to denote stretch marks or scarring.

Tara blinks. Moe sets the last of the blunt in a wet coffee can, then clings to Tara's bicep. Tara hobbles down to the grass. The mandrake climbs higher as she stumbles. "Careful now," she warns. "We don't get a lot of injured humans 'round here. So you're shit out of luck if you need more than a band aid."

Moe does not shift between faces and forms. Tara gives it a minute. She wants to make sure she's stable before she walks around the cabin's exterior, to join the others. After no more hallucinations come, she heads for the campfire.

Seated on her shoulder, Moe asks, "So?"

"What?"

"You're out of orbit, space cadet. Any change in perspective?"

Tara nods. Well, the world's still too big and too small. That's nothing new. So much of her life has been confined to Del Bosque, to northern California. She's perfectly aware that this has made her feel caged and trapped, just as much as she's aware she feels there's too much to ever be seen in one lifetime out here.

The contradiction tore at her. She ran from it. Now all she can do is stew in it. Let it overtake her, until she stares through her fingers at what remains.

June strolls off the front porch above and down to the green. There's something about how the afternoon sun lights her skin, bringing green up from her pale, freckled face. How her carrot red hair glimmers bright poppy orange. How her eyes go from brown to dark, dark violet, like the velvet sheen of an iris.

She has her gloves off. One of her hands has divided, the fingers split to ribbons of jade and sage. The fine, delicate threads like webs between them are almost translucent. Rainbows dance between her dandelion stems.

Tara hunches into herself, hands on her elbows. June's as natural as any tree or animal or plant. She's just as amazing.

Moe rolls her eyes. Tara's awe knocked the mandrake loose, but she rights herself soon enough.

"You're coming up on my record, you know," she says.

Tara squints.

"Took me twelve years. You kids have had ten? I won't forgive you if you beat me is all." Moe jerks her chin toward June. "You shouldn't make it longer than it needs to be."

Tara can guess what 'it' Moe means. "What if I hurt her?"

"You will," Moe says.

Tara glares over at her. "Thanks," she mutters.

"Then what?" Moe nudges. She swings down from Tara's shoulder to the ground. "You're gonna hurt her. Next question."

Tara shakes her head. She never wants to hurt June. She's already hurt June. She wants to protect June. She can barely protect herself.

She understands now. She doesn't have to save June. But what does she do now? Save herself? Save Leah?

"I think," Moe says, "you ask her. Shoot your shot. I can tell you right now, though, she's not gonna tell you to punish yourself."

"I deserve it."

"No one deserves anything," Moe says, slapping a root on Tara's shin. "If you deserve it, I do. And that means she does."

"But she doesn't-"

Moe cocks her head, hands on her hips.

Tara growls. Her face scrunches, searching for a rebuttal.

But all she can do is breathe.

"What have I told you, Priscilla Ann?"

Priscilla Ann Walsh ignores her mother, who has grappled herself to the grate about the unlit campfire. Winnifred Walsh will not take her eyes off her five children, or June herself. June has three little flower girls alight on her arm like a flock of sparrows.

"She ain't even dangerous," Priscilla says. "You're one of us still. Ma lets me play with all the other planted people. That means she don't get to get after me about you."

Winnifred's frown says otherwise. "I dunno about that one," June chuckles.

"I do!" crows Maeve, the youngest. Now that June has outed herself as a fellow mandrake, the kids have gotten bolder to match Priscilla Ann. Maeve climbs up to June's shoulder and surveys her elders. Her sister Ciara dangles from June's growing dandelion stems, swinging there, wee leg-like tendrils pumping forward and back to pick up speed.

June prods Ciara higher and higher with her index. Her mother glares at June. But she softens when June says, "You might wanna reconsider. I'm not from here."

"'Course you are!" Ciara laughs. She's this close to a 360 degree inversion on her makeshift swing. June stills her hand to keep the kid from loop-de-looping.

"We aren't from here, either," Priscilla says. A bee snuffles at her clover. "Right, Ma?"

Winnifred gives her daughter a nod. On June's other hand, her sons climb between dandelions like they're monkey bars. "We're from the other coast," one of the mountain mints says. Finn? June's struggling to keep up with all these new names.

"From out east!" says the other boy.

"We are indeed," Winnifred allows. "Now be careful. How do you expect her to catch you if you won't stop that wiggling?"

June manipulates her stems, plucking a vibration through them like they're strings on a harp. She feels each of them, the root hairs sensitive to every move the mandrake kids make. "I'll try my best," June assures their mother.

It's the longest June has had her stems free, out in plain view. They've always been something she idled with in her own home, where only her or Betty could see. In her room, flexing and unfurling them as she tried to focus on her homeschool homework. At her desk, generating letters that would never be read. Whenever she did show her mandrake side in front of Betty, she'd feign non-reaction. But June could tell.

She could see it in how she stared, like Winnifred does now, concerned as June makes a cat's cradle of her fingers for the Walsh children to play on.

In one smooth motion, Winnifred lassos from atop the grate to stand on June's forearm. She gives June a long, hard look. "Can't believe how grown you are," she says softly. "Age don't come of leaving the forest, does it?"

"I wanna try!" Priscilla whines. She skitters into June's pocket. "Take me with you," she whispers.

"You damn well will not!" Winnifred cries.

"I don't think it really works like that," June admits, and Winnifred is visibly relieved. "I'm like this from being half-done." At least, she thinks. It's the second time she's spoken these words aloud, after a decade of hearing it between her ears over and over again. Not that she's sure the Walshes totally understand what this means. They don't take on the horror her grandmother has in the past, or the guilt Weiss just did.

Weiss and Leah, for their part, don't confirm or deny what June means. They both slump into each other on the log bench, drained from the vision. Leah had to be shooed out of Cottonwood cabin by Moe after crashing at Tara's bedside. Weiss makes a stone lawn ornament of himself so Leah won't fall off the log while dozing.

The Walsh matriarch puts her roots around Priscilla, extracting the clover from June's pocket. "There will be none of that talk, you hear me?" Winnifred insists.

Priscilla groans. As Winnifred hmphs off with her children in tow, Tara and Moe emerge. June waves, letting her hands reel back to a reasonable size and shape. Her gloves stay stuffed in her boilersuit pocket.

Tara gapes, eyes enormous. Is she still high?

The Rathbone wives join together and take a seat on the grass. June's more than a little envious of the couple, for more than a couple reasons.

Then Tara flops down at June's left, sliding down the log to the grass. Her head rests against June's knee. June has to keep from bouncing her leg.

"Are we gonna talk about what we saw?" Tara yawns.

June folds her arms. She takes deep breaths in, out. Even if she wants to explode out of her skin. She's been patient, but Weiss agreed it'll be Tara who will have the answer if June and Leah didn't find one.

Leah stretches. Weiss stirs to life, his claws crackling from their stiff statue state.

"We have to have gleaned something from all that," he mutters. "I didn't have much presence of mind myself."

"Lizard brain," Leah says.

Weiss turtles back into his cloak. "I'm aware."

Leah pats him on the back. "Only teasing, bud," she says. "Did you see anything, Tara?"

June's roots grip her laces. She forces herself not to fidget, digging her softening fingertips into her biceps. Moment of truth. If their efforts are wasted, if Leah came to them for nothing, it'll come with a shrug or a shake of the head.

Instead Tara perks up, and so does June. "Uh. I mostly saw mushrooms. Fungi. But I did see other things."

Other things. June's face burns. Tara had gotten a front row seat to June and Leah in total meltdown.

Tara's not acting embarrassed, though. No more than the other travelers from the vision are, anyways. She just taps her lip, thinking. "I saw some flowers. When we were inside."

"Flowers?" Weiss asks, leaning forward.

"Other than you guys," she says. "We were in this big pile of them in the end. Purple stars, white blooms in the middle? With blue and yellow. They were like jester hats. Do those ring a bell?"

"They could be pincushions," Selina suggests. She has her legs crossed, Moe in her lap. "But you said yellow. Oh! Doesn't clematis have a star shaped petal?"

"Sounds more like blue columbine," Moe says.

"Those colors," Weiss says. He bites his talon and rises to pace. "Why do those sound like aquilas? There can't be more of them. There have never been any in the greenhouse."

Leah arches a brow, straightened up on her log. "You mean *aquilegia*?" she asks.

Weiss blinks. A Eureka expression enters his eyes. "If you saw them in the vision," he rasps, "you must have encountered them somewhere in reality. Where?"

"I saw them when I was here last time, in the house," Tara says.

The master's house, on the garden property. June had never seen much of it herself. No wonder Musten shoved them toward it only when Tara joined the vision. "You looked in the house?" June asks.

"I looked everywhere for Leah," Tara explains. "I thought it was a waste of time, since I never saw anything. It didn't look like anyone had ever lived there, actually."

"No one has. I do not know if the masters could be said to be living," Weiss says. "Regardless, no plant has thrived there that I've ever seen. Aquilas have never occurred to me. They've never been used with mayapples, to my knowledge. What if they're the key to making a mandrake memorable?"

"They do sound a lot like inverted scorpion grass," Moe says. "If they do cancel out the memory effect, it'd make sense they'd be kept as far away from the greenhouse as possible. Hell, far from the ground as possible."

"Sounds like something your masters would do," grumbles Mateo. He's sparking the fire, dusting his hands off once he has some fallen branches kindled. "So humans can't find out where they are and, I don't know, hold them accountable?"

"Exactly," Weiss says. "If an aquila could lead humans to our gate, that must be why the masters did not leave any in the greenhouse."

Mateo takes a seat at Leah's right. "Is that what you saw on your vision quest?" he asks, jabbing her gently. Leah covers her face with her hands. Mateo pats her shoulder. "C'mon, I've experimented. I'm not judging you. I'm just glad to see you all came out okay."

"As am I," Selina says. Moe grunts an affirmative.

They've come out more than okay. They have a lead. Maybe one of the other mandrakes has seen the house in detail? "I think we were in the tower," June says. She glances at Tara. She nods to confirm it.

"The one that crumbled a few years back?" Mateo asks. He flattens his palms on the log's bark.

Leah winces. June and Tara look at Weiss, who puts a stop to his pacing.

"I haven't been caring for the garden like I used to," he admits. "We need to investigate. If there are any of these flowers left, they might be just the component we're looking for."

His tail sways. He's wagging it, and June quirks her mouth.

"We can go tomorrow," Leah butts in. "Tara needs the rest."

Tara does not argue. She smooths small circles along June's halfway hand with the pad of her thumb. June feels Tara's temple against her thigh. Tara needs to put Tara first, if only for a few hours. Especially after the gift she's given them.

Given to Leah and Mateo, anyways. They're the closest to human amongst the mandrakes. Well, current Cottonwood mandrakes. June watches the rapt discussion Weiss and the wives are carrying on. Something about the property of buttercups in magic, or how perennial and annual blooms interact with mayapples? Does June have a place in this? She has the option of staying as she is.

The mandrakes now engaged on the subject do not. June has to temper her enthusiasm. Mateo is amped, speaking emphatically with his hands, but Leah doesn't match how June is feeling. She pipes up when asked to, yeah, but she's otherwise quiet. Must be exhaustion from the vision bogging her down, or maybe she's in shock. June lists toward her. She should check in.

Tara twirls one of June's stems around her ring finger. June squirms, not uncomfortably.

The Rathbones have drawn over to Leah, scooched between her and Mateo.

None of them are minding the girls, now deep in aquila talk.

Tara whispers to June. "Wanna go for a walk?" she asks.

June stiffens. Tara does not seem to notice, taking June's bicep to hobble to her feet. She's more stable than when she first fell from the circle of spores. She hangs onto June's arm as she stands, even so.

Poppies unfurl from June's pomp, her face ruddy. She rises and nods.

Tara takes the lead. They leave behind the conversation, passing under Oak cabin where a group of other mandrakes are shooting the shit, playing cards etched into helicopter seeds, laughing at one another's bad hands. They don't seem terribly interested in the campfire chat, what it might mean to be remembered by society. What's that like? Accepting their lot as they have, just kicking it out here, building an identity away from the world beyond the woods?

Then June is tugged down one of the old camp trails. Gravel, smudged with moss and weeds, thick enough June isn't hearing the earth call her name quite so strong. She wants to be able to promise it's not long now. Perhaps soon, finally, she can plant down and rest without being forgotten.

But she can't bring herself to say it.

"Where are we going?" she asks instead. Tara is forging ahead, her hand warm in June's own.

"Surprise," Tara just says. "How you feeling?"

June puts on a fragile grin. "Great," she gets out. "You? You seem a little…"

Out of it. If Tara can hear June's hesitation, it's not enough to slow their pace.

They keep moving. Past the equipment sheds, past orchards June is certain weren't there in the 2000s, past the opening in the trees where the lake lies. June can see Weiss's heavy tread imprinted on the formerly muddy entrance. So he did go to see the lake, along with the rest of the camp he neighbored all these years.

But his steps are not present on the overgrown trail Tara takes up toward the hills. June lags as the incline gets steeper. Tara slows for her, but June joins her at a steady clip.

A tower comes into view. Not the garden's of seamless stone to the east, but the plywood and two by fours that shouldn't even be standing to the west. June has to crane around the surrounding willow and walnut trees to take in the zipline's three story height, screwing up her eyes to see anything but the ivy that's long since engulfed the structure. How is it even upright, laden in so much time and foliage?

"Didn't think it'd still be here," Tara says, patting the ladder. "You remember?"

June shrugs. She'd climbed this thing half a dozen times in her three years at Cottonwood. Wait. Five times. Twice a summer, and the first she'd been sidelined. June smiles when she thinks of why.

Tara fiddles with a strand of ivy that blankets the boards. English ivy, so not poisonous. "Wasn't so bad after the first time. I thought I was going to get sent home right then, though," she says. "Dumb, when I think about it now. I thought me crying made Leah look bad. Maybe my brain wouldn't have freaked out if Haylee Pierce shut the fuck up."

"God, what ever happened to her?" June snorts. She never ran into the girl after 2009. Never bothered hunting her down on Facebook or Instagram when the idea might have crossed her mind.

Tara laughs, so harsh it becomes a cackle. "Moved away in high school. Got a modeling contract. Probably married an exec already."

"Probably," June shrugs. "I bet she's an influencer now."

'Ugh," Tara groans. "Or an extra." She leans against the tower, arms crossed. "I'm glad this place closed down. Can you imagine her as a counselor?"

"I dunno," June says. She knocks on the flat slats that cover the front of the tower. She doesn't hear a hollow echo, but something inside that thunks. The ivy vines shake awake at her touch, their dead leaves falling loose like dandruff. "I think we could have been good at it. Other than…"

Tara nods. Other than.

She's watching June closely. June averts her eyes. Tara does the same. Does Tara sense June is keeping something from her? Omitting a truth that hangs in the air like a cloying fog?

Anxiety makes the opening. The earth rushes in, raging like a tide in her skull. June gasps. Her fingers coil amongst the ivy vines.

"I'm fine," June lies.

Tara stops testing her weight on a ladder rung. She meets June's eyes. Can she hear the silent urging, too, with the psilocin dancing in the folds of her brain? June has never dared confirm the floral threads lacing her own, each lobe infested every bit as much as her fingers spooling to stems. Maybe she's got thick, damp moss for bronchi, hard white wood for bones, a mayapple for a heart.

Her hand slides under her tank top, just over her bra. Is there a heartbeat? Locating it got harder after breasts came in, padding possibly-pseudo flesh over the organ.

Tara watches from seven feet up the ladder. June lowers her hand.

"You coming?" Tara asks.

June cringes. Out the corner of her eye she sees the splintering tower, creaking audibly as they place their weight against it.

But June calms her breaths. Tara says nothing, propping her foot on the next rotted rung.

Stems curl around June's first handhold.

She chooses each to follow with care, but catches up to Tara quickly. To her shock the tower is holding up to their ascent. Even when one of Tara's steps snaps a rung, sputtering barkdust into June's eyes, her dandelions deftly lash the halves together again. Her mandrake side never fails to surprise her with how strong yet versatile it can be, the stems' dexterity like that of her dominant hand even at extreme lengths. It's not something she gets the chance to play with often, aside from using her inhuman strength to throw freight around the nursery.

Before long, they've reached the top.

When Tara clamors onto the platform, she offers a hand down to June. Both of June's hands are knit into the ivy. She rewinds one to flesh and accepts the haul up.

She doesn't need the help. But she appreciates it, and the fact Tara's not shaking when she looks down beyond June. She hasn't scared herself out of this, lack of harnesses be damned. June hasn't either, much as she knows this climb should have her quaking in her boots.

Yet as June settles on the platform, her nerves are already easing. She and Tara sit on the painted jump-off marker. She feels what's inside the tower: a colossal tree, practically dead but capable of keeping the structure in place all the same. June gets comfortable enough to admire their vantage from the treetops, the canopy around them swaying like rolling waves for miles and miles. Through them, the lake, glittering like white noise, clear and smooth as a sheet of glass without any of the rafts and swimmers and canoes to disturb its surface.

"Beautiful, huh?" June says.

"Yeah," Tara says.

June glances over. Tara isn't looking at the horizon.

June's words dry up. She clears her throat.

"So," Tara says.

"So?" June asks.

"We did it," Tara says, nudging their shoulders together. "Right?"

"Definitely," June says. "You saw the missing piece. How's it feel?"

Tara sighs. She scoots forward, letting her legs dangle over the platform. She kicks them idly. "Good," she says. "I guess."

"You guess?" Tara has potentially solved the problem for everyone in this forest who wants to get out and be remembered for it. She's done it. What June couldn't, what Leah might have managed eventually after further trial and error. She should be jubilating it up.

But Tara kicks her legs. She sighs again, drumming on the platform.

"I'm excited for Leah," she says. "She's going to come home, see our parents for real this time. Get her life back. It's just... I guess it feels too easy?"

"Don't you deserve one easy thing?"

"Maybe," Tara says. "I don't know. I just know I've been so paranoid. It's like I'm never just. Off. It's like this job I've never been able to quit, because no one else was going to do it. But now? I mean, what if this flower they're talking about works? What if my job's over? What do I do then?"

June hasn't even let that concept sink in. Being tied up, disconnected from other people because why try? It'll just inevitably be erased, when she inevitably makes the mistake that plunges her into the earth and loses her every relationship she could dare develop.

Until now. She just has to go for it. And then? "What do you want to do?" she asks Tara.

Tara shrugs. "I wanted her. Or to get away from where this happened, if I couldn't. But Leah's okay now. Kind of. I can let go a little. It's weird. Good weird."

June nods. Good weird. The good weird of climbing this tower, her hands unraveled, her body doing only what her body is capable of. She's never been allowed this pleasure outside these woods. She could say it's safer out there, in her boots and gloves on solid cement, hardwood, linoleum, tile. But it's far from the ecstasy that is this, her flesh and flora mingling, the wordless whispers quieted because they're no longer hungry. They'll have been sated.

And maybe June can be, too.

But how to say it?

"Hey," Tara says.

She takes June's hands. Both of them, knotted and gnarled as they are. She puts her own over them. The pads of her fingertips trail the roots like they're the softest silk, the stems as if they're precious instead of distorted human digits. Slender brown fingers twine June's, river silt slipping through June's frantic grasp, streaming off and away until she's sure she'll never gather all the grains again. Whenever June thinks she's got a grip, everything comes apart.

June comes apart. She can feel herself doing so now. Roots slither through her boot laces, writhing uselessly over the edge. The ground can't devour her from up here.

"In your letters," Tara says. "You said you wrote about stuff you didn't think you could tell me?"

Oh. So she can see it. "Listen, Tara," she says. And falters.

Tara's drawn closer. Her dark eyes linger on June's face, drinking her in.

June isn't ready for this. She's painfully aware of how near Tara is, how much even the smallest give in her facade is obvious and unforgettable. "How did you know?" she asks. "You said you never read them."

"I've always kind of known," Tara says. "Sorta. I'm not sure how I couldn't know. Do you remember that night?"

She can tell the night Tara means by how her hands gather up June's stems. Their last night together, before their ten year hiatus. Tara must have put it together. How incomplete June is, because Tara tore her from the ground too early. She's smart. She would have connected the dots herself.

Tara leans forward. Her nose brushes June's.

There's only a breath between their lips.

"Wait," June says.

"What?" Tara says.

"Are you…" June says, examining Tara further. Tara's gaze goes from languid and heavy lidded to suddenly stricken. Did she just try to kiss June?

"I thought," Tara murmurs. "Oh my god. You said in the letters, you might've-"

"I want to!" June cries. "So much. Yes! But there's, uh. God, I thought you'd figured it out."

"Figured out what?"

"I'm not a real person. Like… a whole human. You know that. It's because I didn't finish growing, because I didn't forget."

"So what? If you go under again, you're going to forget?" Tara asks.

"Not just me. Everyone."

"Okay," Tara says.

"Okay?" June echoes. How high is Tara? How can she say that? "Tara, that means your family will forget. Everyone at the nursery will forget. My gran will forget. She almost did, once. It was horrible. I could have been gone before you ever got there. It's part of why…" June stops, and collects herself. "It's why I tried to tell you in my letters. In case anything happened to me, I knew you'd be able to remember."

"Shit."

"I mean, they were good for me without that, too," June admits. "I got to tell you how I felt about you where you wouldn't see it. Or where I thought you might not see it. And I got to talk about stuff I couldn't tell anyone else. They were important, even if you didn't read them.

"But if I did, I could have helped you."

300

"That's not what I want, Tara," June says. "I don't want to be another secret you have to keep. Back then, it was selfish. I would have just been adding another thing to your plate." If June was half the person she wished she'd been, she would have driven down to Tara's and come clean the second she got her license. She would have searched her up and found her number, called, explained. She hadn't dared cross the wall she saw spring up between them after '09. It was easier to throw words into the void than assure they would be heard.

"I wouldn't have minded," Tara says. "I would have known for sure you knew what happened. That I wasn't the only one. And I didn't want to find out you forgot. It hurt less to just assume you moved on, and I could, too."

June can't move on, though. Moving on means forgetting. Except now it doesn't. It hasn't since she found out this morning it was possible for her to go under and come up with her mind intact. The fact she can now trust Weiss with that, because he's held in check by Leah and Mateo and every other human-brained mandrake. It's new. It means she has a choice again.

"Maybe we can," June says. "For real, this time. If the flower works."

"Yeah," Tara says. "Yeah!"

She takes June by the cheeks. June grins through Tara's palms.

Tara gasps. She brings her hands down. "Oh my god. Sorry. I thought-"

"Yes, I feel the same. Just. Not yet? Not while I'm still…" June says, and wriggles her stems.

"I like it," Tara says. "I like you. All of this."

Tara threads her fingers through the stems. June trembles. She's overcome with the memory again, shrunken and hugged to Tara's chest. For all her fear since, she didn't feel afraid that night. Her focus had narrowed to a pinprick, tunnel vision trained squarely on the friend she'd defend from anyone. That certainty was a relief.

The certainty now sinks in. She extends her stems until they're about a meter long, crisscrossing them in a mesh, building up a one-armed embrace to envelop Tara as she wished to yesterday. Every place Tara shifts against the fibers wrapping her like a shawl makes June's blooms flutter open and closed.

She checks Tara's face, taking her chin and steering their eyes together. Tara's melting. Her heartbeat and slow, relaxed exhales fill June's chest.

"Do you mind if we don't take the ladder down?" June asks.

Tara nods. She gulps, feeling the fear she avoided on the climb up, but tightens her hold on June.

June closes her eyes. She can't rely on her own stems to make it down, but she reaches out to the ivy and the tree they infest.

It's a tough sell. English ivy is invasive, parasitic, and it feels in her palm how many of their brethren she's torn from around arborvitae and trellises at Bug Nursery. But the truce is sealed when she agrees to dismantle the boards that conceal their host upon her return. They braid a dozen or so of their vines together under her hand, forming a rope.

June tugs it. Seems sturdy enough, at least as thick as her wrist. She slips through the boards to the tree within the tower. She ties off. Then she ties it around again, for good measure.

Tara nods into June's tit. She shuts her eyes.

It's not exactly the zipline of their past, because the cord above is absolutely not weight-rated for two adult women. But latched to the tree, the ivy lowers June like a spider spinning down from a ceiling, June gently tapping her boot's sole to the tower to slow their descent.

When they finally reach the ground, June's shoulder aches. There's a hitch in it like she's stretched too far, so she flexes like balling her hand to a fist. The stems she's extended to cover retract, and the ache in her shoulder subsides. She huffs. She hasn't exerted her mandrake side this much before. It feels good. Tara huddled against her looks awed.

On the ground, the not voices pick up again. June and Tara talk over them.

25

Tara opens her eyes, and the sight she's greeted with cannot possibly be real. Why a fat, freckled arm over her belly like Tara's a scrawny teddy bear is more impossible than living flowers and giant beetles, she isn't awake enough to question. She just knows the arm, the hand attached curling gentle fingers into Tara's sweatshirt cotton, the body pressed against hers plush as a pillow- it's exactly the sort of fiction her mind would conjure.

She turns her head. June's face, worry soothed out by sleep, meets hers. The strange reality washes over Tara. Sweeps out. Washes in again. She lets her breaths settle in time with June's. She has the room to do so, now that they don't have a wake-up call.

Today only Benson lays outside the rotting Camp Cottonwood gate. Must be sleeping, not that insects snore or have eyelids to close. Tara won't wake him, or June, just yet. She doesn't want to wake up from this.

Tara shimmies into June's embrace. Damn her stabby shoulders. She can hear June stirring. The sensation of lungs rising and falling against her spine is so alien, whatever the pace. It feels wrong. An apology forms in her mouth, utterly reticent to flee. If the apology can drag its feet fast enough, maybe Tara can believe she's allowed to stay here.

Then June squishes her cheek to Tara's. "Mornin'," she mumbles.

Her smile digs just under Tara's eye. She's getting away with this, isn't she? "Morning," she says.

They say nothing else. Saying something will break the spell. They lie there, just as they've done since they returned to the truck last night. They didn't feel ready to do anything else.

Like this alone isn't more than Tara ever could have imagined. Had she really thought she wouldn't combust on the spot if her kiss had stuck the landing? Cuddling on its own makes her wonder if Musten has dosed her up with their spores again.

She reaches up a hand to trail June's bicep. June's fingers dither at the coarse hair where Tara's neck meets the hard bumps of her spine, tracing her index up and down them until Tara shivers. It's taking everything not to roll toward her, to make sure this is okay, to see in June's eyes that this is real.

Eventually they have to disentangle. June sits up to lace her boots, Tara yanking on her crunchy socks. Ugh, Tara stinks. The chicken soup armpits hadn't crossed her mind, nor did her grubby hoodie or jeans creased with bark dust and loose seeds. They've been out here two days, no showers, in the late summer heat. She sniffs her hoodie and determines it's better off here in the truck.

She folds it over her messenger bag in the cab, though not before taking a glance at her phone- still out of service, into single digit battery life- and collecting up the snacks she stowed from the Ayala household.

The two of them head through the gate. Benson springs awake at June's tap on his shell. He follows after them as they walk side by side, ginger ales and plastic-wrapped goodies in hand. Is it healthy to feed mandrakes potato chips? They don't hurt June as she munches a few. Tara figures if her sister is longing for bread, the other mandrakes will take interest in the other culinary delights the human world has to offer.

Tara pats Benson's shell as they go. June waves at the nettles, arching out and up at their procession. All the while she dances her touch over Tara's forearm, going with the grain of thick black hair Tara has never been quite happy exposing.

As the camp comes into view, she's aware it's hardly the worst growth anyone here is used to seeing. Leah and Mateo are already sitting by a live fire. No Weiss, but the two humanest mandrakes are mid-conversation. Leah fidgets in her baggy Bug-gifted sweater.

She elbows Mateo when she spots Tara and June. "Morning, guys!" she says.

Mateo rubs his sore ribs, shooting Leah a scowl. His eyes light upon the snacks, however. "Yo," he says. "Are those pinguinos?"

June tosses a package over. He fumbles the catch. "Genuine Hostess," June says. "We had some in the truck."

"Yes!" Mateo crows. He tears into the wrapper, his stone nails making short work of the crinkly plastic

Tara grins. "We've got soda, too. Thanks for feeding us," she says. Last night he'd put on a spread of grilled squash and potatoes, heavy on the herbs and garlic since mandrakes only had whatever salt they could steal from the conservation center's breakroom.

"No prob," Mateo says through shelf-stable pastry. "Whoa. How much sugar is in these?" June offers him the whole box, and he reads the label over.

Tara approaches her sister. Leah rubs her eye and smiles, tired. Before Tara can broach yesterday, Leah jumps right in. "Weiss ran on ahead," she says. "We told him we'd wait for you."

"We?" June asks.

"Yup! If this aquila can make us memorable, I'm in," Mateo says. He tosses an arm around Leah, who startles. "I'm going and no one can stop me."

"Hey, we're not going to try," Tara laughs.

"Yeah, Geodude," Leah replies.

Mateo rolls his eyes. He banks the fire. "Har har. Anyways, June Bug, should we get going?"

June has popped open a ginger ale. She gives a thumbs up around the can. The rest of their delivery is placed like a ritual offering on the log, for the other mandrakes to investigate at their leisure.

Leah takes the lead. June, gloveless, keeps her hand woven in Tara's. Dandelions, to fingers, to dandelions and back. Tara relishes the sensation. She can't help fiddling with the stems like she might the strings on her hoodie. Mateo keeps pace with Leah. Any attempts to snag her sleeve or get her attention are brushed off.

So he lags to join the girls. "You're gonna rot my teeth faster than the cupcakes," he says, indicating their bound hands.

Tara chuckles. June sprouts a few poppies, face flushed.

"First Moe and Sel, and then you've got Frank and his throuple. Plus Dom and Gibbs hooked up last spring," he says, listing sources of PDA on his fingers. "Hate to break it to you, but I gotta get out of this love fest."

He speaks a little more hushed as they come across movement in the weeds. A furry orange tail, swishing among the high grass, catches his attention. Mateo brings down his hand, and a cat comes nuzzling, rubbing his hand on its cheek. On its back is a mandrake, who claimed no particular gender and everyone called Kit. "Howdy, Tayo," they call up.

Mateo tips an imaginary hat. He did used to have one, didn't he? And the mustache, now a scraggly mountain man beard.

The cat scampers at Kit's coaxing. Tara watches several more mounted cats follow. She'd met Dom, Gibbs, and a dozen other members of the Union at dinner. Played a round of cards with them, not that she'd been much good at learning the rules with June on her arm. They had described the feral cats they found roaming the grounds as a real godsend for getting around without having to grow to human size.

Moe had explained why she'd stayed small when June asked. Made for an easier time monitoring the animal population, she said. She herself had spent months on the wall of a black bear cave, studying their behaviors so she could be certain they weren't affecting them negatively by keeping the camp as was. Whenever one swiped at her, her body could duck and climb to the roof much quicker than if she had a larger surface area.

Tara decided she could ask more follow up questions later. She has so many, and the fact she has people who can and will answer is new. "What are you going to do when you get home?" she asks Mateo.

He smiles. His thumbs go to his belt loops, only pausing briefly to scratch his moss beard in thought. "Find my family, for one. I may not have a girlfriend anymore, but I had that money saved up for the farm. If the account holder exists again, I can probably open it back up and give my aunt the money. After that, who knows? World's a big place."

"You farmed?" June asks.

"Yeah! Weed, actually. I had a few thousand ready to move, was gonna take my girl and I up north. Medical marijuana looked like it was going legal in Oregon," he confides. "Hey, did that actually go through? We don't exactly get news out here."

"Yeah. Cali, too, and not just medical," Tara says. "Rec. It's basically like alcohol now?"

"No fuckin' way," Mateo says.

"Mateo," Leah snaps.

"What? They're grownups," he says. His hand rests on Tara's shoulder. He gives her a brotherly pat. "I know you're her baby sister, but you're old enough to learn your first swear. Repeat after me: fuck."

Leah groans. She slows her stride to be included in the party.

Tara just smirks. "Well," she says. "Hope this flower is what you're looking for."

"Yeah, me too. Our last strategy was trying to ungrow all the way to human, and that's a lot more complicated than just one flower." Mateo loops an index around his beard. "Could be nice to keep this stuff around," he says. "Whatever species it is, we can't seem to get it out. I'll probably save on expenses if I only eat for fun, too."

Leah shoves him. "What?" he cries.

"That's dumb, you ass," she says.

"It's called being pragmatic," he corrects. "People dye their hair still, right? I could pull it off in public if they don't get up too close."

"Eh, your texture is more like hair, though," June says. "If I keep these," she says, plucking at a blooming poppy, "people won't buy it."

"What do people know, anyways?" Mateo scoffs. "It's a good look on you, kiddo. I think you should."

June's face goes a little green. Tara feels stems tighten around her wrist.

"You really think this will work?" Tara asks Leah.

"Sure looks like it," Mateo mutters.

June tugs Tara close, bumps their hips together. June eases her weight against Tara's spindly frame. She stumbles. Tara's quick to grab her and resume their trek.

Mateo mimes a gag, but he's grinning. Leah stays mum. The creek thins. The thicket they're after shouldn't be much further.

"Thanks, by the way," Tara says to Mateo.

"Yeah?" he asks.

"For watching out for her," she says, jerking her chin in Leah's direction.

Mateo stuffs his hands in his pockets. "You're welcome," he whispers. Then he speaks up. "Here we are."

Here they are. The thicket has only grown, and so has the hole around it. Instead of a tunnel to crawl through, they walk into the bee balm and bluestem without hindrance. June's stems coil Tara's arm like vines up a trellis. The dandelions tremble.

Tara follows the parted grass and heavy footprints into the birch grove. The trees here are unchanged, lofty and ancient as they ever were.

There's something distinctly different, though. In every memory she has of going to the garden, it's a silent journey in total darkness. But above she hears birds crying out to each other. She spots the scurry of field mice underfoot in the meadow grass, snakes slithering out to catch the morning sun.

June has her eyes closed. Does any plant life add its own sounds to the fanfare?

They come to the iron gate. The garden within its walls is wrong.

Maybe not wrong. Everything's where Tara remembers. The hedge encircling the gate continues growing, and growing and growing until it's too dense to slip through like she had when she was a kid. Arborvitae have ballooned until they've formed a single, solid green mass.

The entrance gate is propped open. They enter. Rose bushes eat onto the pebble path, rocks now drowned out by dirt and dust. Mossy hares and furry rabbits bound across what little trail remains. They pass the pond, teeming with algae carp but a few bluegills, too, shimmering under the lilies. Sharp shrieks sound off overhead. Sure enough, up in the canopy are Western scrub jays right alongside those leafy monstera-winged birds.

The greenhouse stands intact, misted glass now foggy with lichen and other such scuzz. Tara's calf stings. The shattered pane where she threw the stones, now standing next to her in human form, has been knocked out completely.

"Who goes there?" shouts a voice.

Mateo rolls his eyes. "These fucking guys," he huffs.

A mandrake, a proper butterfly-sized one, skitters out from the surrounding underbrush. "You!" it says. "You are not permitted here."

"It's just us," Tara says. "Who are you?"

The mandrake is followed by a phalanx of others. They number about ten. They stand humanoid enough to have been people at one time or another. Their eyes are beady blank.

Tara's gut wrenches. She grabs the denim of June's boilersuit, wringing it in one hand. "What the hell, guys?" she cries. "What happened to no more mind control?"

"Call it a mercy," Mateo says. He flips one of the mandrakes the bird. "At ease, pendejos. Go piss off someone else."

"They're still drones," June says.

"You let Weiss do that?" Tara asks.

"Hey, they made that call," Mateo says. "They're Spanish. Like, conquistadors and missionaries and shit from the 1700s. They didn't take the ungrowing well. Got violent."

"Holy shit," Tara says.

"Yeah," Mateo says, drumming fingers on his chest. "I was more mandrake when they stabbed me so it was fine. But they're a real pain in the ass."

"It was their choice." Leah watches the mandrakes mill about. "They put it to a vote. They didn't want to remember, so we were the ones to do it. Weiss wasn't involved."

Tara stares after her sister, who peeks around the greenhouse. The mandrake drones prod at June's boot, Mateo's ankle, Tara's own sneaker as they inspect their intruders. Mateo nudges one gently aside to step after Leah.

Looming just above the greenhouse, the house is a shambles. Tara had explored every nook and cranny, and finally those sleepless nights might pay off.

But she freezes. The tower isn't just crumbled, the roof caved in.

It's obliterated. Parts of the tower still litter the house's roof, the rest of the rubble cascading to the ground. Heavy chunks of stone heap on the pond's shore. Any plants below and around the wreckage are flattened.

No purple or white sticks out from the heap.

26

Whatever peace Tara found in the vision has fled. She's on her knees digging in the debris. Her hands almost get crushed as she tips up a boulder to reveal shriveled stalks, white and dry as flaked bone. "No, no, no, no…" she murmurs. She throws a chunk of stone into the pond. The algae carp and bluegill plunge to the depths at the impact, rippling out to the shore and in again.

"This isn't fair," she says.

June has taken her gloves from her pocket. She brings her flayed hand under her eyes. She breathes in, out. Stems retreat to skin. Yellow smoker's stains at her fingertips, the flesh a little bit too green, but she tugs the fabric over the digits, snapping the hem down her wrist for good measure.

She sighs. She sets a gloved hand on Tara's back.

Tara keeps digging. Mud crusts under her nails, jeans spattered with pond scum.

June bends down beside her. She listens. The earth in the garden is the strongest she's ever heard. Not loud, never loud. But its wants are a bellow. Its primary want is her.

She picks through the noise. She can't do as she usually does, offering a finger full of root hairs for the flora to grip and focus upon. Here in the garden, there's no guarantee she'll be able to resist its summons.

Below the bellow, desperation dulled by time, she hears it. She rolls over a rock. Pinned under the stone, the plant is weak. It's been alone for too long, trapped in a tower and now beneath the ruins of one. Its meager roots paw blindly at her glove.

They fumble a few around her thumb. She's able to bring it from its shallow grave. The last blue columbine is rather pretty, even squashed, though she can't say it's an exact match to the ones at the nursery. They're like the mayapples, a funhouse mirror of a real species.

Only two blooms have managed to pull through. Fighting through the cracks to the sun stunted any growth it might have done otherwise.

But it's alive. That's something.

June takes the plant from the ground. Dandelions scratch at her gloves' rubber fingertips. She feels one of them pierce through and sink into the fragile ball of roots. Her vision goes murky. She blinks it away.

The humans around her have spent this search staring. They don't say anything. They don't have to.

June holds up the aquilas for them to see. Two bruised, purple bunches of petals, the pistils limp. Withered leaves protrude from its base. It's going to require so much recovery, it might never make it to another season. This pair of closed flowers might be all they ever get. This start, and Mateo and Leah, have waited long enough.

They're still staring at her. Aren't they going to take their chance while they have it? How can they stand there and gawk?

Heavy stone footsteps thunder on the soil. June feels them more than she hears them. Weiss emerges behind the gathered humans.

"You found it," he rasps.

June nods. Weiss says what they're all thinking.

"That's not enough."

He kneels at June's side. He examines the aquilas, taking the wounded leaves and parched roots in his careful talons. "What a sorry state," he breathes. "The masters never had aquilas for me to work with. I don't know if I can…" He falters. His grip on the plant goes slack. His crystalline eyes don't understand. He's gone statue, frozen in fear, cradling the blooms in his claws.

June offers her hand. Weiss looks at her glove.

"Who's first?" she says.

Her hand goes behind her back. Stems are splitting the seams now.

"What?" Tara asks.

Mateo watches over June's shoulder. Neither him or Leah are looking at June's hands, or at her boots where roots are wrestling her laces.

"We shouldn't test it out yet," Leah says. "Not if we're not sure it's going to work. We experimented for years to get this much," she points out, waving over her very human body. "We can't risk losing this sample."

"This might be the only sample you ever get," June says. "We're not gonna know if it's what you need unless you try."

Tara's still. "No," she says, shaking her head. "We're not doing that."

"There ain't a choice," June says. And there isn't. She pinches off a bloom. The whole garden flinches. The plant slumps. It's not like it expects to be pollinated in future. It doesn't have much hope to spare. It's just happy to have company again.

"It's yours, Mateo," June says.

Mateo accepts the bloom from June. He looks at Leah. At Weiss, at Tara, at Leah again. Her arms are crossed, her sweater sleeves fluffed against her chest. "Wait," he says.

"No more waiting," Leah says. "You deserve to go home, now."

"So do you," Mateo cries.

"So does June," Tara says.

Leah's arms fall to her sides. "What?"

June winces. She didn't want it to come out like this, but Weiss nods. The first time she's ever seen Tara and Weiss agree shouldn't be on something this shitty, but that's just their luck, isn't it?

"This isn't about me," June says. "It's gotta be you guys. Mateo, you've waited the longest. Leah's been here almost as long. I'll be fine." The glove on her left hand bursts. The rubber cracks as her stems shred through, and the fabric scrap is quickly snatched so it can be stowed in her pocket.

Leah's not having it. She's looking closer now. They all are, seeing June grow out of her boilersuit, the roots in her laces lashing like a serpent after a mouse. "This is not fine," she admits. "But…"

But now what? It could have just been Leah and Mateo, no hashing it out necessary. Instead they have another variable, and that's not what she wanted. How did she mess this up again?

"June?" Tara asks.

June shakes her head. This isn't about her.

"If she plants again, she's like you," Tara explains to Leah. "Right? No one outside will remember except me."

"Then June takes mine," Mateo says. His voice doesn't broker dissent. June hates it. She hates this. "If you didn't come here, we'd still be hanging out with the chucklefuck conquerors. You're the one who got us out of fairyland."

"Weiss did that," June says, pointing a dandelion in his direction. Weiss stays knelt there, thoroughly out of it. Only the aquila start exists to him.

"Kid, you know he wouldn't have before you showed up. Because if he did, none of us would have been here to begin with. Face it, you changed everything. Why do you think everyone here remembers you? You were the first one to treat us like people again."

"I only came because I was following Tara."

"And I came for my sister," Tara says.

"And I came after you, Mateo. Face it," Leah says. "You're the reason we're all here."

Mateo throws up his hands. "Don't pull that shit with me, Leah," he says. "We both know why we're here."

"Because of me," Weiss rasps, still staring at the start.

"Well, yeah," Mateo says, gesturing broadly, "but Leah here is the one who-"

"This is my fault."

"Weiss," Leah says.

He hunches into his cloak.

June crams both hands into her pockets, the right glove eviscerated. There aren't anymore in her backpack, tucked into the truck outside the gates. She hasn't destroyed this many away from home. She hasn't been away from home enough to do so.

The second bloom stays clasped between two stems peeking from her denim. "Look," she says. "You both need this. I'm not even a real mandrake. Mateo?"

"No," he says. "I'm not doing it." But there it is, that hesitation. That waver. He mentioned an aunt. A girlfriend, long gone. Time wasted. Family who can't form his face in their minds, unless this is what they've needed. They're fighting about this and they don't even know if it'll work.

Mateo moves to hand his bloom to Leah, but June raises the other, so his sandpaper stone fingers twirl the petals around.

No one makes any attempt to stop her. The real reason June and Tara came is Leah. Leah is the one who found them and asked for their help. If they don't give it now, if June withholds this chance for herself, what sort of monster does it make her? She can't take this from Leah. She can't take this from Tara.

She can just stay like this. For now. Until she slips. Maybe Betty will be gone by then. Maybe she can will the nursery to someone else, someone who will earn it more than June does if this halfway human is the most she'll ever be.

June reaches out. Leah extends her hand, brushing fingertips over June's dandelions.

June places the bloom in Leah's grasp.

Leah drops it. The aquila flutters to the tower's wreckage. Weiss catches it before it can land among the rubble. Mateo shakes his head, lips pressed tight shut.

Leah levels her gaze with June. Past June's shoulder, to Tara.

"I can't do this," she says. "I'm going home."

She runs. Tara follows.

June steps to go after them, but spun nylon and kevlar tear. Her laces surrender to the roots chewing through them. She can't lift her foot from the ground. She's stuck.

Tara clatters through the garden gate. Grasses part where Leah has fled through the birches, through the meadow, through the hole in the thicket until the trail goes cold and Tara is alone.

Leah must have tread the water. Tara pants, running the creek's shore. Not again. She only just got her sister back. She can't keep going home to Del Bosque empty-handed.

"Leah!" she calls, to no reply. Leah's going home. She must be headed for the Chevy. But how does she expect to drive it? She hasn't driven since '09. How does she expect to make it to town if she can't even ride shotgun without sleeping off nausea?

Why doesn't Leah talk to her? "You wanted me to come here," Tara says. "You found me. I was gonna leave. I was just going to leave you here. If you think I deserve you, I don't. But you don't deserve to pay for what I couldn't do."

She could have stayed that night. She could have swept Leah and Mateo and Moe and Selina into her arms and taken them along. She might not have known how to make them remember, but maybe June could have. Maybe Tara could have cut all this heartache off at the pass.

There would still be Walshes and the criminals and the Union and, yes, the fucking conquistadors trapped within the garden's confines. She would have been where she is now, just with four more people to have looked after while slogging through school and backseat-raising her brothers.

She traces the bends and banks of the creek, racing the paths of her last summer at Camp Cottonwood. Where could she have known? When she first entered the garden and met its keeper? When she'd seen the mandrakes, the fairies who deliberately fled her presence so Weiss could win his game? When she saw the thriving patch of flowers in an inhospitable stone tower?

At every hinge she sees where it could have swung. She could have gone during the day, when Weiss and the other mandrakes were active. She could have gone searching every other night, letting herself sleep instead of wandering the world a zombie who couldn't tell a clue from a dud.

She could have gotten help. She could have just told June when she asked, could have warned her about the danger.

They could have both gotten out unscathed, having reformed Weiss before he made the mistake of planting June. They could have both been planted, with no one to remember or rescue them.

Whenever she changes anything, fresh consequences flood in. What choice could she have made that didn't end in this, or worse? What else could she have done?

What does Leah want her to do now?

She stops. She shuts her eyes, balling her fists. This is why she'd put her head down, thought about her future in Eugene where none of this was supposed to matter. The past was only a bat to beat herself with.

This is why she ignored every letter to grace her mailbox. She wanted to burn them. She wanted to tear them up. She wanted to bite them to shreds with her teeth. They'd taunted her every few months. When she thought June might give up, just when she believed it was over, she would see the new edition of the *June Bug Doesn't Quit* newsletter.

Why did it piss her off so much to see them? She never did destroy them, but her destructive rage pressed her eyes with tears she had to snort down.

The last one arrived when she was eighteen. She'd walked into the apartment, convinced this time- this time- she'd trash it. All of them. She'd throw every single one away. She couldn't focus, and she needed to focus. The boys needed her to learn to drive, so she could take them to sports or school or appointments. She needed to cut down her own bus and bike commutes so she could do more.

Her dad quipped about bills, at the stovetop making dinner. She would have to do the dishes after he made a mess cooking. At least it would be a delicious mess.

She shrugged in reply. Whatever ambitions she had for killing June's letter, they didn't get beyond stuffing the envelope in her hoodie's kangaroo pouch. She sidled up to Tom. On days his pain was bad, she would take over and finish making the meal herself.

Since Tom seemed to be having a good day, Tara shuffled off. Her mom would be home in an hour, and she had homework to do.

Safely in her room, she sighed. She plucked at the envelope's seal.

She tugged open her drawer. Another letter for the box.

What if she read them? What would happen? If June kept sending them, that had to mean something, didn't it? That she remembered. That she liked Tara.

Tara burned. Well. That she didn't loathe Tara.

She let her face fall to the desk, stacked with notebooks and worksheets and textbooks. Somewhere under those, her laptop. She could open up search. Look up June Bug, Bug Nursery. Call the number on the Facebook page, website, whatever.

And then what?

Tara couldn't change it. She couldn't fix any of this.

"Please," she says. "I don't know what you want me to do."

Only Leah's dollar store flip flops, abandoned to drift up in Tara's direction, float toward her in response.

She's come to the end of the creek. The cabins rise into view.

So does Leah, hunched behind Madrone.

Her bun has come undone. Hair hangs loose to her shaking shoulders. Tara can't see her sister's face through the curtain.

She looks so small.

"I'm sorry," Tara hears. "I thought I could do it."

Tara sees how Leah tenses at her splashing steps. She stays this few yards' distance, standing on the sand where the cabin's shadow ends.

"I know. I know what I'm supposed to do," Leah says. She spreads her fingers through her hair, splitting the strands to stringy tendrils. The strands stay keratin and dead skin cells. "I can't do it. Even if I'm like this. Even if it looks the same, even if it feels the same, it's not. I'm not."

Her sister's laugh is a bitter one, choked out around a sob. Tara swallows.

Tara steps into the creek. Her sneakers are soaked. She walks the water carefully, the sound disappearing into the creek's burble.

She comes to sit on the silt at her sister's side.

Leah tosses her head, and the curtain parts. Her russet hair cascades over one shoulder. Her chestnut eyes are puffy and red.

"I should have figured it out sooner. Maybe then you and her wouldn't be here," she says.

"Figured out what?" Tara asks.

"I moved on," Leah says. "This body didn't. I worked so hard to get it back, but it's not mine. I don't even want it."

Leah examines a dusty brown hand. She flexes, fingers jittering with strain, as if sheer will might grow them to gnarled roots, the hair to long tines of plant matter.

"I'm sorry," she sniffs. "It shouldn't have taken this long. If I got there sooner, you wouldn't have had to take on so much. I'm sorry for all I put you through. It must have been so hard."

Tara lays back, letting her legs lie in the creek. Cool water washes over her scar. Her socks are sodden.

"It was hard," she says.

"You had to take care of everything when I was gone. I didn't want that for you."

"I had to do all the firsts again. I had to do everything they wanted."

"Like I did. You had to be perfect."

Tara shrugs into the silt. She didn't know if she'd call it perfect. Just always reliable, always available. Her black hair itches, pebbles biting into her bare arms as they spread wide over the shore.

"I had to be what they needed all the time. Doing stuff they couldn't. I had to watch the boys. They still call me Mom sometimes."

"You used to call me Mom sometimes."

"Yeah," Tara says. "I remember that. I stopped when you got cool, though. When you stopped acting like my mom. You were just my cool older sister. Trying to get me to have fun. Taking me here."

Tara has spent so long in Leah's shadow. As she says it she knows she's done the same thing to David, to Alex. Protecting them, projecting how primed and poised to take on the world she was so they didn't have to. She even tried being cool for them when she reached Leah's age and got the Nissan. David, who she takes to animated movies he pretends not to like until he's gushing on the drive home. Alex, who she encouraged to draw and now shows her every doodle he's ever done. So they can have what she didn't get the luxury of.

She'd been the best new Leah her parents couldn't have asked for.

She almost got away with it.

To what? To be miserable and perfect in another state? Getting away to Oregon wouldn't have saved her. Wouldn't have answered why the last ten years running ragged to make up for what happened ate her alive.

"I didn't think I'd ever see you again, " Tara says. "That's what was hard. I had to act like none of this ever happened, and it was my fault. I could have done the other stuff fine."

Tara glances up. Leah looks down at her.

"I missed you," Tara says.

"I did this to you, Tara. Everything forced on you? I did it."

"Our parents did that to you."

"Dad couldn't control getting sick. Mom didn't control when she had us. They didn't plan on needing me like they did."

"Then the world did it to them so they could do it to us," Tara tries. "I don't know."

"But-"

Tara sits up. Leah falters.

"I know, Tara."

"Know what?"

"When I saw June wasn't human, that's where I had this theory," she says, rushing the words out. "She told Betty, and because she's a mandrake it still stuck. I didn't know for sure until the vision."

Her arms wrap around her knees. "I called the house, Tara. I could have told them then. I could have told them since I got my memory back. I could always go home, and I didn't.

330

It's my fault they did this to you. It's my fault you didn't have a childhood."

Tara stares.

"Don't you get it? I ruined your life. I could have come back at any time, and I didn't, and they made you the new me instead."

Tara chuckles.

"What? What, Tara?"

She scoots closer. She strokes Leah's back, just between the shoulder blades. Leah used to do the same when Tara had nightmares.

Leah heaves. She tries reining it in, but the sobs overtake her, shuddering into her knees. Tara lets her go. She trails her fingers through russet curls, divvying them to braid out of her face. Her sister can come up for air when she's ready.

Tara takes time to process what she's said. Aside from the same sort of shit Tara's told herself all these years, of course. God. Is this what Tara has sounded like? How Tara has moved through the world, waiting for everyone to berate her for not being a goddamned psychic mind reader?

No, she hones in on the theory. "So," she says, "you can't go out there and be remembered right now. But you could. If you plant again."

Leah wheezes. She's cried herself congested. "Yes. I think so. I should have sent Mateo home before. He's going to be so-"

"You don't want to go back, do you?" she asks.

Leah averts her eyes.

"I wish I did," she whispers. "I thought I did, until I got there. I saw them."

"Yeah?"

"They're just… fine. Happy, even. They don't even need me," Leah laughs. "And I don't want them to need me. With these people, it's different. I want to keep looking out for them. Not because I have to, because I want to. Because they look out for me, too."

"I get it," Tara says. "Why do you think I was leaving?"

"I'm sorry."

Tara leans up on her elbows. Sorry isn't what she wants to hear. She doesn't think she can say it back.

"They seem like cool people," she says. "Really. If you want to stay, I'll come visit. I don't think I can go to Oregon now that I know you're all here, anyway."

"I'm holding you back."

"No," Tara says. "I… I don't think I was going for the right reason. I mean, c'mon, a communications major? Me? What a joke. An *expensive* joke."

Leah smiles a wobbly smile. "Shut up. That's my sister you're talking about."

"No, seriously," Tara says. "I didn't even want to be honest with myself. Forget other people. I don't know what I want. I know I want to see you again. Even if you never come back to stay, I still want to see you."

Leah nods. A sort of recognition enters her eyes.

She nods again, sniffing up more snot. "Good," she mumbles.

"What's wrong?"

"I thought you were going to hate me. You should hate me. If I don't come back, I'm leaving you to deal with them alone."

"This isn't alone, is it?" Tara says. She puts her arm around Leah. "Even if Mom and Dad don't know, I still get you. That's more than I thought I'd get. That's what I want. Not all the stuff you did for me. You. Okay?"

Leah's face crumples. She does some more crying.

Tara pats her sister's back, letting Leah sob into her shirt.

28

How am I? I've been holding it together.

Dandelion stems emerge from her pockets, spilling down down down. They're meant to reach up, hungry for light, but not now. Can't live on light alone. They need water, need dirt, need space to unfurl in the dark. Trying to reel the roots in is like trying to suck blood back into a wound. The only way through is out, not in, and attempting otherwise just earns her an ache in her brain. Poppies spray from her scalp, her ears. Wildflowers threaten to burst from beneath her eyelids.

New guy's nice. I think he wants to be friends. I can't do that to him.

There's a grasp on her biceps. Her roots rip from the ground, and she blinks. Firm granite claws, tipped in obsidian talons, hold her arms and lift. Panicked crystal eyes bore into her. "June Bug?" Weiss rasps.

Mateo stands behind him, his aquila bloom between his thumb and index. Its start rests in the crook of his arm. The aquila's leaf pets at his hand. It's never met something like him before. What is he? It hasn't met something so like itself before, yet not, a plant who walks and talks and thinks. It's only ever met the masters, or the human girl who admired them. They had consoled each other, a respite from the loneliness they'd been assigned.

Weiss lifts June to the top of the rubble. With three feet of rock between her and the garden, not just mere centimeters of rubber and leather, she can breathe. She rubs yellow dactylions in circles on her temples. "Thanks," she says.

Weiss's stone shoulders settle. Under her he frets and fusses, so unlike his unreadable facade ten years prior. He paces, stops, paces again.

He flops down at the tower's base. His elbows rest at his knees. "I'm sorry," he says. "I've failed you."

"You tried," June says.

"Fuck yeah, you did," Mateo says. "I might get to go home again."

June smiles. Good to see one of them can.

Mateo joins them on the heap, the start balanced like a baby on his hip.

As June unravels, she thinks about the letters.

2010.

What am I even scared of? Gran can't miss me if there's no me to miss. I can't miss me if there's no me to miss. It won't feel bad. It's not about them, is it? They're going to forget, and I'll forget. So why am I so afraid?

2012.

This is all my fault. I was stupid and trusted someone I shouldn't have. Now I don't trust anyone, so I learned my lesson, right? That's a lie. I trust you. That's not your fault either.

2015.

I know it's coming. I hear it a lot. I'm not going to be around forever. Neither is Gran, but if I can make it until she's gone then it's not so bad. She deserves that. But they don't. The whole point of making it until I lose Betty is so no one's left for me to leave behind. No one can forget what they never learned. Is that terrible? Is all of this terrible? I think I'm terrible.

The words are burned into her mind, the carefully chosen phrases she wove like a net. They never caught anything. They were her heart and soul and they were never opened, never read, never understood. She shoved all her feelings in an envelope and shipped them away, an hour away, a million miles away. Forever away. Bon voyage. If she could get rid of them, she could keep going.

Her stems dig into the rock. She realizes it's Weiss's torso she's scratching up with her dandelions and retracts. He isn't angry. He's scared. His fear pours off of him and mingles with her own. It's like the vision. It's like that night.

It's like feeling someone else's scream in her own chest.

"I have to do something," Weiss rasps, his voice down to a whisper as his wails bleed from his head into hers. "You're going to stay. I won't let this happen."

She laughs. It's a lie. It's a lie! She can feel it as clearly as she feels his anguish. He has no idea what to do. He thought this flower would be some magic cure against what he's done.

Mateo winds his hand into her dandelions, crunching a bouquet to hold. Her boots have slipped off. The roots stretch longer.

"You're taking it," Mateo says. The bruised purple bloom, he's fighting to tie it to one of her weeds. "I'll figure it out. Leah and you, that's what matters."

June wriggles her stems back, curling them to herself. "I had my time," she says. "I didn't make great use of it. You're gonna keep it, okay? You're gonna do better. Make new friends. Do new things. Alright? Keep it."

She can't take this chance from him. Mateo has waited the longest of them to get his life back. She hates that she can't give any of the time he's wasted back. She hates that can't give the same to Leah, or Tara, or anyone else. Even herself. She can't do anything. She's so stupid.

"That's not true," Weiss growls. Their agonized looping has tangled together. "You did not do anything wrong."

June did everything wrong. She couldn't even keep her last promise.

The final letter burns through her.

2017.

There's no more after this. If you want to hear from me, you know where to look. I'll put down my number. Address. Everything. Ball is in your court.

I graduated yesterday. Had a ceremony and everything. They almost didn't let me wear the gloves and boots. Something about making the school look bad, but Betty gave them what for and they shut up. I don't know what I'm gonna do. There's college courses online now. But why? What would spending all that time and money do?

I want to make sure I'm here for Gran. It's been eight years. She's still pretty spry, enough to chew people out and get around and all. Her hands are going. Eyes are fine. I think she'll be here at least another decade. So I'll tough it out. Save her funds for healthcare, because God knows I'm gonna be a mess when we're looking at the end. If they try to take her.

I just don't think it's going to go good, is what I'm saying.

I don't want you to worry. It's not your job to keep me from planting.

I love you, you know? I want you to be happy. I don't want you to see me like that. Remember me like that. You gave me more than I could ever ask for. I get time, because of you. I would still be in the garden if not for you. My grandmother would be alone if not for you. You don't need to do anything else. You did so much for me. If you blame yourself for any of this, don't.

I wish I could give her back. I wish I could give them all back.

I wish it was her. Not me. You should have saved her instead. Betty would've known I was gone. You could have had your sister.

I can see why you never wrote back.

"Focus," says Mateo. "What can we do? June? Tell us what you need."

Tara. But she can't say it. Tara saved her once, and it's not her job to save her again. She shouldn't be saved. She needs to go under. She needs to grow up.

She touches dirt. Somehow, she relaxes even more. Hairs spring up on what once were toes, now coils unwinding for minerals, burrowing into the earth below this island she's been atop.

"I'm going to bring you back," Weiss says. "It won't be long. Just enough to grow out what- what I-"

What he did. He regretted it from the second he did it. She knows that. It doesn't change what happened, what's going to happen. But it means it won't happen how she imagined. She won't be alone, before or after.

She reaches for Mateo and Weiss. Stems patter at their arms, their shoulders. Why is she holding off the inevitable? She resigned herself to this.

"It's not going to be me," she says.

"I know," Mateo says. "I'm sorry, kid."

"I can try to ungrow the rest of this," Weiss hisses. He uses his clawed foot to dig some roots from the soil. She cringes, the rip not painful but not pleasant either.

"Even then," she mutters. The person she is now is going to be gone. Whoever's next, even if it's in this body, even if it's got her mind and memories, will be the person who comes up. That's been her fear. She will never be the person before the mayapple. Before the garden. Before Tara and Leah.

A ruckus. She can feel them before she sees them. Huddled together, the Ayala sisters leaning on each other's weight. Leah stumbles as Tara takes up a sprint. Her sneakers pound against the dirt.

"Oh shit," she says. "Shit, shit. Shit! June?"

Hands on her cheeks. Fingers trailing through her petals. She smiles. "June," she hears. It's going to be okay. Do you hear me? Blink if you can hear me."

June does so. Brown eyes, like loam. Sharp face. A shock of black hair. She trails a flower down Tara's jaw.

"It's gonna be okay," she repeats. "We figured it out. You can all go back."

"How?"

Tara presses their foreheads together. Her breath, June's lack thereof. "You just have to tell them. Okay? When you come up, we'll go tell your grandma. And anyone else you want to tell."

"The aquila-"

"It doesn't matter," Leah says. June can't see her. She can only see Tara. "We'll talk about it when it's over."

When it's over. Done. After. That's different. "I'm sorry," she tells Tara.

Tara brushes an index down June's lip. "Don't be," she says.

"It's not your fault," June says.

"It's not our fault," Tara echoes. She smirks. She's arched over June, who gets smaller by the second. She peers around Tara. Mateo has sidehugged Leah, her face ruddy from crying. She's here, too.

Dread is finally, finally melting to anticipation. She's going to do this. They'll be here when she resurfaces.

"I'll be right back," June tells them. She takes Tara's chin in her stems. "Wait for me?"

Tara nods. She's releasing her hold. Before she can let go, June pulls her in.

Their mouths meet.

29

Tara feels June's lips curved against her own, quirked at their corners. June tastes like honeysuckle. The heady scent of nectar floods Tara's senses.

She slumps.

June slumps, too, until Tara yanks her by her tank top's straps under the boilersuit, balling her fists around the cotton knit. A cat's cradle has formed across her hands, binding her up in June's silken stems. Poppy pollen tickles Tara's nose. She breathes it in deep. She plunges into the kiss, letting every ounce of longing she's pent up over the past decade across their divide.

Maybe, she thinks, June doesn't have to go under. Maybe they can just stay here, consumed in each other like this, forever.

Mateo whoops. Tara's eyes are closed, but she can feel her sister's stare against her back. Weiss's, too, more confused.

She has an audience. She can't convince herself to care, letting the meat of her palm graze June's bra and her tongue flick the leaf behind the mandrake girl's teeth.

But eventually June's grip loosens. Tara's does, too. She can't help the guilt. Tara should be the one paying for all of this. She should be taking the blame, and therefore the punishment.

June removes her glasses. She tucks them and her keys in Tara's pocket. Tara finds her footing. No. That's not what this is. This may involve reaping and sowing, but this is just a consequence.

The lost pressure leaves her floating on air. She lays her head on June's chest. June lets her cheek rest against Tara's hair.

"Thanks," June whispers. "I'll see you."

Tara nods. She steals one more kiss, pecked on June's neck. The skin burns. June's flushing, suddenly aware of the witnesses for her burial.

Leah's laughing into her hand. Weiss squints, one claw raised like he might ask, but Mateo shakes his head.

Tara lets go.

June sinks. Tara can barely catch the moment itself. The dirt acts with the momentum built up over ten years, desperate to snatch June into itself before anyone can change her mind.

A breath in. Out. Again, and again, and again. Tara's alright with this. She's happy for June.

She is still fighting the urge to get down and dig her out.

"We'll have to do this twice," Leah says. She's come to stand beside Tara. "First to finish the original planting. After that, she'll need a mayapple."

Weiss takes a sprig from his cloak. "And this," he adds, and hands it to Tara. "She'll need it to remember herself."

They all stare at the disturbed patch of earth. Nothing yet.

"If we're right about this, talking to the humans as a mandrake should make other people remember her," Leah explains.

"And if it doesn't?" Mateo asks, hefting the aquila start onto his arm again. He tweaks the bloom between his fingers.

"We'll be here," Tara says.

She takes up vigil where June sat on the crumbled tower.

The four of them watch. They wait.

"It might be hours," Leah is saying, just as the eight spoked leaf pops out of the ground.

Leah, Mateo, and Weiss look.

Tara kneels down. She gently takes the stem. She pulls it up.

The other three spectators lurk over Tara while she dusts the little sprout from its soil. Tara sees the sprout yawn. It rubs its eyes, blinking up. Tara drops the mandrake in her hand. It's no bigger than the leaf that announced it.

"June?" Tara asks.

The sprout says nothing. She's waiting to be given orders.

"I need you to hold this," Tara says.

The sprout grabs the sprig from her. She stands there on her many roots, poppies flared like a lion's mane. She cocks her head this way, that. Does she recognize Tara?

"Now what?" Tara asks.

"We go to the greenhouse," Leah says.

Tara rises. The sprout stays on her hand, lashing around her wrist for a more stable seat.

Weiss leads the way. He strides on, gaze locked firmly ahead.

They enter the greenhouse. Inside still soars into sunflowers, but the color-coded spiral is a contorted rainbow now. The mayapples aren't filed at the center in yellow. They're the first plant they see as they walk in, grown up and out at varying heights, varying sizes of leaves and fruit. The ground before them looks freshly stirred.

Leah bends down and beckons the sprout's attention. "You've just got to touch one of those," she says.

Tara kneels beside her sister. The sprout eyes the round, yellow fruits curiously. She won't leave Tara's hand.

"I'll be right here," Tara tells her. "I'm not leaving."

With this, the sprout disentangles. She touches her roots to the dirt, balancing atop instead of burrowing in. Tara nudges the sprout toward the mayapples.

The sprout ambles a few inches. She has the sprig clutched to what qualifies as a chest. She's just a seed. A little drone of the gardenkeeper, planted for his convenience. She's not going to ask questions.

Still, she hesitates there, unsure. Tara curls a finger around the sprout's middle. A very small hug, but a hug nonetheless.

"You're doing great, June," she says.

The sprout's flowers fluff. She crawls closer to the mayapples. She points to a fallen one, as large as a golf ball. "This one?" she asks. Her voice is a high whisper.

That Tara can't answer.

"Gardenkeeper?" asks the sprout.

Tara glances where they came. Weiss has long since closed up his edelweiss, his arms shielding his stony chest. He won't watch, turned to face the greenhouse windows.

"You planted me, didn't you?" the sprout asks.

Weiss is a statue. Mateo bites his lip.

"We need you to plant yourself," Leah soothes. "Can you do it?"

The sprout's rooty mouth scrunches. "Maybe. I just touch one?"

"A big one," Leah says. "The big ones make you bigger."

"I get to be bigger?" the sprout gasps.

Tara nods emphatically. The wonder in the sprout's voice makes her snort. Her eyes sting, but she can't keep from laughing.

Her bray makes the sprout blink. The beady black eyes, blank and empty, shine. "Big ones make you big," she mutters. "Big ones. I like this one. Ooh, but this other one's really big!"

She mumbles away at herself. The sprout's like a kid in a pumpkin patch. She wants the very perfect mayapple.

The sprout's expression gets anxious, though. Her roots fidget and finagle, worrying at each other, twisting into knots.

Tara lets the sprout twirl a tendril around her pinky. "Just when you're ready," she says.

The sprout hums. She touches a lumpy little mayapple attached to a branch. The tendril around Tara's pinky goes limp, drawn into the soil with the rest of the sprout. Now to wait.

She can't decipher exactly when xylem and phloem discover a certain spark buried deep in their cells. A reminder, somewhere, that the seed planted all those seasons ago used to be something very strange and special indeed.

There is no gradient. Just a moment where she's a sprout anchored in the soil, then another in which she has a name and a home and a self somewhere beyond. There's no surfacing to visit them just yet. She has time down here.

So she unwinds. She stretches, sprawls, spreads her roots as far as she can see.

The world below has been dim and indistinct for so long, a crowd at a distance she could barely hear the gasps of relative to what she's experiencing now. She absorbs the discordant not-sound at its true volume and vibrancy. It's blinding, deafening, suffocating in intensity.

Then it quiets. It's a lot. But it's not the nothing she anticipated. She'd been afraid of it, once. She's not sure why. Because she'd be alone?

She's not. Footsteps echo six feet above her. Snatches of speech, muffled. The motion of what moves on the earth's crust plays to her faded senses, conversation from another room, and they're comfort enough that she's safe to gravitate to the underground where so much sings.

She expands her roots further. She's not an isolated, impermeable body but a network, the strings of her spilling forth through the dark, touching everything, tasting everything.

It's like dancing. She travels out and out and out until she taps birches and bee balm and bluestem, into blackberry and bracken just beyond.

She alights on a web like her own but not. There's the feeling of moisture and misted, muggy thoughts. Spores in her lungs. Does she have lungs? She's without stomata, so she must have something else at the center. But the something else is packed with soil.

Not to worry. Clearly she's alive enough to communicate here. She meets the web.

Mycelium hyphae, microscopic compared to her clumsy fibrous roots, flare awake. As if they're ever asleep, but she's collected their attention. She gets an answer, without words. A wave, the mycelium igniting like a fuse, sending stimulus after stimulus out along its millions of billions of connections.

They collide with her own one right after the other.

The house in the garden, brilliant and brimming. The masters of the house, in forms she can't quite comprehend or contemplate, always sniping snapping scheming. Confrontation. A banishment, an exile. Why did not matter. What mattered was this master was alone, and they were a web. And they were vast.

When their fellows departed, they were still barred. They could tell something remained. Animals, humans, entered and did not exit. In the center of their vastness, for many centuries, an island. A lone enclosure they could not access or ascertain.

They thought the sisters might be their key. They were wrong.

She takes the hint. Their tissue binds to hers, the threads intertwining, and she tugs.

The border about the garden bursts. The web fruits a body above. She reels, releasing them. She has more connections to make.

Beyond the garden, beyond the border she's broken up, she feels.

She nudges the Union. The men and women of the work, brought here by broken promises. But they've bonded here, and she takes in the sight of each as they were, as they have been, as they are. She beckons them.

She finds the family, the Walshes brought under those same lies and half-truths. She sees Winnifred after her husband's demise, dragging her kin to the west if it kills her, too. Her children, all five frozen in time. An invitation to them, too, a pull on Priscilla Ann that her siblings and elders pursue.

Next the thieves, secure in their new home. They love and linger and that's enough for them to be at peace, but she feels the urge to call them close if they desire.

She pitters a few roots at the Rathbones. In a wordless shout she calls them, and Moe picks up. She pulls at Selina, who dithers. The wives are on their way.

She thanks each. She listens. There's buzzing. Insects, worms, arthropods of every sort. A king among bugs, a beetle too big to live as anything but a mandrake, bounds along the creek that cuts the camp. The water deposits into a lake she can recall laying across in the sun. Oh. The sun sounds nice. She'd like to see it soon.

There's something else, too. Someone? Several someones.

Stream of consciousness congeals to something a bit more solid. June Bug. That's her name! This is what she does! It's not all she is. She's getting more names. Weiss, the gardenkeeper, is obvious. But there's Mateo Valdez. Leah Ayala. Tara Ayala, Leah's sister who June Bug has just kissed.

She hugs the memory of her kiss close and clings. She wants to do it again! But with what?

A snap. The roots rattle home to their core, rebecoming.

A dandelion grows from the dirt.

She feels a fingertip press the petals.

Four more flowers spring up to form a hand, wrapping like fingers around a wrist.

SPRING

David and Alex Ayala do not recognize the woman who knocks on their door. She does look vaguely familiar, though, someone they might have met when they were little. She tells David she's come for Tara.

Tara tumbles down the stairs and jumps into the woman's arms. The woman is tall and wide, a massive mane of coiled orange curls swaying past her butt. Is it hair? It clusters in slips like folded silken paper. Tara kisses her freckled cheek and introduces her as June Bug, her girlfriend.

Alex hugs the girl, too. He doesn't need to know her to know she's Tara's friend, and so he likes her already. She wears overalls, a flowy white shirt like a pirate's underneath, and strappy hiking sandals.

"I'm taking the boys," Tara says, shouting to their father in the living room. Tom looks up from the bread he's kneading and accepts a sidehug. Rebecca reminds the boys to listen to Tara, making June blush as she tells the girl how much she's grown. Both of the Ayala parents have been in good spirits since Tara declared she wouldn't be going to Oregon after all. At least not yet. She would be staying and saving her money until she chose her new major. Maybe art?

They don't care. They can't remember a time she was this happy.

Tara pulls one of Tom's jackets from the closet under the stairs, one that smells strongly of weed and campfire smoke. She'd taken to wearing his old flannels over the previous winter, paired with sturdy jeans and heavy black boots. Hiking and camping every weekend until the pass froze, and now she could finally take her brothers to her favorite spot. The same place she and June used to go as kids, she tells them.

David dimly remembers his sister leaving for summers when he was a tot. Alex doesn't, but Tara promised them a surprise so he's sold.

They climb not into Tara's Nissan but a teal Chevy truck. They have to squeeze together to fit in the middle seat. They're doing their best, under Tara's side eye, not to jostle and punch each other the whole way to wherever they're going.

When David flicks Alex in the forehead, there's a tap at his shoulder and he yelps. A brown hand with slate gray nails has reached through the rear window, a man with moss green hair and a beard laughing in the truck's bed at their reaction. June Bug says he's Mateo, and he's not the surprise.

Mateo talks excitedly to Tara about his family and his journeys over the winter, around and actually outside California. He looks too old to be someone Tara goes to school with, yet they talk like old friends.

Weird. David and Alex are much quieter for the hour to follow. The freeway becomes backroads becomes forested gravel broken up by succulents and weeds. They trundle past Del Bosque Conservation Center, where one of the staff sees the truck and waves.

David's eyes play tricks on him. It sure looks like a flower on the windowsill waves, too.

There's no time for a second glance. They continue into the forest, until they pass under a gate that reads Camp Cottonwood.

The plant life parts to let them in.

The truck reaches the camp itself. A number of impossible figures stand on the crumbling curb. A beetle bigger than a minivan. A giant stone lizard, lashing its tail. Dozens of plant people like what David saw in the window, all roots and vines and blossoms who flock to June as she grows to look more like them. Her hands stretch long and green to embrace them.

A person with lavender-blue wisteria sprouting from their head, a moss cloak draped across their shoulders, tea roses peppered down the cloak's length, watches. A baggy purple sweater hangs off them like a poncho. They're all loose fabric and loose "hair", and they're familiar.

"Hello," they say.

David cocks his head. Follows the shapes of their face, how much they match his own and his brother's, his mom's and his sister's.

Alex runs right up to the lizard. He grins. The lizard's bare stone shoulders stiffen, covered in white felted flowers that flare to attention. "Are you a dragon?" Alex asks.

The lizard only looks slightly affronted. He sniffs. "I do not believe so," he rasps.

"Whoa! You talk!"

The lizard smiles sheepishly.

David can't stop staring at the witch. That's what they seem like, anyway. Tara and June take each of the witch's arms. "What do you think, David?" the witch asks.

"Who are you?" he says.

The witch tells him a story. The memory of the mandrake lodges in his brain like it did for the Valdez family, like it did for Betty Bug. His sibling is kind and calm, like they've prepared for this. Alex tugs on their sleeve, and they glance down. He hasn't met them. Not like David has. But his oldest sister is gone, and they'll both have the day to get to know this new person.

Tara and June make the rounds. The Walsh girls have grown, now at Tara's hip in height. The thieves accept their spoils from Mateo, Dom from the Union filling him in on their introduction to the conservation center next door. Good ties with the neighbors are important.

It's at the campfire that Musten rests upon their amanita throne. Their time spent with Leah and Weiss in mediation has made them more welcome, even if the feelings both have toward the mushperson are hardly simple. Tara gives them a nod as they head for the tower.

June kept her word to the ivy, who flourish without the boards blocking their host. The tree itself has been convinced to accept a few grafts, growing branches of its own where the platform once blocked it off.

In the grass they lay back and watch the cottonwood seeds drift by. They've bloomed early this year.

ACKNOWLEDGEMENTS

This book would not exist without the following folks: Anna McCluskey, who invited me to my first convention and made me finally take the possibility of publishing seriously. Asher Olsen, who read my drafts and offered some of the best feedback an author could hope for. Karelia Stetz-Waters, Rosiee Thor, Al Hess, and Danger Slater, who made me feel like making art about my experiences that would reach people's hands could be possible.

Thanks to Cherry and Sophie, without whom this book would be a dream in a draft buried deep within the bowels of my Google Drive. Thanks to Knell, Alice, and Joe for listening when I ranted about running out of new ways to say dirt and root.

Thanks to Oni, Shiranne, and Moss for putting up with my bouts of hermetic self-exile while I drafted. Thanks to Mocha, Leena, Abby, and of course Smokey for being fantastic editors (stepping on my keyboard and/or biting my hands).

Thanks to my parents for always supporting my creative endeavors, and apologies to my parents for using that support to dissect my childhood and print it for people to read.

THANKS TO MY COVER ARTIST, SARA DEVOE! HOLY SHIT! Close this book and look at the cover again. Did you look? It's incredible. Those little cutie patoots don't even know what horrors await them. You can see more of her work at cosmignon.info and read her comic Runaway Drakaina online. Thanks too to the fantastic Bennett Gould and attalady for their skill in bringing the grownup girls to life. They can both be found at @sm0kebreaks and @attaladyart respectively.

SPEAKING OF...

Thank you for reading!

About the Author

The person known as Rose Giacomini disappeared into the Oregon forest long ago. Only their cat remembers them. All others live in the illusion that Rose is a writer and baker from the Willamette Valley. They can be found on Instagram and Tumblr @giacofmanytrades, and in earthly embodied reality when you go to the woods and listen for birds.

About the Cover Artist

Sara DeVoe, also known as Cosmignon, is a passionate and energetic illustrator and comic creator. She has been drawing seriously since the 6th grade, when she swore with determination in her tweenage heart that she would be voted the school's most artistic student (and she was)!

She graduated from the University of Redlands with a B.A. in Studio Arts in 2019. Since then, she has been looking for illustration, character design, and comic work! She is especially interested in the fields of book cover illustrations, children's books, and graphic novels.